THE LAST
Treasure

OTHER BOOKS BY JANET S. ANDERSON

—

GOING THROUGH THE GATE

THE LAST
Treasure

JANET S. ANDERSON

SCHOLASTIC INC.
New York Toronto London Auckland Sydney
Mexico City New Delhi Hong Kong Buenos Aires

ISBN 0-439-69993-2

Copyright © 2003 by Janet S. Anderson. All rights reserved.
Published by Scholastic Inc., 557 Broadway, New York, NY 10012,
by arrangement with Dutton Children's Books, a member of Penguin Group (USA) Inc.
SCHOLASTIC and associated logos are trademarks and/or
registered trademarks of Scholastic Inc.

12 11 10 9 8 7 6 5 4 3   5 6 7 8 9/0

Printed in the U.S.A.   40

First Scholastic printing, February 2005

Design, map, and family tree by Tim Hall

For all Smiths everywhere, but especially my own
—

⊰ ACKNOWLEDGMENTS ⊱

This book has been a long time in the making and has gone through many changes since the Smiths and their Square first presented themselves to me. During that time, I've been grateful to many people who listened, answered questions, looked things up, and contributed to this story.

Thanks first of all to the Andersons who helped: my husband, John; our daughters, Kate and Alix; and my mother-in-law, Martha. Next, thank you to neighbors, friends, and colleagues: Bob Lynch and Bob Coffey; Karen Beil and fellow writers in the Capital Area; Bev Shepard, and the Friends of Hamilton Meeting; Margallen Fichter, Sue Clark, Steven Taylor-Roth, and the Friends of Albany Meeting. And thank you to Donna Brooks and Meredith Mundy Wasinger at Dutton, whose reading and ideas contributed so much.

My greatest thanks, however, go to my editor, Susan Van Metre, for her support, her unstinting care, her clear eye, and her patience in pointing me again and again in the direction the Smiths needed to go. Everything she did made this a better book. I was reminded so often of the ending of the Shaker song "Simple Gifts":

> *To turn and to turn*
> *Will be our delight*
> *Till by turning, turning,*
> *We come round right.*

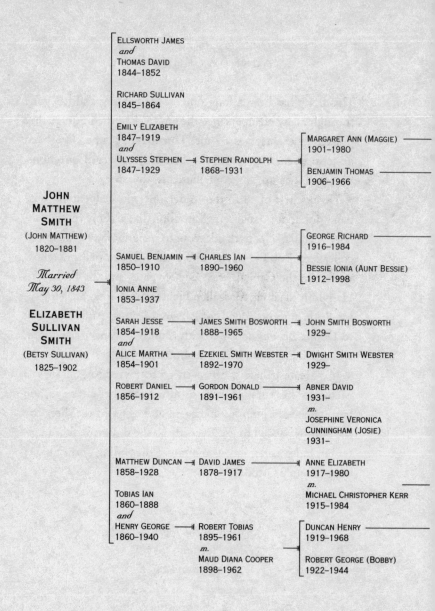

ELLSWORTH JAMES
and
THOMAS DAVID
1844–1852

RICHARD SULLIVAN
1845–1864

EMILY ELIZABETH
1847–1919
and
ULYSSES STEPHEN ──┤ STEPHEN RANDOLPH ──┤
1847–1929   1868–1931

MARGARET ANN (MAGGIE) ────────
1901–1980

BENJAMIN THOMAS ────────
1906–1966

JOHN
MATTHEW
SMITH
(JOHN MATTHEW)
1820–1881

Married
May 30, 1843

ELIZABETH
SULLIVAN
SMITH
(BETSY SULLIVAN)
1825–1902

SAMUEL BENJAMIN ──┤ CHARLES IAN ────────
1850–1910   1890–1960

GEORGE RICHARD ────────
1916–1984

BESSIE IONIA (AUNT BESSIE)
1912–1998

IONIA ANNE
1853–1937

SARAH JESSE ────── JAMES SMITH BOSWORTH ──┤ JOHN SMITH BOSWORTH
1854–1918   1888–1965   1929–
and
ALICE MARTHA ────── EZEKIEL SMITH WEBSTER ──┤ DWIGHT SMITH WEBSTER
1854–1901   1892–1970   1929–

ROBERT DANIEL ────── GORDON DONALD ────────┤ ABNER DAVID
1856–1912   1891–1961   1931–
                                      m.
                                      JOSEPHINE VERONICA
                                      CUNNINGHAM (JOSIE)
                                      1931–

MATTHEW DUNCAN ──┤ DAVID JAMES ────────┤ ANNE ELIZABETH
1858–1928   1878–1917   1917–1980
                                      m.
TOBIAS IAN   MICHAEL CHRISTOPHER KERR
1860–1888   1915–1984
and
HENRY GEORGE ────── ROBERT TOBIAS   DUNCAN HENRY ────────
1860–1940   1895–1961   1919–1968
                   m.
                   MAUD DIANA COOPER   ROBERT GEORGE (BOBBY)
                   1898–1962   1922–1944

— SAMUEL STEPHEN
1921–1924

— CATHERINE ALICIA (KITTY)
1939–
m.
DAVID MACLEOD ——— EMILY ANNE SMITH-MACLEOD ——— JESSICA EMILY COLBY (JESS)
1938–1972   COLBY PETERSON (EMMY)   1989–
                          1966–

— MATTHEW SULLIVAN
1955–

— ELIZABETH CHRISTINE KERR
1952–

— RICHARD CHARLES (R.C.)
1941–
m.
ISABELLE MARY LEWIS ——— BENJAMIN ROBERT   ┌ ELLSWORTH DUNCAN (ZEE)
(IZZY)   (BEN ROBERT)   │ 1990–
1942–2003   1971–   │
                         m.   ┤ THOMAS ROBERT
                         SARAH JANE CUTTER   └ 1990–1990
                         (SALLY)
                         1971–1990

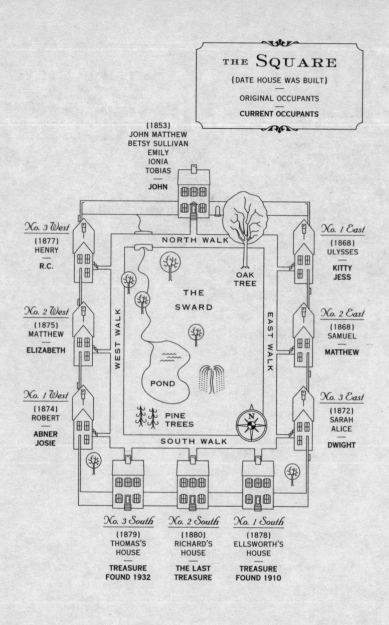

THE SQUARE

(DATE HOUSE WAS BUILT)
—
ORIGINAL OCCUPANTS
—
CURRENT OCCUPANTS

(1853)
JOHN MATTHEW
BETSY SULLIVAN
EMILY
IONIA
TOBIAS
—
JOHN

NORTH WALK

No. 3 West
(1877)
HENRY
—
R.C.

No. 1 East
(1868)
ULYSSES
—
KITTY
JESS

OAK
TREE

No. 2 West
(1875)
MATTHEW
—
ELIZABETH

THE
SWARD

WEST WALK

EAST WALK

No. 2 East
(1868)
SAMUEL
—
MATTHEW

POND

No. 1 West
(1874)
ROBERT
—
ABNER
JOSIE

PINE
TREES

N

No. 3 East
(1872)
SARAH
ALICE
—
DWIGHT

SOUTH WALK

No. 3 South
(1879)
THOMAS'S
HOUSE
—
TREASURE
FOUND 1932

No. 2 South
(1880)
RICHARD'S
HOUSE
—
THE LAST
TREASURE

No. 1 South
(1878)
ELLSWORTH'S
HOUSE
—
TREASURE
FOUND 1910

❧ CONTENTS ❧

THE LAST
Treasure

The Haunting

It is night, just after midnight on June 8. Somewhere in the Midwest on a rickety bed in a cheap motel, a boy who never dreams is dreaming. His dream is crazy, and he thrashes restlessly, trying even in sleep to shake it into sense. Miles away, almost half the country away, in a tract house in a California town, a girl who dreams too often is sinking into nightmare. She's had other nightmares, but this one is different. This one is worse.

The two, one thirteen, one almost so, are distant cousins. They are so distant that they've never met. They are so distant that they've never even heard each other's name. But that might change soon. John Matthew Smith is working on it. He has to. His family, *their* family, is falling apart, and he's finally understood that this time he can't save it himself. The dead, after all, can only do so much.

John Matthew has been dead since 1881. He's survived as a spirit, of course. He's stayed close. Every June, in fact, on the anniversary of his death, he makes his way from the cemetery two streets over in his eastern mill town and walks his Square. He walks slowly, and it takes him a long time. Nobody's ever seen him, though. For many, many years, nobody even sensed he was there.

During all those years, his routine never varied. He'd start at the north end, where everything started, at the house he and Betsy shared for so long. It was not a house that had been built for show. It was a house that had been built for family. It was four stories high from cellar to attic, and each tile of its strongly pitched roof, each brick of its mellow facade, each window shutter, black and heavy, had been chosen to shelter and protect. Radiating out from it on either side was a tall brick wall, covered and softened by a net of ivy that wove itself thicker and greener with every passing year.

From this house, his house, he would turn and, keeping the wall to his left, walk east along the Sward, the grassy, treed space that centered his Square. Dark and leafy and full of shadows, it would whisper of green things and growing things; it would echo with voices and laughter and footsteps. It would seem to him alive with children, his children, for whom he'd planned and planted it so many years before.

Reaching the corner, he would turn right down the slate walk and make his slow way south past more houses, three more houses, connected by more brick wall. At first glance they were all the same. They looked identical not only with his own house but with the three to the south and the three to the west: ten identical houses in all, backing onto the Sward and the pond.

To him, though, they only looked the same. Each *felt* different, as different as his children, one from the other. Oh, how he'd loved them. Serious Emily and responsible Ulysses; mischievous Samuel and energetic Ionia; Sarah and Alice, so inseparable that even marriage and children hadn't torn them apart . . . Robert, who loved art, and

Matthew, who loved gardens . . . Tobias, so shy, and Henry, so bold . . . How happily he'd watched all of them grow and most of them move, some to his houses on the east, others to his houses on the west.

And on the south? No children had ever lived in those three houses. But he would linger there perhaps longest, remembering them finally without sorrow, his three oldest sons all dead before their time: valiant Ellsworth and stubborn Thomas, and Richard . . .

Richard . . .

But much as he loved them, loved all his children, it wasn't just for them that he came. He came for the family there now . . . The Smiths there *now* . . . As he walked past the seven houses where Smiths still slept, he would stand for a moment, listen, nod finally, and move on. They rested peacefully enough, he'd think. He'd provided for them well.

With what? you ask. With treasure. And not only the treasure of his love and his hope . . . In each of the three empty houses that weren't empty at all, he'd hidden something solid and earthy and wonderful to keep his family close and together forever.

For almost a century, then, John Matthew had walked and looked and been a spirit at peace. That's not to say that things never went wrong for his Smiths. People got sick, people failed, people died. But always, too, they married, had families, held celebrations. There were always children to run down the slate walks into one another's houses, to wade in the pond, to play hide-and-seek among the tall trees of the Sward. And twice, when times got hard, when the money ran out, there were children to go into a south-ernmost house, unravel John Matthew's puzzle, and come out again with treasure.

But then something happened. Nobody knows what, exactly. Nobody knows why. Maybe anything unchanged for too long finally chokes up. Dries up. Starts to die. All we know for sure is that about thirty years ago the weddings began to dwindle. Children began to leave and not come back. Smiths started first to quarrel with one another and then to avoid one another, and finally you could hardly call them family at all.

It was then that John Matthew's spirit darkened. Peace gave way to grief, and grief to despair. The Square, each June 8, became a haunted place. Pacing down the long walks, he'd drag the wind up behind him. Faster and faster it would surge, swirling through the trees, riffling up the pond, banging the shutters. On one such night twelve years ago, it tore the great oak at the north end of the Sward up by its roots and left it to die, hopeless and terrible as a beached whale.

A clear-enough message, you'd think. But not clear enough. Things are much worse now, and time is running out. So tonight John Matthew's wind blows harder, blows farther, until finally, finally, it reaches the last remaining branches of his family's tree. Tonight two of his many-times-great-grandchildren dream dreams they never have before. Tomorrow night they'll dream again, and the next night, and the next. Until they hear. Until they listen. Until they come.

Until they do, John Matthew will have no rest.

The Birthday

The morning of his thirteenth birthday, Ellsworth woke up from a crazy and increasingly familiar dream about water burning and saw that a new crack had formed in the wall opposite his bed. He lay there for a long minute, sweating, waiting for the dream to fade and his pulse to stop pounding. Even with a fan, the room was cooking. There was no point opening his window. With the overgrown bushes outside, hardly any air got in, but the nightly racket of motel regulars reeling back from a hard evening at the racetrack came through loud and clear. Once in a while the racket would swell to uproar, and his dad, working the night desk, would have to call the cops.

He finally sat up, untangled the damp sheet from around his feet, wadded the pillow behind his head, and studied the wall. It was a new crack, all right. A big one. It started in the north corner, the parking-lot side, disappeared behind his old David Copperfield poster, reappeared between his ELECTRONICS: A TO ETERNITY chart and his LIFE'S A PUZZLE: SOLVE IT sign, and was finally sucked down into the motel's matted brown carpet. Trevor would probably say it was an omen, a crack behind Copperfield on his thirteenth birthday. Ellsworth didn't believe in omens. Or at least he never used to. Just lately, though, things were going on that he didn't quite get. The dream was part of it. But bigger, much bigger, was his father. Something was eating Ben Robert, and Ellsworth didn't have any idea what it was.

By the time he'd thought of floating it by Trevor, it was too late. Trevor was gone, away with his family for the summer. It had taken Ellsworth at least a week to realize he missed him. He'd never missed a friend before because he'd never had one. He'd moved too often. It was hard to believe that settling down for a year, even in a motel, could change things so much. A year ago he wouldn't have known what it was like to hang around with somebody, get invited for meals, be part, almost, of a family. Trevor's mom had even called him "honey" once, and Trevor's little sister had practically choked him a couple of weeks ago when he'd hooked up a new bell on her bike. He guessed she'd meant it for a hug.

Now, though, he was alone again, alone with his dad. But it had always been just the two of them, and they'd always been okay, even though Ben Robert had gloomy spells from time to time when his book hit a snag. And since February or so, he'd been jittery. That's when he'd stopped smoking. That would make anybody nervous, Ellsworth kept telling himself, but he still couldn't shake the feeling that there was something more going on, something bigger, something that had nothing to do with smoking or Ellsworth or the book. Ben Robert had always been Ben Robert, and now he was . . . well, he was . . . different.

Ellsworth kicked off the sheet, slid out of bed, and plopped down in his desk chair. He didn't want to think about it anymore. It was his birthday. And here was Hugo, looking for breakfast. He'd won Hugo at the school Fun Fair a year ago. Everybody else's fish had died the first week, but Hugo was still swimming. Now Ellsworth watched with satisfaction as the little orange fantail zigzagged to the surface and sucked down his breakfast as fast as it appeared.

Sitting next to the fish tank was something else good, something he'd found at a garage sale a week ago. It was a Heathkit for an old-fashioned radio receiver, the kind you build yourself. "My son's," the old lady had told him calmly, sticking his dollar in her apron pocket as they stood together on her cluttered driveway. "He bought it thirty-one years ago and started to build it and then he got drafted and was sent to Vietnam and he never came back. So it's all there. He'd like it getting used, I think. Good luck."

Luck, sure. He'd need some luck. But it *was* all there—he'd matched every bit of it against the parts list—and he understood enough of the directions to get started. He'd build it, all right, and there was no question about it. It would blow Trevor away.

Right now, though, dishes had started clattering in the next room, and finally it could *feel* like his birthday because his father was obviously back from work and was putting together one of his traditional over-the-top birthday breakfasts. Cooking was the one thing besides writing that Ben Robert loved to do. So maybe breakfast would be blueberry pancakes. Or maybe French toast spiced with cinnamon, with tiny sausages sizzling on the side.

The door suddenly opened, and his father appeared around it. He was grinning, and Ellsworth, feeling even better, grinned back. Everybody always said how much they looked alike, both on the short side, both skinny with big noses, dark blue eyes, and brown, curly hair, but now his father's hair was sprinkled with flour, and there was a spatter of grease on his cheek. "Hey, Zee," he said softly. "Happy birthday. Ready to eat?"

It was a lot cooler in the living room–kitchenette that faced the back. Here the two windows were propped open, a scarred box fan vibrating in front of the biggest. In one corner stood the sofa that turned into Ben Robert's bed and the plywood and filing cabinets that made up his desk. It was neat, as always, his old typewriter exactly in the center, typed pages beside it.

Above the desk hung the two drawings that had followed them forever. One was the Smith family tree, with John Matthew and Betsy Sullivan at the top and their thirteen children, spread out to two or three more generations, below. The other was John Matthew's Square, its ten houses backing onto a shared park, the Sward, with a pond at one end. Below the drawings was a small corkboard littered with notes. It was all somehow going into the book that Ben Robert had been writing ever since Ellsworth could remember.

Breakfast turned out to be blueberry waffles, honey-cured bacon, and a whopping bowl of strawberries with whipped cream. As Ellsworth wolfed it down, he couldn't help studying the packages piled up on the dinette's extra chair. Two were small, probably books, but one was huge, covered clumsily in the same striped paper his dad had used a couple of years ago to wrap a bike.

"Okay, Zee," Ben Robert said as they both scraped up the last of the cream. "I can't wait either. You'd better open it."

It was a computer.

⊰ 3 ⊱

The Letter

"You know what I know about those things," Ben Robert said, fiddling with his spoon as Ellsworth stared at him, speechless. "Not much. But I think it's okay. Is it okay? The guy I bought it from said it's about three models back but that it had a modem and should hook up fine to the Internet. I figured you'd scope it out somehow. And the guy gave me his phone number in case you have questions—there's some stuff already on it, I guess."

Ellsworth finally came back to life and stood up so fast his chair skittered against the wall. He grabbed his father in an awkward hug. "Thanks. I don't get how you did it. But, boy . . . You know . . . Thanks." He couldn't say any more, but he knew that his dad understood. A computer! There were computers at school and at the library, but somebody was always waiting, so he couldn't ever really get into them. He could never just . . . fool around, play with them, see how far he could push them. But now he had his own. He circled it, touching the screen, tapping gently at the keyboard.

And then, suddenly, watching his father's fingers drumming on the table, he knew how Ben Robert had done it. Being night clerk of a crummy motel might be a perfect job because it gave his dad time to write, but it paid peanuts. Peanuts didn't buy computers. It was cigarette money that had paid for this present.

"Thanks, Dad," he said again hoarsely. For a moment, Ben Robert's face relaxed into the playful smile that Ellsworth hadn't seen for months.

"My pleasure," he said. "That thing's got a word processor on it, doesn't it? So when I finish my book, you can type it." He pushed back his chair. "You going to be okay today? I'd better crash for a while, but I'll be up in plenty of time for pizza."

"Sure," said Ellsworth. "I was just going to check the mail and then try and figure out what's wrong with Mr. Rocco's clock."

His father, halfway across the room, turned back. His eyes were somber again. "Zee? There might not be a card from Elizabeth this year. If there isn't, it's my fault. I'm sorry." Before Ellsworth could respond, he had vanished into the bathroom and shut the door.

The motel's parking lot was a crumbling expanse of aged blacktop, tacky in the July heat, and a thin sprinkle of gravel that always ended up in the treads of Ellsworth's sneakers. As he crunched his way to the office, he saw that the Lake Breeze had done good business the night before: every one of the sagging, old-fashioned cottage units had a car parked outside, some of them newish vans and SUVs loaded with beach stuff for the swimming area down the road. This meant, Ellsworth knew, that Mr. Rocco would be in a lousy mood. The more tourists he had, the more complaints about broken showers and stuck windows and TV sets that didn't work.

"What do they think this place is, the Ritz?" he said before Ellsworth even made it through the door. His face was in its usual clench of irritation under his shapeless hat, and he was pulling distractedly on the wrinkled shirt that always hung two sizes too big over his skinny chest. "They want more than one towel each, they should bring them from home." He repeated that sentiment into the phone and hung up. "Your father says it's your birthday, Ellsworth. Happy birthday. Here's your mail. Watch the desk for a few minutes, will you, while I take those characters in unit six a fuse. Don't run the coffeemaker with the toaster, I tell them, but do they listen? No." He stomped out, slamming the screen door behind him.

There were only two pieces of mail. One envelope was junk advertising GOOD USED CARS!! The second, though, was for him, right on schedule. Why had he doubted, even for a second? He didn't really know Elizabeth—she was some kind of cousin who lived far away—but she'd never missed his birthday, not once. She only ever sent a card, but it was always a good one, a big one with things to punch out or color when he was younger, and, more lately, funny ones with bad jokes. She always wrote the same thing. "I miss you, Ellsworth. I miss your father, too. Stay well. Root yourself in my love, and grow and thrive in the Light." That Light business was Quaker talk, Ben Robert had told him. Ellsworth wasn't quite sure what it meant, but it felt okay.

He never rushed opening the card. It was too special. She'd used a big stamp this year. She always did flowers, and this one was bright and wild, orange and green. "Bird of Paradise," it said. Slowly turning the envelope over, he squeezed it gently. It was a really fat one this year—it must be a winner. Then he stopped squeezing and blinked. On the back, in careful black print, was a return address.

There'd never been a return address. Ellsworth had asked his father about it two years ago when it finally occurred to him that maybe he should write back, thank her for the cards, just . . . be in touch. "Better not," Ben Robert had said gruffly. "Trust me on this, Zee, okay? Just leave it. It's better."

"Two West, the Square," he read now. "Smiths Mills, New York."

The Square . . . His father's Square . . . John Matthew's Square . . . Quickly memorizing the address and zip, he tore the envelope open.

He hardly noticed the card. You don't look at cards when inside them are three one-hundred-dollar bills. And a letter. He stuffed the money into his pocket and opened the single sheet of pale gray paper.

"Dear Ellsworth," he read:

Eleven years ago, when Ben Robert finally got back in touch, he made me promise to send nothing more than one card every year, on your birthday. It was all, he said, that he could stand.

I'm breaking that promise now. First, because you're not a child anymore. At thirteen you've got to be allowed, if you want, to know your family. To claim your birthright, if that doesn't sound too old-fashioned. To claim the Square John Matthew left for us all, and maybe, if you want and can, to solve the puzzle of his last treasure.

Second, Ellsworth, we need you. Tell your father that we need you here, more than I can say. Come home, Ellsworth. If only for the summer, please, please come home.

4

The Decision

The afternoon had lasted forever. For most of it, Ellsworth had ridden his bike methodically around town, stopping every once in a while to finger the crisp one-hundred-dollar bills in his pocket and trying to remember everything his father had ever told him about the Square.

It wasn't much. Once or twice Ben Robert had described it, how it looked in winter with the weathered brick of the houses warm against the snow, the trees sparkling with ice, the pond frozen solid enough for skating. Or on a warm summer night, alive with fireflies and frogs and crickets and the moon floating above the trees. He'd talked a little about the houses themselves, about big cool rooms downstairs and up, and back staircases to kitchens, and attics jammed with trunks that might hold anything.

He'd told some stories, too, old stories from the family's past. He'd told about John Matthew, who with his share of the Smith whaling fortune had moved west to New York, built his first textile mills on the banks of the Hudson, and never looked back. He'd told about John Matthew's marriage to Betsy in 1843, their first house and their first children, and then about the terrible fire that had destroyed the house and their two oldest boys: the *first* Ellsworth, age eight, and his twin brother, Thomas.

He'd told about the "new" house built in 1853, with its

grassy Sward behind, and about the decision, fifteen years later, to slowly build nine more like it to complete the Square. And then, finally, he'd told the stories Ellsworth loved most and wanted to hear again and again. About the wonderful treasures hidden in two of those houses in honor of that first Ellsworth and Thomas . . . About how nine-year-old Maggie Smith had discovered one in 1910, and two decades later, ten-year-old Bobby had dug up the second . . . About how they'd found them when the grown-ups couldn't . . .

Ellsworth had imagined it all so often. *Him* walking into those houses at the south end of the Square and solving the puzzles. *Him* emerging triumphantly, treasures held high. And in his mind, the whole time, a shadowy but admiring group of Smiths was standing all around him clapping and clapping. "Ellsworth!" they were shouting. "Our hero! Ellsworth!"

And the third house? The third house and the third treasure, hidden for the third son, Richard? Ellsworth had asked over and over for that story. But Ben Robert would never tell it. He would never say much at all about Richard, except that he'd been killed in the Civil War and that his treasure had never been found. "It's Richard I'm writing about," he'd say. "Someday you'll read it all, Zee. I promise. But for now, Richard is *my* story, and I just don't want to talk about him."

There were so many things he didn't want to talk about. His parents . . . Ellsworth's mother and brother, dead since Ellsworth's birth . . . His decision to leave the Square, take Ellsworth with him, and never go back . . . "We're the

Smith family," he would say over and over again. "You and I, Zee, the two of us. We're all the family we need."

Ellsworth had finally stopped asking. And after a while the Square had felt more and more unreal, like a place in a book, his father's book, peopled by ghosts who were mostly long dead. Except for Elizabeth. She was real. She was alive. Every year when he got her card he could almost see her, a tiny old lady sitting in a big room filled with flowers, writing out an envelope addressed to him and smiling.

And now it was Elizabeth who'd made it real again. The Square, the house, the treasure . . . It was a real place to which he could really go. By the time Ellsworth was finally pedaling along the lake back to the motel and his birthday pizza, he had his questions all lined up in his head. How soon could he leave? How would he get there? What should he take if he was going to be away the whole summer?

But by the time the pizza was nothing but an uneasy mass in his stomach, he still had no answers. Ben Robert had listened to him in silence and read Elizabeth's letter in silence and eaten his pizza in silence except for crunching down extra hard on his special crispy crust. Then he'd pushed his plate away and shaken his head.

"I can't let you go." He looked into Ellsworth's face and then settled himself more firmly in his chair. "Listen," he said. "I understand why Elizabeth wrote this. But there's too much you don't know, and I'm not even sure if I can explain. It's just that it would be like . . . throwing you off the end of a dock when you didn't know how to swim. You might be okay, but the odds are you'd drown. I can't take that chance."

Ellsworth sat for a minute trying to turn this into sense and then shook his head, too. "I don't get it," he said. "What does swimming have to do with it? It's the Square, Dad. And the treasure. The last treasure. Why can't I go help them find it?"

Ben Robert's face twisted into an expression Ellsworth had never seen before, and he gave a short, hard laugh.

"The last treasure? Yes, well it's probably there, all right. But you can't find it, Zee. Nobody's ever going to find it. Because at the end, John Matthew guessed wrong. He thought he knew what his family was like. Well, maybe when the Square was finished in 1880, he did. But the family's changed since then. It's been changing for a long time, and now. . . . Now . . ."

Now Ben Robert was up from the table, pacing around the room, breathing deeply. He finally slowed, slumped back down, and continued, more gently. "Look, Zee," he said. "There's lots of reasons I never told you about that last house and why I don't want to tell you now. Partly— and I've said this before—it's not your story. It's mine." He gestured over to his desk and his pages of manuscript. "It's my story, and when it's finally all down I'll be rid of it." He sat very still for a moment, staring into the corner. Then he nodded to himself and turned back to Ellsworth. His face softened even more as he looked at his son, and his voice with it.

"I even *wish* you could go. At least part of me does. So you could see the Square. Meet Elizabeth. She's a good woman, Elizabeth. A good person. But the problem is that there are other people living on that Square, too, and some of them are people you don't want to know. Especially now." He rubbed his hands down over his face, hard. "Believe me, Zee. If there was something there I thought you needed, we wouldn't have left when your mother died. And your brother . . ." His eyes now were full of familiar pain, and he reached over and gave Ellsworth's shoulder a hard squeeze. "It's like I've always said, Zee. We're all the family we need. Okay?"

Ellsworth tried to nod, but felt his head shaking instead, something stubborn in him resisting what, for the first time with his father, didn't feel right. "Yeah, but it's not just the treasure. Elizabeth says they need me. Didn't you always tell me you should help people out when they ask you? And the thing is, see, I want to go. That counts, doesn't it?"

His father was silent for a long moment. "What are you trying to say, Zee?" he said finally. "That you'll go even if I say no. Even if I say you can't?"

"She says they need me," Ellsworth repeated stubbornly. "She sent the card when you said she wasn't going to. And her address. And money. So, yeah . . ." He was feeling more and more miserable, but he had to keep going. "Yeah," he repeated. "Maybe I will. Maybe I *have* to, Dad."

Abruptly his father pushed back his chair and stood up. "I've got to get ready for work." He struggled for a moment, trying to regain his composure. "I never thought I'd have to say this to you, Zee. But I'm your father. I brought you up. You're *my* son, and I'm not going to give you up, not to Elizabeth, not to anybody. Never."

He didn't wait for an answer. Ellsworth heard the bathroom door rasp shut and the pipes begin to rumble with water. Then he stood up, too, very slowly. He could barely move. His body felt stiff, like machine parts that had seized up and rusted shut. Finally back in his room, he pulled out his desk chair and stood there holding it, hardly seeing Hugo drifting in and out of his gently waving grass. He could hardly see anything or feel anything because his brain was churning everything inside him into one lumpy question. Would he go?

He reached down into the pocket of his jeans and tugged out the now crumpled bills and his answer. Yes. He'd go. If there was a treasure waiting for him, he had to go find it.

Okay. He took a deep breath and let it out again. Good. So what next? A bus schedule. Before they got their old car they'd always ridden buses, but he didn't have any idea how to get to Smiths Mills, New York. In all their travels, they'd never gotten farther east than Ohio.

So a schedule and tickets . . . Clothes, yeah, probably, and a couple of books . . . Then something flickered in front of him, and his careful logical plan collapsed. Hugo! He couldn't leave Hugo. But how could he take him on a bus? How could he carry him? He swung over to the desk chair and stared down into the fish tank, his thoughts now skittering frantically. A bucket? Maybe he could borrow a bucket from Mr. Rocco. But what if Hugo jumped out? He needed a lid, something with a lid. But what?

He shook his head, but it didn't work. It was as though somebody had clamped a big hand down on top of it, hard. The thoughts had skittered away, and what was in there now wasn't a thought at all. It had nothing to do with Hugo, nothing to do with treasure. It was an image, the one that had been glowing more and more brightly every night in his dreams: a wide expanse of water glittering with fire. He shut his eyes against it, but it didn't so much disappear as recede, as though someone were moving back from it with a wide-angle lens so that he could see, finally, what surrounded it. It was a Square, green around the bright water, giant trees shading giant houses, lights shining from windows, faces shining from doors. Faces, the faces of his family, who had lived there forever and whom he had never known. They were smiling faces, waiting faces. They were faces waiting for him.

They slowly dimmed. In their place came a breeze, a delicate, flickering, cool breeze from someplace that couldn't be his window because his window was closed. For just a moment it played gently over him, quiet and calming, and then it, too, faded, and he walked slowly over to his bed, undressed, and slid down under the crumpled sheet. For another moment he heard cars crunching over the gravel outside, and car doors slamming, and from far away, the plunk of early fireworks set off from cottages around the lake. He didn't hear anything more until early the next morning when his father tapped gently on his door.

"Zee?"

Still half-asleep, Ellsworth slowly shifted his legs so that his father could sit down on the bed, and then he looked up into Ben Robert's face. It was pale and his eyes were pouched and tired.

"Zee?" repeated his father. "Do you *have* to go?"

Ellsworth tried to shake himself more awake. Did he? Did he have to go? He nodded groggily. "I'm sorry, Dad."

Ben Robert tried a smile and then gave it up. "Okay, then. I knew it right from the beginning, I think. I just didn't want to admit it. So I came so close. So close to . . . screwing things up the way this family does best." He shuddered, then found Ellsworth's ankle with his hand and held it tightly for a moment before letting it go.

"But around three o'clock this morning, something stopped me. I don't really know what it was. I just suddenly remembered, *really* remembered what it felt like to be forbidden something that every part of me needed. So, listen, Zee. You can go. And all the things I should have told you?" He held out an envelope. "I've written it all out here. Read it before you get there, though, okay? It's important."

Then he turned and looked directly into Ellsworth's face. "But there're two things I've got to say. So listen to me, Zee. First, Elizabeth says they need you. Maybe they do. But families aren't like . . . clocks, Zee, or lamps. You can't just . . . fix them. It doesn't work that way. You've got to remember that. And second?" His voice was suddenly hoarse, and his face tight with strain. He reached over and touched Ellsworth gently on the cheek. "You'll come back to me, okay? Promise me, Zee. No matter what happens there, when the summer's over, you'll come back."

Ben Robert's hand was cool, but it wasn't his touch that made Ellsworth shiver. What was he saying? Come back? Of course Ellsworth was coming back.

Why wouldn't he?

5

Smiths Mills

Two days and four buses later, Ellsworth would have given almost anything to be just that: back at the Lake Breeze in his small hot room hearing his father tapping away. This trip he was on, this trip he was *still* on, had turned into one of those "vacation" movies that always seem so funny when you're watching it. There's always a silly mother and a dumb father and two stupid kids and a dog, and things start out bad and get steadily worse and you laugh and laugh and laugh.

He'd met that family, yesterday, or maybe it was the day before, he couldn't remember, and they hadn't been funny at all. He'd also met one bus with no shock absorbers, one with no air conditioner and no toilet, and two bus stations from the dark lagoon. Worse, much worse, on the very first bus, just as he'd hauled out Ben Robert's envelope, he'd suddenly fallen asleep. "Fallen" was the wrong word—it was more like somebody had yanked him into a long dark hole and kept him there until the bus had reached its station and jolted to a stop.

He'd woken in a panic, and in his desperate squeeze down an aisle crammed with the whole state of Indiana, lugging a backpack and a duffel and Hugo sloshing in a big red picnic thermos borrowed from Mr. Rocco, he'd left the envelope behind. He'd realized it two seconds after he'd

24

watched the bus pull out of the station. Everything that his father had wanted to tell him was gone.

So now, on this last bus lumbering down a long hill into Smiths Mills, Ellsworth felt sick. His stomach roiled with thirty hours of jouncing, his eyeballs ached, and he smelled. He knew he smelled. The spilled pop and ketchup weren't so bad, but those two little kids who'd been piled in next to him for most of a very bad night had leaked.

And then, to top it all off, he had to admit it: he was scared. In just a few minutes, the bus was going to grind to a stop, and there would be . . . who? Elizabeth? Probably. But maybe other people, too, people who "needed him." And he didn't know anything about them. The family tree over Ben Robert's desk stopped in the fifties, so he hardly even knew names. They'd be like . . . the Heathkit without an instruction book. He knew, now, what Ben Robert had been talking about. He was at the end of that dock, all right, and he was somersaulting in, and he didn't have the foggiest idea how to swim.

The treasure didn't even seem real anymore. Real was Smiths Mills and its narrow main street and its tall crowded-together old-fashioned stores. Real were flags drooping from lampposts and flowers drooping from concrete urns. Real was the driver putting on his turn signal and pulling over into a space in front of a coffee shop. Real was here.

There was a mild bustle around him as two or three other passengers gathered their belongings and trailed down the aisle. Ellsworth couldn't move. He felt clamped to his seat. Then, suddenly, the window beside him started shaking. Somebody was pounding on it. He dragged himself upright. Below him, a large old woman in a blazing orange jogging suit was waving violently. Her hair was as bright as her outfit. Her lipstick was brighter. Now she was pointing at Ellsworth and screaming something to somebody behind her whom Ellsworth couldn't see.

Trembling, he screwed the top of Hugo's thermos partly back on and shrugged himself into his backpack. Was this Elizabeth? Could it be? Well, who else, this person who thought she knew him? He wound himself slowly up, and finally, his stomach still churning, stumbled past the driver and down the steps of the bus.

He was hit immediately by the heat and then, the next second, enveloped in an enormous, unavoidable hug.

"Ellsworth! This is wonderful! Elizabeth felt terrible that she couldn't meet you, but she was in pain this morning with that knee of hers, and when she's like that, she just can't drive. And I said that of course I'd come instead, except that I was a little worried that I wouldn't recognize you, but of course I did. You're the spitting image of Jess here, isn't he, honey?"

She released him, and Ellsworth staggered back, gaping. The girl she pulled out from behind her like a magic trick could have been his twin. She had the same mop of curly dark hair, the same blue eyes and big nose, the same wiry build. Except that where Ellsworth had always thought of himself as kind of ugly-ordinary, this girl was . . . Well, she was . . . beautiful.

Beautiful except that she looked like she'd like to take both Ellsworth and the beaming old woman, stuff them into the bus, and push it over a cliff.

"Uh, yeah," said Ellsworth. "Hi." She was staring at him, her eyes getting bigger and bigger, and she was slowly backing away.

"Jess?" the woman said. "Jess, aren't you going to say hello to your cousin Ellsworth?"

But Jess was already gone, skirting her way rapidly around the small pile of suitcases the driver was unloading from the hold. She stumbled over a break in the sidewalk, righted herself, and broke into a run.

"Jess? Jess! Honestly!" The old woman shook her head, and taking out a Kleenex, she dabbed at her sagging face. "I'm so worried about that girl. It breaks my heart the way she just picks at her food. And the nightmares . . . 'HELP, FIRE!' she screams. 'MOMMY! MOMMY!' But her mother isn't here, of course, she's back in California with that new husband of hers, fighting with the insurance company . . ." She shook her head again. "Still, that's no excuse for her behavior now. Rude, just plain rude, and—"

"No," interrupted Ellsworth. "Scared. I mean, she was scared, at least that's how she looked." He suddenly felt desperate, as though everything he didn't know was closing like quicksand over his head. "Listen," he said. "Listen, who *is* she? And you know, I'm sorry, right, but who are . . . *you*?"

She looked at him in bewilderment. "Why, Ellsworth," she said. "I'm your cousin Kitty. I was your grandmother's closest friend. And Jess, of course, is my granddaughter. She's been here two weeks now, and she was just tickled to find out she was going to meet somebody her own age. We worked it out last night, you know, and the two of you are *fifth* cousins. Isn't that exciting?"

Luckily, she didn't wait for an answer, but kept right on going. "Heavens, though. We've got to get you home. The car's over here. No point waiting for Jess, she can walk when she's finished sulking, it's not far. I'm sure Elizabeth's dying to see you. She never wants to see me, of course. No, we've never been close, Elizabeth and I. Gardening, landscaping, the Quakers—that's all she's ever cared about. And I must say, I was just so upset when I found out she'd been in touch with you all these years and never said a word. And then to hear you were coming! Why, I nearly fainted!"

Ellsworth, on the other hand, was suddenly feeling better. He was feeling almost cheerful, actually, as he tossed his gear into the trunk, squeezed into the broiling front seat, and placed Hugo's thermos carefully between his feet. He was here. Somebody had met him. Maybe Kitty talked too much, but he'd already learned some important stuff. He'd learned that Elizabeth *did* like flowers—she liked to garden. She had a bad knee, too, and she could keep secrets. And he'd learned that this Jess had just come, too, Jess who was his own age and looked just like him and already hated his guts. That should worry him, but somehow it didn't. Girls were like that. Although he didn't know much about girls, come to think of it. He hadn't really been friendly with any since the fourth grade.

Kitty had turned off the main street and was driving down another lined with tall trees and big white houses and a park. Then she turned again, and again, and the next moment drove through some wide iron gates into a cemetery, dim and much cooler under its canopy of trees. She'd been quiet, concentrating on her driving, but now, slowed by speed bumps, she started talking again.

"I always like going this way, although it's terrible now, everything so dry, global warming, you know, we haven't had rain for weeks. Our plot's in the oldest section, of course, but Jess can walk you over tomorrow if you want. I've showed her where everybody is. John Matthew and Betsy Sullivan . . . All thirteen children . . . Four sets of twins, you know, among them—not every family can claim that. Not to mention actually raising most of them and keeping them here—that was a big accomplishment even back then, when everybody's families were big." They were out of the cemetery now, turning slowly down narrow side streets. "Later, well, the Smiths scattered, didn't they? But a lot of them, the dead ones, of course, are there in that plot where they belong. And most of the rest of us are still where *we* belong. On the Square." She lurched to a stop beside a crumbling curb. "And here we are. Welcome home, Ellsworth."

He hardly heard her. He was staring down a street that looked ordinary except that the three houses on the right were all the same. They were brick, a dark weathered red brick with black shutters, and they were big and square and solid and old and were joined together by a high brick wall. Set into the wall to the left of each house was a heavy wooden gate with a small inset door. The gates were all closed, held shut by long bolts, their short driveways a jumble of leaves and sticks and crumpled paper. They looked like they hadn't been opened for years.

"We never drive in anymore," Kitty said, as though reading his thoughts. "At least, not on this side of the Square—Matthew and Dwight and I. We just can't be bothered. Lock and unlock, lock and unlock, it's too much trouble, and there aren't any garages, are there, so what's the point? No, we just park on the street."

She heaved herself out of the car, and in a moment had her front door open and was ushering him in. "Now, the downstairs bathroom's right here, under the stairs. You just come along to the kitchen when you're ready. I told Elizabeth I was going to feed you before I sent you over."

Ellsworth slowly plopped his duffel down, shrugged off his backpack, and set Hugo's thermos on the hall table. He knew where the bathroom was. He knew where everything was. The plan for John Matthew's houses had been taped to his father's desk, and it was basically the same for them all.

Ellsworth knew where the bathroom was, all right, but he didn't need it. He didn't need the kitchen, either. Hardly noticing Kitty as he passed through it, he pulled open the back door. He made his way steadily across the small porch, clattered down three steps, and landed, for the first time he could remember, onto the Square.

⊰ 6 ⊱

Home

It hit him the same way his first pop-up book had when he was little. It was like he'd been looking at Ben Robert's drawing, all flat and neat, and then turned the page. *Whoomp!* One dimension to three in the blink of an eye. And there was so much of everything. There were so many trees and bushes on the big grassy Sward. And the houses. They were so . . . real. So ordinary, kind of, and lived in. They had porches and fences and yards. They had sprinklers and hammocks and lawn chairs and tables, and every bit of it was winking and glittering in the hot morning sun.

For one second, it was dizzying. It was too much. Then he took a deep breath. Okay. It was kind of a shock. But the drawing could still help. It could still tell him things. Like where was he? If he looked across the Sward he could see three houses, or at least the parts of them not hidden by leaves. But to the right, there was only one. So that had to be north. And that had to be John Matthew's house, the first one, or at least the one he'd built to replace the one that burned.

If that way was north, then the other way was . . . south. South, where the treasure houses stood . . . But he couldn't see them. There was too much stuff in the way. Well, he could solve that. In a minute, Kitty's yard was behind him, and he was walking across the wide slate walk and into the very center of John Matthew's Square.

And then suddenly he was hit again, even stronger. This time it wasn't thought. It was feeling. It seemed to come, somehow, from the Sward itself, from the trees and the bushes and the grass. That made it even crazier. That kind of stuff had never interested him, never at all. Anyway, the grass here was like straw, and the leaves were drooping, and half the bushes looked dead. But it didn't matter. It didn't matter what it looked like. It only mattered how it felt, and how it *felt* practically knocked him down. It felt like *his*.

And the houses, and the wall that connected them, one to the next? As Ellsworth, hardly thinking now, turned and turned so that he could see them all, he felt like everybody who'd ever lived in them was sweeping him up and holding him close and welcoming him home.

Then he heard his name, and there, trotting briskly toward him, was Kitty.

"Ellsworth," she repeated, reaching him and thrusting a bag into his hands, "I know you're anxious to see Elizabeth, but you looked like you were going to faint out here. You've got to have something to eat. Now, here's some muffins and bananas for you and a loaf of my special zucchini bread for her. Nobody can say I don't try. And, Ellsworth? What's in that thermos you left on the hall table? I started to pour it down the sink, but then—"

"Hugo! My goldfish!"

"Now don't get in a state. I *thought* I saw something move down in there. He's fine. But he certainly needs a better place to live. Let me think now. My daughter, Emmy, had a fish once, and that tank is right down in the cellar. I know right where it is. You won't find anything in Elizabeth's house, that's for sure, which is why I don't understand why she won't let you stay with me. Much more sensible, but no, no, she wants you all to herself. So you'd better run along. But don't you let them try and send you into that treasure house."

Ellsworth's attention, drifting with Hugo, jerked back. "What? Why?"

"It's dangerous, of course. It's jinxed. Anything in there should just stay in there, as far as I'm concerned. It's certainly not worth a life."

"Jinxed?"

But Kitty was plowing right on. "And certainly not a child's life. Because those treasures have always needed a child's eye, you know. Matthew goes on and on about it, as though the rest of us haven't heard those stories since the day we were born. Matthew, who never even moved to the Square until five years ago! And then he thought he could get Jess looking! My Jess! I put my foot right down, of course. I've warned her not to get anywhere near that house, to just plain stay away from the south end of the Square. Oh, but now, there's the phone. It's probably Elizabeth wondering where you are. You know which one is hers? Go right around that clump of trees and you'll see it. Number Two West. Go on now, and then you can come back later and pick up your things."

Ellsworth took two steps and almost fell over the stump of a big tree. He gazed at it blankly. He felt like the first time he'd tried to fix a lamp without unplugging it; he felt zapped. This treasure wasn't just in Elizabeth's letter, then, the way he'd started thinking on the bus. It *was* here. And if it was here, he could find it, just like those other kids had found those earlier ones. Of course, he'd have to get his hands to stop shaking first. He stared stupidly at the bag he was holding and then yanked it open, wolfed down two muffins and two bananas, and immediately felt better.

He had to go and see that house. He had to get a closer look at it, just for a minute, so he could get it clear in his head, and then he'd go find Elizabeth.

He wanted to run, but there were too many dead branches littering the ground, and the dry grass was long and shaggy with clumps of spiky flowers sticking out of it. As he picked his way along, he got glimpses of the houses on either side. He wished he knew who lived in them. His father's drawing wasn't much help, because it only showed who was there in 1881, and all of them were dead. Maybe he'd make his own drawing and bring it up-to-date.

Suddenly he slipped on something and found that he'd reached the pond. There was a mess of slimy mud between what water was still left and the rim of ragged grass that probably used to be the edge, and dotted around the rather scuzzy surface were lily pads. Weren't there supposed to be frogs on lily pads? Hugo might like a frog.

But the lily pads were bare. Looking around the pond's edge, he saw a bench and some of the biggest trees he'd seen yet. Huge trees. One was the kind with branches that droop down so far they touch the ground. The other two were so tall that he had to crank his neck back to see all the way up. They were pines, evergreens, but they hadn't been green for a long, long time. Their branches were scaly and brittle-looking, and most of their needles had fallen off. Once, maybe, he could have climbed them and looked out over the whole town. But not anymore. They were absolutely, rock-bottom dead.

They made him feel funny, and turning away, he shoved through the overgrown clump of bushes beside them and stumbled out onto the smooth slate walk at the south end of the Square. He stood there for a long minute, staring at the three houses looming over him. They made him feel even funnier. He wasn't sure what treasure houses should look like, but not like this. Not . . . shabby. Not . . . dirty and shuttered and blank. The two on the ends were the worst. Ellsworth's house, the one he'd always thought of as his . . . And Thomas's . . . They didn't just look empty. They looked dead. They looked as dead as the pine trees.

And the middle house? Richard's house? That was better, but it still didn't look like treasure. Well? So what? Frowning, Ellsworth straightened his shoulders and took a firmer grip on the bag. Was it such a big deal, how it looked? What about the first time he'd seen a computer, right? It hadn't looked like much, either. It had just been a gray box and a black screen, and then somebody had flicked a switch and touched a key, and it had come alive.

No. Who cared about outside? It was inside that mattered. Because *inside* could be anything at all.

Elizabeth

He knew it was Elizabeth's yard the second he saw it. It was full of flowers. They were all jumbled together, every size, every shape, every color, every smell, and they were crawling with bees that looked and sounded like they were in some kind of bee Disneyland and never wanted to leave. Ellsworth, who suddenly didn't mind taking his time, went down the walk cautiously, trying not to bump into anything that might sting.

His name leaped at him from the screen door. It was written in big caps on a Post-it note. ELLSWORTH! WELCOME! He pushed open the door, but for one confused second thought he was still outside. The kitchen was full of plants, crowding every window, hanging over the sink, filling half the counters. But then he saw it wasn't just plants. It was full of everything, books and dishes and knitting and fruit. A huge tiger cat, sound asleep on a pile of newspapers, took up most of the table, and two more, black and orange and much smaller, lay curled around each other on top of the refrigerator and looked up sleepily when the door slipped out of Ellsworth's hand and banged shut.

"Ellsworth? Is that you? I'm in here. In the library."

As Ellsworth crossed the kitchen and continued out into the hall, the hand holding Kitty's plastic bag was suddenly slippery with sweat. What if he hated her? What if she hated *him*? But when he finally peered through the open door and saw the woman waiting for him, he knew that everything was going to be okay.

She wasn't anything like he'd imagined. She wasn't tiny and she wasn't old. She was a tallish middle-aged woman, her graying hair cut short, and although she wasn't quite smiling, her eyes were warm and welcoming. She shifted the cane she was holding and held out her hand.

"Hello, Ellsworth. I'm Elizabeth. I feel we know each other already." Her hand was large and slightly rough; her grip brief but strong. "I'm very glad you're here. I'm sorry I wasn't at the bus. But I can't drive now, with my knee, and when Kitty volunteered, it seemed like a good plan. You could meet two other family members right off, one of them your age." She smiled. "And now I know who Jess has been reminding me of. You both have the Smith nose. Just like Ben Robert." She'd been maneuvering herself slowly into a rocking chair and now gestured him toward the battered plush couch that stood in front of the window. "Although you're probably tired of sitting, aren't you? You've been sitting for days. How was your trip?"

The couch felt better than it looked. Now that it was his turn to talk, though, his mind was blank. "It was okay," he said finally. "I mean, I didn't miss any buses, and nothing broke down. But you get kind of tired of sitting, like you said, and there's not much to do. It gets kind of boring."

"You're not a reader, then, like Ben Robert? No. It's hard to remember him without a book in his hand." Her smile faded. "I've missed him very much. How is he, Ellsworth?"

How was he? How was his father? Ellsworth took a new grip on Kitty's bag and tried to think. "Well, he's usually okay." He stopped and thought some more. "Except lately, the last few months. It's like he's been worried about something. He's not writing so much. He hardly ever talks. He just kind of wanders around. I don't know what it is, but I've been kind of wondering if something, you know, maybe's wrong." He nodded. Yeah. That's what he'd been thinking, all right.

Elizabeth nodded, too, and then, without trying to hide it, took a Kleenex out of the pocket of her skirt and wiped her eyes. "The last few months. Yes. Do you know, Ellsworth, I can remember so clearly the day he was born. It was two days before my nineteenth birthday, and the forsythia and daffodils had just come out all over the Sward, and I picked the biggest armful I could carry and walked with them right through town to the hospital and into Isabelle's room and plunked them down on the bed and burst into tears." She put down her Kleenex and laughed shakily. "The only thing the nurses could find big enough to put them all in were buckets, so who knows how any floors got washed for the next few days. And there were R.C. and Isabelle and little Ben Robert, and I think it was the happiest day of all our lives. . . ."

R.C. and Isabelle . . . His grandparents. Ben Robert had never talked about them, never at all. And Ellsworth had lost his letter before he could read it. So he didn't know anything, and suddenly he felt tired enough to ooze right off the couch and onto the floor. He heard another quiet laugh, and looking up blearily, he saw Elizabeth reach for her cane.

"I'm sorry, Ellsworth. I'm talking, and what you need is sleep." She hauled herself to her feet, took an experimental step, and shook her head. "Stairs aren't too easy just now, so I won't go with you. But Matthew—he lives across the Square—made up a room for you upstairs. It's the second one on the left at the top of the landing. He's anxious to meet you, by the way. You probably haven't heard of him—he came after Ben Robert left—but I think you'll like him, especially if you're interested in history. He teaches it at the high school, but it's more family history I'm thinking of. He's read as many of John Matthew's journals as he could get his hands on, and he's given a lot of thought to the treasure houses. Especially the last one. I know he'll want to talk to you about that."

Instead of going back out to the hall, she was leading him slowly toward the half-open sliding door that separated the library from the front room beyond. He was just about awake enough to see that the library, like the kitchen, was full of stuff. Books were everywhere, and a big computer desk between the windows on the north wall was flanked by filing cabinets and covered with stacks of papers. The northwest corner of the room was hidden by a tall screen covered with flowers, and built into the west wall itself was a wide brick fireplace set off by a mantel of dark wood. Over the mantel hung a picture.

It wasn't a large picture, but it stopped him because it almost looked too big for its heavy gold frame. Elizabeth, nearly at the door, turned.

"Ah," she said. "Yes, well. The picture. I wasn't going to mention the picture until you'd had some sleep, but that picture, Ellsworth, is one of the reasons I wanted you to come home now before the summer is out. You probably know what it is."

Ellsworth shook his head and took a couple of steps so that he could see it more clearly. Only a couple of steps, though, because too close and he had the funny feeling it might suck him in. He'd get wet, too, because the whole middle part of the picture was a pond. It was a very flat and blue pond. Ducks floated on its surface and frogs sitting on lily pads stared out in a flat froggy way. Around it stood ten houses, and in front of the houses . . .

Ellsworth blinked. In front of the northmost house stood an old couple. A child stood between them, holding their hands. Their other hands reached out to two more children, who reached out to others, forming a circle, a whole linked dancing circle around the pond. Ellsworth took another step and peered more closely. How many of them were there, anyway? He worked his way around, counting. There were thirteen, thirteen kids and two adults, and it finally came to him who they were.

"It's them, isn't it?" he said. "John Matthew and Betsy Sullivan and the kids. Is that Ellsworth and Thomas, those little guys there, dressed the same? And that one there. Is that Richard? What's he wearing?"

"His uniform," said Elizabeth. "She would have felt that's how he'd want to be remembered, no matter how it made her feel."

"Her?" said Ellsworth. "Who?" Now Elizabeth looked puzzled.

"You are tired, Ellsworth, if you can't recognize Betsy Sullivan's last picture. I'm sure your father's described it to you many times—he loved it, especially when he was little. He'd go to whatever house it was hanging in at the time and just look and look. Well, it's beautiful, isn't it? All that energy and color and joy. Hard to believe that they didn't know how good she was. John Matthew, I think, only had those pictures framed and hung to please her. Our Matthew could give you the whole quote, I'm sure, from one of the journals, but it was something like 'how it broke my heart, watching her daub out her grief in paint.'

"Now it's worth a truly incredible amount of money. At least that's what Cousin Abner tells us, and he's an art dealer so he should know. Certainly the other nine did very well after one of his gallery friends 'discovered' Betsy Sullivan just about the time I was born. 'A new Grandma Moses,' was how he put it. A genius, at any rate, and lucky for the family that she was. Selling those pictures has kept the Square going for the last fifty years. Kept the houses going, anyway, and the Sward. I'm not so sure about the rest of us."

Now, as she shifted painfully on her cane, her eyes for the first time were clouded. "No, I'm not sure. Six months ago, you see, when our sad financial state became perfectly clear, we voted to sell this picture in the fall. We 'voted,' as though a decision to get rid of something so important to the family could be made without consensus. The last picture and our only real clue to the last treasure, and its fate was decided by one vote." She closed her eyes for a moment, and when she opened them they were clear again but very grave. "I'm not sure why I'm surprised at the result. The family's been through some hard times over the years, but never like this. Things now are just about as bad as they can be."

Looking Back: 1910 and the First Treasure

It is 1910, and things are nearly as bad as they can be in a number of ways for the Smith family of Smiths Mills, New York. One of those ways is money, and the lawyer, old Wilcox Gorham, has just sent a letter to Ulysses Smith telling him so. Ulysses Smith is John Matthew's oldest living son, and he has watched part of the Smith fortune slide into that great sinkhole known as the Panic of 1907 and part of it go up in flames when the biggest of the Smith mills caught fire one freezing February night, 1909. The family isn't going to starve anytime soon, but "according to the terms of John Matthew Smith's will, the time has come to open the house known to you as Number One South and recover that which has been placed therein for you. I will remind you," the lawyer continued, in typical lawyerly fashion, "of the counsel left you by your beloved father to aid you in the retrieval of his gift. 'The search should be conducted by at least two members of my family, one of them, at least, a bright child with a sharp eye. God bless you all.'"

In 1910, Ulysses Smith is only sixty-three years old, but is, when he receives this letter, in no shape to do anything about it. Two months earlier, the carriage bearing him and his favorite brother, Sam, home from a political meeting overturned on a sharp bend on a foggy road and sent both of them into the river. Ulysses managed to pull himself up the muddy bank and is still recovering from the pneumonia he contracted from his dunking. He is still also in shock, as Sam, having been tossed headlong onto a boulder when the carriage went over, had been instantly killed.

Stephen Randolph Smith, Ulysses's eldest son, is forty-two years old and a lawyer himself. Despite this, and despite worrying about his father and mourning his favorite uncle, he can't help but feel a thrill as he reads old Gorham's letter. He remembers his grandfather well, because he was thirteen when John Matthew died in 1881, and they'd been close from the day he'd been born. He'd watched the houses to the south go up, brick by brick, and although John Matthew had never divulged their secrets, he'd made it perfectly clear to Stephen Randolph that what he'd hidden in them were no sentimental tokens. They were treasures. Real *treasures*. Stephen Randolph had never stopped dreaming about finding one of them, and nine years ago, when his daughter, Maggie, was born, he'd begun sharing his dream with her.

So it came about, one damp cool morning in June 1910, that a tall man with graying hair and small girl with brown curls were standing on the back porch of a locked house dedicated to the memory of the first of John Matthew's sons and getting ready to turn its key for the first time in thirty-two years.

" 'Ellsworth James,' " Maggie read from the engraved brass plate at the right of the door, " '1844 to 1852.' He was only eight when he and Thomas died, wasn't he, Papa? He wasn't even as old as me. It's not fair, is it? But if we find his treasure, he'll be happy, won't he? And Grandpa Uly will be happy, too. He'll get well again, won't he?"

"I hope so, Maggie. I hope so."

Quietly they tiptoed through the dusty rooms, pointing out what they could see in hushed excited voices. There wasn't much. In the front hall hung a chandelier that looked exactly like every other hall chandelier on the Square, and in the back room, the room used variously as a second parlor or a library, was a solid wooden bench. It stood in front of a bricked-up fireplace, and Maggie and her father immediately sank down onto it and looked up. Hanging over the fireplace was the only other thing the house contained. It was a picture.

"Oh," said Maggie. "Oh, Papa, look at it. It's a Great-Grandma Betsy picture isn't it? I wish it was in *our* house. Oh, Papa, isn't it the most beautiful picture you ever saw?"

Actually, Stephen Randolph thought it was no such thing. Every house on the Square had a Grandma Betsy picture in it, and every adult, at least, thought they were dreadful and only left them hanging out of respect for the old lady they'd all loved so dearly. This one, to Stephen Randolph's eyes, was the most sentimental one yet, but he could see well enough why Maggie liked it. It showed a little girl about her age kneeling on a seat under a window. It was a big window, made of little panes, and she was looking out. Through all the panes but one was a dull view of a wet garden on a cold November day—all brown and gray and sad. But through one pane, the one in the highest left-hand corner, streamed the most brilliant light. It was almost an explosion of light, of golden sunlight, and it filled the pane with rainbows of color. The little girl was reaching toward it with everything she ever hoped to be shining from her eyes.

"Very pretty, Maggie," he said. "Why don't you sit and look at it while I do some measuring. You know what I think about

Grandpa John Matthew's treasure. I've told you how he loved to build and how I've always been sure that what he built into this house was a secret place to hide his secret treasure. If I just can measure carefully enough, I'm sure I'll find it."

So over the next few days, Stephen Randolph measured. He measured every room. He wrote numbers down and compared them with other numbers until he could hardly see. He knocked on walls and tapped on floors and crawled around the cellar on his hands and knees. And he didn't find anything, not anything at all. During all that time, Maggie followed him dreamily around, writing messages in the dust, or sat quietly looking up at the picture on the back-room wall. She loved it. She loved that one pane of glass dancing with light.

Finally, at the end of a long muggy day, coming one last time down the dusty staircase, Stephen Randolph sighed and gave up. "I'm sorry, honey," he said to Maggie, who was waiting for him below. "I'm sure John Matthew's treasure is here. But I guess I didn't know him as well as I thought I did, because he's hidden it too cleverly for me. Maybe somebody else in the family will have more luck."

But Maggie was hardly listening. Instead, she was gazing up to where the late-afternoon sun, finally out after days of rain, was streaming through the small west window in the hall and striking the glass chandelier. Suddenly her face, too, was alight. "Look, Papa!" she called up to him. "Rainbows, just like in the picture! Just like in Grandma Betsy's picture!"

Stephen Randolph looked. Sure enough, the chandelier had turned into hundreds of prisms splitting the sunlight into hundreds of rainbows. And as he looked, even though he was a lawyer, even though his own plan and his own search had turned to dust, he began to laugh. Because he had to remember now what John Matthew had said. "A bright child with a sharp eye . . ."

"That's my Maggie," he said. "It's been hanging here in plain sight all along, hasn't it, and it took you to see it. Let me go get some help and we'll get the thing down."

They got the thing down and took it apart, and there, in among the crystal prisms, were thirteen perfect little diamonds, one diamond for each one of John Matthew's children. All of them were in one place, hanging and shining together.

Together, they were worth all the money the family needed. And Ulysses? Ulysses got well, and eleven years later was able to hold Maggie's firstborn son in his arms.

Jess

Ellsworth had been dreaming of stars, glittering stars like diamonds, forming constellations that kept changing just as he began to recognize them. Now he woke from his nap with a start. A shaft of early afternoon sun had sneaked through the tangle of tree branches outside his window and was dancing over his face. He pushed himself upright. One last pattern was still shimmering in his head, trying to tell him something . . . something . . . something about a treasure. But even as he tried to grab it, it faded away.

It didn't matter. He didn't need dreams. What he needed, first of all, was to call his dad. Elizabeth had said she'd let him know that Ellsworth had gotten there, so that was okay, but Ellsworth needed to talk to him, too, as soon as Ben Robert woke up. What time was it, anyway? He didn't have a watch, and neither of the two clocks in the room worked. The only thing he really knew was that it was time to eat. Past time. Elizabeth had told him to help himself to anything in the kitchen whenever he came down. She was going to be holed up in the front room until midafternoon with some kind of Quaker committee meeting she'd scheduled weeks ago and hadn't been able to change.

He swung his legs over the edge of the high bed and bounced gently, looking around. He'd never seen anything like this room. Trevor would love it. The two nonworking clocks, to begin with, one in a wooden case beside the bed and the second a tall grandfather one between the windows . . . He couldn't wait to get his hands on them. And then there was a radio, one of those big old floor models, and what had to be—he dropped down to the floor and padded over to examine it more closely—yeah, definitely one of the first TVs ever made. Talk about treasure . . . Even better was that the whole house seemed to be like this. Elizabeth's *mother* had been born in it, she'd told him, and she'd lived in it her whole life and hardly ever thrown anything away.

Even the broken stuff she obviously didn't know how to fix. It was funny. His dad couldn't fix things either. "That's one Smith gene I never got, Zee," he'd said once. "Too bad, considering what the name means. Smiths have always repaired things. Made things. Blacksmiths and goldsmiths and silversmiths making horseshoes and bracelets and bowls. Well, I guess I make things with words, but words don't help much when the toaster's packed it in."

This TV had definitely packed it in, but for now it'd have to wait. Heading for the door, he noticed, for the first time, a small ink-lettered sign tacked to it. WAY WILL OPEN, it read, in strong black letters. He looked at it for a minute. What way? Open where? Slowly, a bit cautiously, he turned the knob and pushed. The door opened a little stiffly, but the only thing out there was the hall, just like it had been earlier. The bathroom was still there, too, with its old-fashioned tub, and he did the best job he could of cleaning himself up, considering all his clothes were still over at Kitty's.

Then, figuring he'd stay away from the front part of the house, where Elizabeth was having her meeting, he found the back stairs and clattered down them into the kitchen. The cats were gone, but in the tiger cat's place on the table, a loaf of homemade bread was sitting on a board under a bowl. He hacked off two thick slices, and finally discovered two jars in the refrigerator full of lumpy peanut butter you had to stir and runny strawberry jam. He poured himself some milk, and carrying the plate in one hand and the glass in the other, used his foot to snag open the door to the back porch.

He almost dropped the milk. The girl, Jess, was sitting on the top step. On the walk below her stood Ellsworth's backpack and duffel, and beside her, a small fish tank complete with orange stones and Hugo. Hugo was racing around trying to figure out where he was, but otherwise looked just fine.

"Hey," Ellsworth said. She didn't answer, so he squeezed in on Hugo's other side and carefully set his glass down behind him. "You brought my stuff. Thanks."

Jess edged away, still silent. Ellsworth sat for a minute, and then, not knowing what he was supposed to do now, took a big bite of sandwich. A glob of jam immediately dropped into his lap. Jess didn't seem to notice but then turned to him abruptly, her eyes accusing.

"Do you smoke?"

Ellsworth's mouth was full of the stickiest peanut butter he'd ever eaten, so he had to concentrate for a minute on working it down. He shook his head, and then stopped, remembering. "Yeah. Well, once. I tried one of my dad's, once. He caught me and gave me the pack. I threw it away."

Her gaze didn't soften. "So do you read in bed? With a candle? Or cook?"

"Cook?" He didn't cook. His father cooked. "What do you mean? I heat stuff up, sometimes. And brownies, from a box."

This time she nodded. "But you don't fry things? Or leave things plugged in that shouldn't be? Or make big piles of stuff, you know, like newspapers and old rags, like you've been painting with?"

Ellsworth suddenly understood. "You mean fire," he said. Her legs jerked and her hands twisted in her lap. She slid down a step, and when she finally turned back to him, her eyes were dark again with the fear he'd seen in them that morning.

"It's so scary," she said. "I've never met you, I'd never even heard of you before this summer, and you look just like me. We could be twins." She shuddered. "Don't you see? Don't you know those stories?"

"You mean the twins," said Ellsworth. "The twins and the fire . . ."

She shuddered again. "I've been dreaming about fire. I thought it was our fire, at first . . . The one at home. That was a cigarette, it was his sister's, she said she'd put it out, but how could she have, it was her chair it started in. And we almost . . . We all almost . . ."

She stopped, her eyes so wide now that they seemed to fill her face. Then she shook her head and kept going. "But in this dream, it's different. It's someplace empty and the light's all funny and the fire's all over, it's everywhere. It's everywhere!" Her hands were clenched now, everything was clenched.

Ellsworth half choked on the second of two swallows of milk. It sounded all too familiar, a dream like that, lately. "Well, so what?" he said gruffly. "They're just dreams, right? It's not like they're going to happen, or anything." He ignored her shaking head and plowed on.

"And, anyway, look, we're *not* twins, right? I'll bet you're older than me. I'm thirteen, I just had a birthday a couple of days ago."

So much breath came out of her she seemed to collapse like a torn balloon. "Okay, then," she said. "I'm almost fourteen. But you're sure you're not older? You seem older."

Ellsworth nodded. Other people had told him that, too. "Yeah, well, I guess it's because I spend a lot of time with my father."

"You're lucky, then. I haven't seen *my* father for almost two years." Jess's voice was bitter. "Well, what do I care, right? And what do I care about this place either? There aren't any kids at all; everybody here's ancient, not that you get to see them much. The only ones I've really met are Grandma and Matthew and Elizabeth. Matthew's okay, I guess, except he's a teacher, and you know how teachers are. And Elizabeth, well, she's okay, too. I mean, she's completely not with it, but at least she's quiet, and she's got all these flowers, like home . . .

"The rest of them, though . . . I mean, they hardly ever come out. One of them never does, not anymore, so I've never seen him at all. And two old guys just come out twice a day to walk their dogs. This John guy, he's got some kind of terrier, and Dwight's is this black cocker with floppy ears. One of them goes one way, and the other one goes the other way, and sometimes you think they're going to bump into each other, but they never do. They just kind of growl at each other and turn around. And then once—that's all they've been here—there was this really tall old couple, they looked like something out of a movie, all dressed up. Abner and Josie. Do you believe the names around here? Yeah, well, with your name, I guess you do. And I tried to talk to them, but they just gave me this 'hello' and this phony smile and kept on going."

Ellsworth was trying to take it all in. "All of them live here? On the Square? My dad never told me. . . ."

Jess's mouth twisted. "My mother told me, all right, except she didn't know what she was talking about. 'It'll be so great, Jess, finally meeting everybody. Finally meeting the *family*.' Sure. Like that's even why she and that dork she just married sent me here. I think he was almost glad about the fire. He never liked our house, that's for sure. It was never fancy enough for him. And why did she think I'd like it here when she's hardly ever been back herself?"

Ellsworth put his sandwich down and flexed his fingers. He wished he had something else to hold—something to fiddle with. Something that he could take apart and put back together again, like those mechanical puzzles he and Trevor had been fooling with all spring . . . There was a horseshoe one that Ellsworth really liked. You had to twist and flip it just right so that the ring holding the two shoes together would just . . . slip off. It was easy, once you got the feel of it. Once you let your hands just kind of . . . take over.

It sure was a lot easier than sitting here trying to figure out what to say next. Jess's mother. That made him think of *his* father, and suddenly he was swept by a huge wave of homesickness. Or not so much homesickness as wanting his father sitting right there with him, right this minute. "I wonder if they knew each other," he said awkwardly. "My dad and your mother. Or if she knew *my* . . ." No. He couldn't say it. It just didn't work to say "my mother" about somebody he'd never known and never would.

Jess shot a look at him, and then away. "I don't know. My mom knew your dad, though, except I think he was still pretty little when she went away. Can you believe it, Grandma sent her *away* to high school, to this girls' boarding school, because she said she wanted her to be *safe*? Doesn't she know what those schools are *like*? No wonder my mom's so screwed up. But then your dad left, too, didn't he, when he wasn't very old? Yeah. So what do they do? They send *us* back."

"Well, okay," said Ellsworth. "Except my dad didn't send me. Elizabeth wrote asking me. Listen. What do you know about that treasure? The one in the middle house? You know, the last one?"

Everything in Jess that had relaxed while they were talking immediately stiffened, and she jerked herself to her feet.

"I don't know anything," she said. "Besides, that house is dangerous. Grandma says it's messed things up, big time."

Messed things up? "What do you mean? How? When?"

"A couple of times. Grandma told me to stay out of that house. You'd better stay out, too. Didn't I tell you I've been having these dreams? You go in there, something will happen. Something bad, I know it will, just like it always does. Just like it always does, and it will be all my fault." She jumped off the steps, and before he could say another word, she was off and running across the Sward.

❧ 10 ❧

Ben Robert's Gift

"Hey! Wait!"

Jess didn't even look back, and Ellsworth, who'd jumped up to go after her, slowly sank down again. He'd probably better let her cool off a little first. He just hoped it wouldn't take too long. He hadn't even started on the list of things he needed to know. How did the treasure house mess people up? Had somebody already been in there? And who was this guy who never came out of *his* house, never at all? Ellsworth chewed down one last bite of sandwich and thwapped his empty plate against his knee. Why hadn't his dad ever told him any of this stuff? Why had he just given him a letter that could get left, unread, on a bus?

So he'd call him. But now? Right now he'd probably still be asleep. Trying to decide, Ellsworth made several trips in and out through the screen door with his plate and glass, his duffel and backpack, and then, carefully, with Hugo's small tank.

The cats had magically appeared again, and nudging his way slowly through their insistent weaving bodies, he carried the tank up the back stairs to his room and, with some difficulty, got his door closed with them outside instead of in. They obviously wanted to get to know Hugo much, much better. Setting the gently sloshing tank on the dresser, Ellsworth sprinkled in some food and spent a few minutes watching the little fish dart up and away from the surface, over and over again. Like always, it did something to him, that movement, something he could never quite figure out. It seemed to put one part of him to sleep and wake another part up, the part that sent ideas bubbling up and out.

But not much was bubbling now. Leaving Hugo, he eyed his duffel. Maybe he should take one minute and dig out some clothes? And his toothbrush? It felt like a long time since he'd brushed his teeth.

He dumped everything onto the bed. He always packed his toothbrush and paste in a sock because it kept them together, and it only took him a few seconds to excavate the familiar lumpy shape from the tangle. Upending the sock, he shook out what he thought was going to be a half-squeezed tube of toothpaste and his old red brush. But it wasn't. The toothbrush was there, all right, but what dropped out with it was something he'd never seen before. It was a small cube almost completely covered with a yellow Post-it note.

Ellsworth sank down on the bed. It took him a minute to unwrap the note, partly because his father had taped it down and partly because his fingers, suddenly, weren't listening to his brain. Finally, jerkily, he pulled off the top sticky edge and smoothed out the small square. It was filled with his father's tiny script.

"Zee. Last-minute decision. You'd better have these. They meant a lot to me once. If you need help, show them to John and Dwight. You can trust them, and they'll give you a hand, I think, for old times' sake. But one thing, Zee. If you do get into that treasure house, don't go alone. And watch your step."

Ellsworth could almost see his father writing those words. He could almost hear his voice. It was almost, for a minute, like having him sitting beside him on the bed the way he had a few days back, telling him it was okay to go. Ellsworth swallowed hard and then, folding up the note, shoved it deep in his pocket. Then he picked up the object Ben Robert had sent and turned it around in his hand.

It was a small wooden box, no more than two inches on a side. It was rough in some places, smooth in others, and although the wood had been stained, it had been done unevenly, so that no two sides looked exactly the same. But the edges fit together well enough, and it was closed on one side by a tiny metal clasp. Ellsworth nudged it up with his finger and then pulled open the lid.

Inside was a small gold pocket watch. When he opened the case he found a round face, little arrows for hands and for numbers, Roman numerals thin as threads. Opposite, on the inside of the case, three initials had been engraved, so elaborately that Ellsworth couldn't make them out no matter how he turned them around. But the date was easier: 1832. There was a key with it, too, a tiny key for winding it up. He looked at them for a long minute and then put them both back into the box and stuffed the whole thing into his pocket along with the note.

A minute later he was closing the door behind him. Turning, he found the cats sitting in a row in the middle of the hall and watching him with identical green eyes. The tiger, huge and handsome, gave him a baleful look, and then, with a contemptuous twitch of his tail, ambled into the bedroom across the hall and jumped up onto the bed. The little orange-and-black ones, though, stood up together as though they were synchronized and began to wind again around Ellsworth's legs, and as soon as he reached down to scratch their heads, started to purr. "Hi, guys," he said. They were sleek and cool, and he picked them up and cradled them against his chest. They clambered up to his shoulders, and one of them, smelling sandwich, reached down and licked at his hand with a rough pink tongue. A thrill went through him. They were so small and alive and friendly. They liked him.

They purred steadily as he balanced them carefully down the stairs, their warm breath and whiskers tickling at his ears. It was almost like they were trying to tell him what to do next. Except he knew what to do next. Ben Robert's note had told him. He had to go talk to John and Dwight. They were the guys with the dogs, weren't they? But where did they live? There was only one way to find that out. He'd have to go ask Jess. Even if she was still mad, she could tell him that.

A few minutes later he'd left the cats staring piteously at him from behind the screen door and was heading down Elizabeth's walk. Halfway across the Sward, though, he heard something that stopped him. It was the sound of a dog barking, and it was coming from the north end of the Square. He detoured around a couple of overgrown bushes and then, suddenly, was standing right in front of what had to be the "new" first house, the one John Matthew and Betsy Sullivan had built after the fire in 1852.

It was like all the others, big and brick and old. It was where most of the original kids had grown up, but there didn't seem to be kids in it now. Instead there was a dog, a little white dog behind a white picket fence, yelping enthusiastically. Behind him was a shed, sturdy and well built, the sound of sawing coming from its open door. As Ellsworth crouched down to scratch the dog's neck, the sawing stopped and a head poked out, a head with a white beard and close-cropped white hair. "Woolman?" the man said. Then he caught sight of Ellsworth. "Oh," he said, and ducked back in. A second later he ducked back out, stared hard, and then raised a hand in an awkward salute. "Hello, there," he said. "Uh, hello." Then he was gone again, but now there was silence. The sawing didn't resume.

Ellsworth didn't know much about dogs, but Woolman sure wasn't a black cocker with floppy ears. So according to what Jess had said, this man was John. He didn't seem very friendly, though. Ellsworth waited one more minute, just in case, but the doorway to the shed stayed empty. Even Woolman had lost interest and was curling up again in the shade. All right, then. It would have to be Dwight. That meant Jess again, for directions, and it was with great relief that, turning the corner onto the east walk, he saw her coming down the steps of her grandmother's house. She was carrying a bulky package wrapped in newspaper and definitely looked calmer. She looked almost glad to see him.

"Oh," she said. "So *you* can carry this. Grandma's on this cooking kick because she says Mom never taught me. Bread was okay, but now we're doing casseroles, and you should see the stuff she puts into them, like fourteen cups of meat and cheese and sour cream. Well, at least I don't have to eat them. This one's for Dwight because he's got a cold or something. That's where I'm going now. He lives two doors down, and I'm supposed to leave it on his porch."

"Okay," said Ellsworth. "I want to talk to him, anyway." He took the package she shoved at him and shifted it awkwardly. Even in its layers, it was hot.

"So, uh, listen," he said. "So you're not mad anymore, right, about that house? Because there is something in it, I'm sure there is now, and my dad even told me, kind of, to look, so that means it's not dangerous. That's why I want to see Dwight, because maybe he can help me." Then he realized that Jess had kept going and was already halfway down the Square. He hurried to catch up. "But listen. My dad says I shouldn't go alone. So would you do it? Would you look in there with me?"

She just kept walking.

"Look, it's *treasure,*" he said. "It's real, it's really there, just like the other two were, and we could find it. I mean, your house just burned, right, and some of your stuff? So you need money, right, and my dad and me, well, we could sure use some, and then, and then . . ." And then came something that must have just been sitting there in the back of his mind. "And then, if we could find something really good, they wouldn't have to sell the picture."

11

Dwight

She stopped so suddenly he almost crashed into her. She whirled around. "What picture?"

"The one Elizabeth has. You know, of the houses and the pond and all the kids."

"I like that picture. She showed it to me last week. Who says they're going to sell it?"

"She does. Elizabeth. She told me. They need the money."

"How come she told you and not me?" She was definitely upset again. "It's like I don't really count around here, except to Grandma. It's like nobody wants to see me or really cares if I'm here or not. Like I don't really belong."

Ellsworth stared at her. John had kind of made him feel the same way. "Well," he said slowly. "If you helped find that treasure, you'd belong. We'd both belong. You know?"

Jess stared down at the sidewalk for a long minute and then nodded. "Yeah," she said. "Maybe." She turned, and neither of them said anything else until they reached Dwight's yard. An old black dog, lying most of the way under the porch steps, raised her head to greet them. Jess went to pet her, but Ellsworth saw something that interested him more.

"Look. He's got sundials. I've read about sundials. They've been around forever, and they work like clocks. You just have to have some sun. Look, come here, hold on to this for a minute, okay? What time is it? I want to check them out."

"Twenty-one past two. On the dot." The voice coming from the shadowy figure behind Dwight's screen door was gruff. "But that's daylight saving's, of course, so the dials are an hour behind. They run on sun time. Real time." The door opened, and a man stepped out onto the porch. He was short and stout and old, and what hair he had left was grayish white and straggled limply down his collar. He sneezed a couple of times, pulled a huge wad of Kleenex out of his pants pocket, and noisily blew his nose. Then he stuffed the Kleenex back in. His pants were slung low under his stomach and were splotched with oil. "Don't come too close. I have a lousy cold, and a summer cold's the worst kind."

"What am I supposed to do with this, then?" said Jess. "It's for you; it's a casserole."

"That's from Cousin Kitty, is it? Hardly worth the bother—I'm not hungry, and I can't taste a thing. Nice of her, though. Just put it down there, and I'll bring it in later." His gaze moved to Ellsworth, who was making his methodical way from one sundial to the next. "Guess I don't have to ask who you are. You're Ben Robert's boy, aren't you? You look just like him."

"He looks just like me, too," said Jess. "Right? We could almost be twins, except I'm older." Dwight gave her a brief glance.

"Maybe." He turned back to Ellsworth. "Ben Robert liked my collection here, too. Liked all my collections. The rest of them are inside—the place could be a museum if they'd let it. Old John Matthew's mechanical toys. Clocks. Watches. Ben Robert liked them all. Not that he had any idea how any of them worked." His short bark of laughter turned into a prolonged bout of coughing, and his wad of Kleenexes came back out, got used, and was stuffed back in.

"Watches?" said Ellsworth. "Wait a minute." He fumbled in his pocket for the little box and shook out its contents. "You mean like this?"

"What you got there, then?" Dwight made his ponderous way across the porch and down the steps. "Not so close. Not so close. Put it down now and then get back. Let me see." He picked up the watch and examined it carefully, and then stared off into the distance. "Never thought I'd see this again. It's John Matthew's, from when he was little. Your grandfather gave it to your dad on his sixteenth birthday. Ben Robert wanted me to get it going again, so I did. Had a good time, we did, with this watch. He give it to you?"

Ellsworth nodded. He held up the little box. "It was in this."

Dwight's eyes narrowed. "Oh, yeah. I know all about that box. John sees us having a good time that summer, Ben Robert and me, and has to butt in. Says he should stop hanging around me and come see him. Says he has to teach him about wood. Wood. Ben Robert could no more make things out of wood than a pig could fly. Ugliest little box I ever saw. No, John was just jealous, that's all. Never thought he was like that before. Jealous. Greedy. After that, though, I knew. . . ."

"Listen," said Ellsworth. "Listen. My dad wrote me a note, to go with the watch. He said maybe you'd help me. Both you guys, you know, John and you, he said maybe you'd give me a hand. I want to go into that last treasure house, and my dad says it's okay, it's okay for me to go, but I need the key. Do you have one?"

Dwight's face didn't turn pale. It just went from red to blotchy, and the Kleenex came out yet again so that he could swab it down. "The key. The key to Richard's house. I don't feel so good; this is all too much for me. Listen. You talk to John about this yet? You go to him first?"

Ellsworth shook his head.

"Okay," said Dwight finally. "Listen. You did right coming to me, but I don't have the key. Nobody does. R.C. threw the first one away forty-some years ago, and I dumped the second one myself." For a long minute he stared out over the Square, and then, slowly, he shook his head. "No. It's just asking for trouble, somebody going treasure hunting in that house again after all these years. I should know. There isn't any key, not anymore, and after last time, I'd be nuts to make a new one."

Starting to cough again, he turned and shambled back up the steps. Then he turned again. "Sorry," he said. "Hate turning you down. But it's best. Best for everybody if you just plain leave that house alone." The screen door slammed behind him.

Ellsworth stared after him. No. He'd said no. So he wasn't going to help after all. But what else had Dwight said? Ellsworth turned to Jess. "What did he mean, 'going treasure hunting in that house *again*'? Like, you know, like somebody's been in there before. . . ."

But Jess wasn't listening. "Did you see that? It was like I wasn't even here. And he didn't even take the casserole. It took me half an hour this morning to chop all the onions for that casserole. Okay. Who needs him, anyway? You want to get into that house and find that treasure? Well, you just meet me there tomorrow morning. I'll show you. I'll show them all."

Now Ellsworth was really lost. "What do you mean? How can we get in without a key?"

Jess was already stomping away, but she turned and gave him one more glare. "I told you. I'll show you. Tomorrow morning. Be there early. Be there at seven. Don't be late."

It was midafternoon and hotter than ever. Everything on the Sward looked beige and bleached and brittle, like it would crumble if you touched it. That was kind of how his brain felt, too. There was only one thing that made any sense right now. Go back to Elizabeth's and call his father.

As he climbed the steps to her porch, the screen began to tremble, and when he pulled it open, it was heavy with cat. Two cats, actually, clinging to it with eight legs and talking loudly. He pried them loose with some difficulty, and slinging one over each shoulder, looked around the kitchen for a phone. There didn't seem to be one. Maybe it was in the library. As he headed into the hall, he heard the soft murmur of Elizabeth's committee meeting coming through the partly open door farther down. As quietly as he could, he slipped into the library. Good. The sliding door into the front room was shut. He wasn't in the mood for more strangers. Almost immediately he spotted the phone sitting on the filing cabinet to the right of Elizabeth's desk, and he slid the cats gently off him and onto the floor.

Then it came to him. He didn't know the number. He didn't know it because he'd never used it. Mr. Rocco hated calls because they had to come through the office, and the office phone was for one thing only: reservations. But Elizabeth must have it. She must have written it down. On the desk, maybe? Not that he could see, and if it was somewhere in one of those piles, it was too bad. He didn't dare touch them. Avalanche, big time.

What he did notice, though, was another of those little signs. This one was taped to the windowsill over the phone and was even more mysterious than the first. SPEAK TRUTH TO POWER, it said. He gazed at it dumbly for a minute. He kind of liked the sound of it; it sounded like an arrow thunking into a target. But what did it mean? And then he felt the hairs on the back of his neck stand up, and slowly raising his eyes, he saw that there was a man standing at a window in the next house staring down at him.

He was standing very still, his edges clear-cut and unwavering. The light was too bright for Ellsworth to see more than his outline. But he didn't have to see more. He knew, as though the knowledge had been jammed directly into his brain, that this was somebody he belonged to. The feeling of connection was so immediate and so strong that Ellsworth's hand rose automatically. Hi. It's me. Here I am.

For a moment, there was no reaction. The man simply stood there. And then, as though yanked by a giant hand, he lurched away and the glass went blank. Ellsworth found that he was clutching the edge of the windowsill, willing him to come back, to walk back to the window and pull it up and call his name. Because he could almost hear it, if he strained, hear a voice, except that the voice that was echoing in his head was high, like a woman's, the saddest woman's voice in the world. "Ellsworth," the voice was crying. "Ellsworth." Suddenly he was shaking so hard that only his grip on the sill was holding him up, because he knew, too, and without a shadow of a doubt, that the woman who was calling his name so urgently was dead.

12

The House Next Door

He tore himself free and stumbled through the library, across the hall, and into the kitchen. Fumbling in the sink, he found his glass and filled it with water. Most of it slopped out. He couldn't stop shaking. Why was Elizabeth still in a meeting? She was the one who'd asked him here. Why wasn't she beside him, right now, to tell him what was happening? She'd said they needed him. They didn't. John sure didn't; Dwight either. And whoever lived next door didn't want to look at him at all.

"Ellsworth?" Elizabeth, leaning on her cane, was standing in the doorway. "We were just finishing and I . . . I suddenly felt I needed to see you. Did you get some sleep? Did you find something to eat? Are you all right?"

"I don't know," said Ellsworth. He was still clutching his glass. Slowly his hand relaxed, and letting out a big breath, he set it down. She *was* here, after all. "I saw somebody. In the house next door. I just want to know who he is. My dad, he never told me. We never talked about anything here, not really. He wrote me a letter about everybody, to read on the bus, but I lost it. . . ." It was such a relief, letting it all spill out, that he hardly noticed that she had limped over, taken his arm, and was leading him toward the table.

"Sit down," she said. "I have to go back to my meeting, but I'll just be a minute, just to tell them to finish without me. I'll be right back. I'm so angry with myself. I should have known it would have been too hard, too hard for Ben Robert . . . Look, here's some zucchini bread—it's Kitty's, isn't it, so it's bound to be good. Have some of that, and I'll be right back."

Ellsworth sank down into the chair and, after a long minute, looked dully into the bag Kitty had given him this morning. Zucchini bread. He'd never heard of zucchini bread. He put his nose down to it. It smelled all right. After one careful taste he chewed down three thick slices, feeding the crumbs to the cats, who had clambered back into his lap. Things were okay now . . . Elizabeth would be back in a minute, and she'd explain everything. He slumped down farther into the chair, letting the cats lick his fingers clean. It was all okay.

But when, a few minutes later, Elizabeth was sitting across from him, talking to him in her quiet voice, the only things that still felt okay were the cats. He could hardly understand what she was saying. She was saying that Isabelle, his grandmother, had died only months before and that his father had refused to come home for her funeral and that R.C. had quit his position at the bank and locked the door of his house behind him and the only way they knew he was still alive was that the groceries they left for him on his back porch every few days were gone the next morning.

She was saying that the man he had seen at the window, the man next door who was grieving himself nearly to death, wasn't just a man named R.C. He was Ellsworth's grandfather.

"My grandfather?" Ellsworth said. His mind felt blank, the word sliding off it, meaningless.

"Oh, Ellsworth," she said. "Your father couldn't even bear to tell you that much? Or that your grandmother died of a heart attack, totally out of the blue, in February? I called Ben Robert as soon as I could track down the number of your motel. I told him we'd wait, we'd put the service off until you both could get here. We'd send money if he needed it. I begged him. But he couldn't, he said. He just couldn't . . . forgive his father. Face him or forgive him. Still.

"It was all just about as bad as it could be. Because R.C. couldn't forgive, either, and this made it worse." She shook her head. "So many years. The two of them angry at each other for so many years, starting before you were even born." She was silent for a minute. "That story, I can't tell you, not if Ben Robert hasn't. But for him not to come to his mother's funeral . . . You have to understand. They'd only ever had Ben Robert. He was their only child. They'd wanted children, lots of them, but they couldn't seem to have them. That happens to lots of people for lots of reasons, but R.C. blamed it all on the house, on Richard's house and what happened there."

Ellsworth still couldn't seem to take any of this in. "Richard's house? What? What happened?"

Elizabeth sat quietly another long moment, as though deciding what more she could tell him. "What happened . . ." she said finally. "Yes. It was in 1960, what happened. I was just a little girl then, believe it or not." She sighed. "I only hope I can tell you so it makes some sense. You see, in 1960 the family was told that somebody had to go into that house and bring out the picture. The last picture, the last one Betsy Sullivan painted, the one that's hanging in my library right now. It was something about insurance, I didn't understand it then, but insurance companies don't like you leaving valuable things in an empty house. And by 1960, Betsy Sullivan's pictures *were* valuable, like I told you earlier. They were worth a lot of money.

"So R.C. volunteered to go, and Isabelle went with him. They actually invited me, too. Isabelle loved kids, and I was crazy to go with them, a treasure house, what could be more exciting than a treasure house when you're nine years old? But my mother wasn't well at the time. Her arthritis was much worse than mine, much earlier, and her pain made her nervous, and she said no. So R.C. and Isabelle went alone.

"And while R.C. was taking the picture down, Isabelle went exploring. Of course she did. She was nineteen and newly married and happy and she loved the stories about the treasures. They were all new to her, and they were thrilling! It would be so wonderful, she thought, if she and R.C. could find the last treasure, Richard's treasure, even though the family didn't really need it yet, even though they weren't supposed to be looking, not officially at least. But wouldn't it be wonderful if they just . . . happened to find it and bring it out along with the picture?

"So she went exploring. And she fell. She never could really explain what happened except 'it moved.' Something moved. Something moved and she fell, fell just the wrong way and broke a hip, and then it wasn't set right, and then it got infected. It took a long long time to heal, and during all that time, years and years, they couldn't seem to start the family they both wanted so much.

"I told you about the day Ben Robert was born. Their first child. And, it turned out, their last. And R.C. decided that if he was only going to get one son, his life would have to be perfect. . . ."

She looked up and saw Ellsworth's face and stopped. She reached over and touched his hand. "I'm sorry," she said. "I don't know what I'm trying to do, telling forty years' history in five minutes. It's too much, isn't it? Way too much. But maybe you can at least see why I asked you to come. R.C. *is* your grandfather, and he's going crazy with grief, and nobody can reach him. It just came to me, was given to me, that maybe you could."

Ellsworth stared down at the table and then shook his head. "He saw me. I even waved, but he didn't wave back. Then he just disappeared. But there's something else I don't get. You said 'forgive' . . . What did he do to my dad that was so bad?"

Elizabeth shook her head. "As I said earlier, Ellsworth, it's not my story to tell. It's not a . . . terrible story, don't be thinking that. It's just a sad one, about fear and . . . rebellion from it. Things . . . misunderstood, other things gone badly wrong. Too many words said in anger and grief . . . Call Ben Robert. Call him now. Ask him to tell you as much as he can, and then, if he agrees, I'll tell you anything more you want to know."

Then her head turned suddenly, and her voice changed, almost comically, to exasperation. "TigerLily, no. Get down from there. Just because your uncle Hodge thinks he can loll all over the table, you don't have to. It's very bad manners. Ellsworth, grab them, will you?"

It felt like oxygen had just been pumped into the air. Ellsworth scooped the wiggling cats off the table and back into his lap. "Hey, guys," he said a little shakily. "Which one of you is TigerLily?"

Elizabeth smiled. "Both of them. Well, one is Tiger and one is Lily, but they're always together, so together they get a beautiful name. They look a lot like their mother, Hodge's niece, except she was more orange. Sadly, she was killed by a car a year ago, so Hodge and I were left to bring them up. Hodge, for some reason, tolerates them. I think they amuse him. They don't threaten him, that's for sure. There's still no question about who's top cat. There he is now—he always seems to know when I'm talking about him, don't you, you old monster?"

Hodge, at the bottom of the stairs, stared at her accusingly over his wide white bib and then padded over and heaved himself up into her lap.

For a long moment, the only sound in the kitchen was a steady purr. Ellsworth knew Elizabeth was right. He should get the motel's number from her and call his father right now. Ten minutes ago that's what he'd wanted, but now he just wanted to be alone. Because she was right about that, too. It was all too much. "Jess brought my stuff over," he said finally. "Maybe I should go unpack or something. And is there a shower I could use? Upstairs there's just that tub."

"Yes, the shower's down here, under the stairs. And of course you can use it. That sounds like a good idea,

Ellsworth. Get cooled off and settled in, and I'll start some supper. And please don't worry too much. I have great faith in you, great faith that things will work out. Way will open. It always does."

"Way will open," said Ellsworth. The cats jumped off him and he stood up. "That was on the door, upstairs. What does it mean, anyway?"

Elizabeth blinked, thinking, and then nodded. "Yes, that's the one in the guest room, isn't it? My friend who made them, those little signs, had a wonderful time putting them around the house in what she called 'telling' places. My favorite one is next to a big ceiling crack in the front hall, except you need to stand on a chair to see it. My very own 'weighty Quakers' *I* call them, which is a very silly joke.

"But 'way will open'? I always envisioned that as . . . fumbling, in the dark, against a high wall covered with, oh, I don't know, thorns and prickles and maybe ugly bugs that bite. No way through except, suddenly, because you've kept fumbling, kept trusting, your hand touches a knob, and you turn it, and then, well, then, a door opens, doesn't it? Into light, of course. Light, and lots of other good things, most of which you didn't expect. Make any sense?" She peered up into his face and smiled. "Well, maybe not now. Someday maybe. But do go and unpack. I'll be here if you need anything. And we'll have some supper about five. Nothing fancy, but I'll try not to let you starve."

It was hot upstairs. Only two of his four windows were open, and Ellsworth soon figured out why—the two on the north side stuck. He wondered if Elizabeth had any

WD-40. Probably not. He shoved at them for a few minutes and then gave up. Rubbing his reddened hands, he looked out and then down into the yard of the house next door.

It wasn't just one of the houses now. It was R.C.'s house. His grandfather's. You didn't have to look very hard to see where Elizabeth's yard stopped and his began. Partly because of a hedge; partly the way it looked. Ellsworth could see the outline of two round flower beds, a bird feeder standing in one of them, a birdbath in the other, but the feeder was empty and the bath was dry and the beds had nothing in them but dead leaves and weeds. As he stood there staring, it suddenly came to Ellsworth that his father had lived there. There, right there, he'd been a kid just the age Ellsworth was now. Maybe it had been his job to fill that feeder and pull those weeds and rake those leaves.

Something flickered in the upper window just opposite, but as quickly as Ellsworth looked, it was gone. He stood there another long beat, but nothing moved again. And if he went over there and knocked, he knew that nobody would answer.

Reaching into his pocket, he pulled out his father's little box and began to turn it over and over in his hand. He just had to face it. His grandfather didn't want to see him. But what if . . . What if he found that treasure? R.C. would maybe think he was worth seeing then. It was just like he'd said to Jess earlier. If they found the treasure, everybody would want to see them, and everybody would know they belonged.

So they would find it. They just would. Tomorrow.

13

The Treasure House

Ellsworth woke up the next morning to small paws patting his face. Tiger and Lily were sitting, one on each side of his pillow, purring loudly. "Hey, guys," he said, sliding up and scooping them into his lap. "How did you get in here, anyway?" One of them nudged his chin with her head, and as his eyes came up, too, he had his answer. His door was open, and sitting on the dresser, looking down at Hugo with great professional interest, was Hodge.

"Hey! No! Get out of here!" As Ellsworth scrambled out of bed, Hodge dipped one paw deliberately into the water, shook it in Ellsworth's direction, and then leaped heavily down to the floor. Tail high, he headed out the door. Ellsworth peered anxiously into the tank, where Hugo was swimming frantically but safely in circles, and then felt two tails flick against his bare feet as the little cats slid by him. They were leaving, too. Their job was done. He was up.

It was light outside, but dim, and the air coming in the windows was almost cool. Still, early though it was, he must have slept for a long time. The evening before, Elizabeth had fed him, and then they'd spent an hour or two on the back porch talking and watching the light fade over the Square. It had been nice just sitting there, telling her about himself and his dad and all the things they'd done the last few years.

But he still hadn't *talked* to his dad. When he'd dialed the Lake Breeze number after supper, he'd expected Ben Robert to answer—he should have been there, on the desk. But nobody had answered, not even the machine. The phone had just rung and rung. All evening it had just rung and rung. He'd have to try again today.

Now, digging through a drawer for socks, he remembered the last thought he'd had before he went to sleep. Flashlights. The house had shutters—it would be dark in there and they'd need some light. He felt a shiver that had nothing to do with the morning air. He was meeting Jess there this morning. Seven, she'd said. Seven. Maybe it wasn't so early now after all. Maybe it was already way past seven, and she'd gotten tired of waiting and left. Worse, maybe she'd got tired of waiting and . . . gone in.

When he slid down into the kitchen two minutes later, though, he saw it was okay. It was only 6:20. There was no sign of Elizabeth, but all three cats were lined up expectantly, Hodge looking like *his* patience, at least, was wearing very thin. Ellsworth finally found a sack of dry food in a cupboard. As he filled Hodge's bowl, he saw that TigerLily had made their way to the top of the fridge. They were nudging at something, and a second later, an empty margarine container clattered down. They stared at him intently, purring loudly. "Okay," he said, finally figuring it out. "You guys eat up there, right? Yeah, I can see why. Here you go."

Cats fed, he started rummaging through Elizabeth's drawers and finally found a flashlight under a pile of screwdrivers and a pack of not-too-long-expired batteries the next drawer down. Sticking the light into his pocket, he wolfed down a big hunk of corn bread and a banana and headed for the door.

The storm door that went with the screen was locked, and as he fiddled with it, he saw another one of Elizabeth's friend's signs taped to the back. WALK CHEERFULLY OVER THE WORLD, this one said, ANSWERING THAT OF GOD IN EVERY ONE. Okay. He wasn't so sure about the last part, but the first part sounded easy enough. At least this morning it did. He made his way quickly through both back doors and out onto the porch, but when he got to the steps "cheerfully" disappeared. What replaced it was the feeling, strong and urgent, of being watched.

But nobody was there. Nobody was there on the porch or on the Sward at the end of the walk, and when he glanced sharply up at the windows of the house next door, they showed only clear and blank in the early-morning light. Then something thunked. His gaze, swinging in the direction of the sound, was just too late. But he knew what he'd heard. It was the sound of a screen door shutting. Somebody had been watching him, all right. Somebody right next door.

In a minute he was off the porch and wading through the damp tangle of Elizabeth's flowers. He clawed his way through the overgrown hedge bordering R.C.'s yard, skirted the bird feeder and bath, and stood, finally, panting for breath, on R.C.'s walk. But he was too late again. Both doors were now firmly shut.

It just didn't make any sense. It looked like R.C. *did* want to see him. So why was he hiding? Ellsworth didn't know, and he didn't know what to do about it except keep on going. Prove himself. Find the treasure.

When he rounded the bushes at the end of the Sward, he saw he'd been right to hurry. Jess *was* already there. She was hunched down on the top step, her arms wrapped hard around her knees, and he got the bad feeling that she'd changed her mind again. He was right. The day was already beginning to warm up, but she was shivering, and the minute he was close enough, the words started spilling out as though she'd been rehearsing them over and over in her mind. "We can't go in there. I had another dream last night, and we can't go in."

"Look—" he started, but she forged right on.

"You don't get it, do you? My dreams sometimes *do* come true. I somehow make them come true. Like that cigarette. She swore she put it out. And the ashtray wasn't even on the arm of the chair. It was on the table beside her. So how . . . how did the cigarette light itself and then . . . jump down into the chair? *How?*"

"I don't know what you're talking about," said Ellsworth. And then he did. She was talking about her house that had burned.

"I hated that house," whispered Jess. "With him in it instead of my father. And then his sister coming, and she was awful, one of those people who thinks she's so good with kids, and you just want to throw up. Did you ever read *Carrie*?"

Ellsworth shook his head. He'd never read *Carrie,* but he knew what she meant. "Come on," he said. "You're telling me you did it? You lighted that cigarette in your head and then stuffed it into the chair and then . . . *whoosh*?"

Her eyes were huge as she stared at him. "Maybe," she whispered.

"No way," he said again. "Look, there's all kind of stuff I don't get. But moving things around with your head? Uh-uh. I mean, I don't even believe what you said yesterday. You know, that you could get into this place without a key."

She was silent for a long minute. When she spoke again she sounded calmer. "You're the one that said that, not me. Sure we need a key. I *have* one. It was what we did this year in technology, okay? We had this unit on locks, and Mr. Glenn showed us how a lot of them work and how some of them are just junk if you know what to do. Especially old locks because they're so simple, there's these skeleton keys that almost always work. So we each made a set and did a lot of practicing and stuff, except we had to sign this thing about how we'd never rob anybody with them or anything."

"Yeah?" said Ellsworth. "Really? I always wondered how—"

Jess wasn't finished. "So I probably could get in there, but I don't want to. I told you. It's dangerous in there. We could really get hurt."

Ellsworth couldn't believe it. She probably could get in there, she knew how important it was, and she didn't want to. He'd had enough.

"Okay," he said. "You don't want to go in there? That's okay with me. But I *am* going in there. I don't know how, but I am. Let me by, okay? Maybe that door's already open, even. Come on. Move over and let me by."

She shook her head. "Don't be mad. I can't help it if I get scared sometimes. I know you don't believe me, but my dreams do happen sometimes. They really *do*. So I have to be scared. I have to."

He didn't answer. She obviously wasn't going to let him up the steps. Well, so what? He'd go over the railing. He grabbed for it and pulled himself up onto the edge of the porch.

"You can't go alone," she said. "Don't you get it? You can't. If you go, I have to go, too."

"All I get is we're back where we started." He clambered over the railing onto the porch. He tried the door, but it didn't budge. There was no way around it. The only person who could get that door open right now was Jess. "Listen," he said. "I've *got* to get in there. I've got to start looking. Come on, okay?" No answer. He gave a big sigh. "Remember yesterday? What you said about showing them? And belonging? Well? So? This is the *way*."

She sat there, staring at the ground. Then, suddenly, she stood up, reached into her pocket, and pulled out a key chain. On it were three long keys with stubby ends, all different. "Okay," she said. "But you've got to do it. Not me. If you can, it means maybe we're meant to. If you can't, you've got to promise you won't try again. You've got to promise."

Ellsworth gazed at her helplessly. "That's crazy. I've never used one of those things before. And I can't promise that. Look. Forget it. I'm getting Dwight. I'll talk him into it. If he sees how important it is, he's *got* to help."

"Okay," she said. "But he's going to want to go in, too, right? So it won't be like you finding it. You know what I mean? He'll just be the boss, the boss of it all. . . ."

Ellsworth felt like somebody was driving nails into his head. She was right. He was trapped. He gave up. "Give them to me," he said.

"You promise?" she said.

He grabbed the keys out of her hand. "Yeah. Yeah. Okay. I promise."

They felt cold and clammy and dead, and his hand was sweating and shaking, and the first key wouldn't even go in, and when it finally did, nothing happened, nothing at all except maybe, just maybe, as he jiggled it, he could see what it was *trying* to do. It was trying to push down on the inside of the lock just right so that a little metal piece in there would move and let the catch slide back. It just wasn't the right shape. He rubbed his hands down his jeans and knelt so he could get closer and tried number two. It was kind of cross-shaped, it didn't look like a key at all, but he pushed it in and wiggled it, and then he could feel it almost catch, almost catch, almost catch, almost catch . . . And then it caught. He was sure it caught, but it wouldn't turn, he couldn't get it to turn, the lock was too old, it was too stiff, he couldn't do it. But he had to. He had to. He pushed with every bit of his strength, the metal biting into his fingers, and then, with a sudden *thunk,* the catch went back, and the door was open.

"I did it," he said, sagging back on his heels. He could hardly believe it. "I did it."

Jess nodded.

"Okay, then! We're going in?"

She nodded again. Then she reached down and put a hand on his arm. She didn't look frightened anymore, but her grip was so hard it hurt, and somehow now, she was scaring *him*. "What? *What?*"

"I'll go in. But you've got to promise me one more thing. You've got to promise me there won't be a fire."

Ellsworth took a deep breath, stood up, and said what he hoped was true. "No fire," he said, and pushed open the door.

⚁ 14 ⚁

Inside

It was scary how dark a place could be when it was daylight outside and how strange noises were when there was nothing to muffle them. The sigh of the door as it closed behind them was almost human. Ellsworth could hear his own breath and Jess's and every step they took as she followed him slowly into the room. He moved carefully, testing the wide planks as he went, but the floor felt as solid as though it had been laid yesterday instead of more than a hundred years before.

They were in. They were really in.

He'd turned the flashlight on and was circling it around the walls. In the other houses, the lived-in ones, this was the kitchen. Here it was only a shell, an empty shell that echoed with every move.

"What do you—" she started, but he held up a hand.

"Be quiet, okay?" he said. "I got to look. Maybe you should just wait here."

"Yeah, right," she said, but she was quiet. They moved slowly out into the hall. The light shone up, flickering from the dulled wainscoting to the high cobwebbed ceiling and back again. Her arm brushed his, and then jerked away.

Ellsworth tried to slow his breathing. He wasn't afraid, exactly. He didn't really think something was going to jump them or swallow them up. It was more like having antennae, all out and ready, or like *being* one, one of those big ones that sucks everything in. He could almost feel that something was here.

He made his way, step by careful step, down the hall, swinging his light up and around and down at the paneling, the heavy oak woodwork, the dull sheen of the mahogany banister guarding the stairs. The air was floating with dust, and Jess sneezed twice behind him and then blew her nose. "Sorry," she whispered. The dust didn't bother Ellsworth, but there was a smell under it that left a funny taste in his mouth. It was a dull, dry, dead kind of smell, as if things he didn't want to think about were lying in the walls.

He swung his flashlight up again, and light gleamed back, a reflective gleam of metal and glass. A chandelier. A chandelier here, too. In the first house, Ellsworth's house, it had meant diamonds. But here? No. The picture had always been the clue, and the one from this house, the one at Elizabeth's now, didn't fit. At least he didn't think it did. That picture wasn't about jewels or gold or anything like them. It showed the houses and the pond, and the family dancing. It felt . . . alive. Nothing had *ever* lived here.

He blinked, shivering, and then swung his light away from the chandelier, moving it up one side of the heavily carved front door frame. Then he held it steady, moving closer. "What's that?"

"I . . ." she said, and then stopped.

"Come on," he said. "Now I'm asking, okay? Can you see it?"

Now she pointed up into the flashlight's beam. "I think

it's an initial," she whispered. "See, right in the middle of all those viny things? It's an *R*. For Richard, maybe? Because it's his house?"

Ellsworth felt a sudden surge of energy. He swung his flashlight around. "Look, there's another one. Up there, on that arch into the front room. See?"

"An *E*. It's an *E*. An *E* for . . . for . . . Ellsworth? Maybe. You know, the first Ellsworth? So maybe all of them are here, all the kids' initials, and it means something. Something important. We've got to look!"

Ellsworth was already moving into the front room. "Look, sure. Look at that!" He was training his light onto the floor. It had been formed by small pieces of wood fitted carefully together into ever-smaller squares. Right in the center of all the squares was a circle. "Is it like that in all the houses?"

"I don't know," said Jess. "At Grandma's, the hall is wood, but all the rooms have rugs, and I don't know what's under. And I don't think I've ever been in this room at Elizabeth's."

"I guess I was yesterday," said Ellsworth. "For a minute. But I don't remember . . ."

"I don't like it," she said. She suddenly sounded nervous. "It looks like a . . . hole. Maybe these floors aren't safe."

"Come on," said Ellsworth. "It's wood. It's not a hole. And listen." He stomped hard on the floor, then again, sending up a drift of dust. "Solid, see." Still, he found himself stepping over the circle rather than on it as he started toward the next room. He looked back, lighting her up. "Are you coming?"

Jess was too busy sneezing to answer.

"Sorry," he said.

She glared at him. "I think you did that on purpose." Even wheezing, she sounded mad now instead of scared. "Okay, so it's not a hole. Okay, so you know everything. So why don't you just dig up this treasure now so we can get out of here."

"Digging was the second house," said Ellsworth. He was feeling more and more cheerful. The floors were solid and Jess was mad. Mad was lots better than spooked. "Thomas's house, not this one. Let's go, then. Okay. There's another letter, going into the library. A *U,* right? So who was *U*? I can't remember. But there's a circle in this floor, too." He played the flashlight up again. "And, see? You see there? That must be where the picture was."

Jess was right beside him now, and he saw her nod. On the west wall of the library, just like at Elizabeth's, was a fireplace. Here it was bricked up, and the surface of its mantel was a craze of tiny cracks. Over that was a shadowy emptiness, lighter, even after forty years, than the plaster around it. They both stared up at it for a long moment.

"Okay, listen," Jess said suddenly. "Listen. The picture, you know? The one that was here, that Elizabeth has now? It's of the pond, right? At least the center part of it is. So what's a pond? It's a hole, a big hole in the ground. And the way these floors look? Maybe they don't have holes, but that's how they look. So it's got to mean something. It's got to."

Ellsworth suddenly felt like he was doing one of his mechanical puzzles, where you have to let one piece go before another one slides free. He'd never known it worked with people, one person saying something that opened an idea in somebody else's brain. Holes. Holes in the floor, connecting to the picture. He wouldn't have gotten that himself. But now he got something else.

"Elizabeth said she fell. My grandmother, when she came in here with R.C. She went exploring and she fell because something moved. Maybe one of these circles *is* a real hole, not big enough to fall in, right, but just to trip on. And maybe at the bottom . . ." He crouched down and felt around the inlaid circle, trying to get it to move, looking for a catch. No. Nothing there. They went back into the front room and tried that circle, too, but the only thing they ended up with was dirty hands.

"The dining room, maybe?" said Jess. "And maybe there was one in the kitchen, too, and we just didn't see it."

They trudged back into the hall, but just as they got to the stairs Ellsworth saw something that made him forget all about holes. His light, shining down now, caught on a large metal plate that almost completely covered the tread of the bottom stair.

"What's that?" he said. He trained his light closer. "It's got writing on it. Lots of writing."

"What does it say?"

"I don't know. It's all fancy; I never can read stuff like that."

"Give me that thing for a minute," said Jess. "No. See? It's just the first letters that are fancy. The rest is okay." She crouched down and wiped the plaque with her free hand. "Okay. Look. 'These stairs.' That's how it starts. Yeah.

'These stairs are . . . are . . . not to climb alone.' " She stopped, studied the words for a minute, and then started reading again, nodding to herself as she went.

" 'Two by two, hand in hand, helping each other, supporting each other: that is the way to the top. There, all together, you will find my last; you will find my best. You will find the greatest treasure of my heart.' " She stood back up and let out a big breath. "Wow."

"Yeah," said Ellsworth. "Yeah, but why did he put it there? What's he really saying, you know?" He bent down and traced the first words with his finger. " 'These stairs are not to climb alone.' So what if . . . what if that's what she did? My grandmother. She tried to climb them alone and she fell?"

Jess shivered. "So there's something wrong with them. That's what I was afraid of. Leave them be."

But Ellsworth had already taken the flashlight back and was squatting down for a closer look. He felt along the tread, pushing at it bit by bit. The metal just felt like metal. The wood just felt like wood. But then, at the far right, he felt something give. His heart starting to beat faster, he pushed harder, as hard as he could, and the whole side of the stair sank down two inches. And when it did, the other side swung up, releasing a fat puff of dust.

"Whoaaaa," he said. "Look at that!" Jess, though, was too busy sneezing, so he tried it again, and the exact same thing happened in reverse, one side going down, the other up. "See? It's like a seesaw." He was lying full out on the floor now so that he could peer in under the tread. "Right? There's got to be fulcrum or something there, right in the middle. Yeah, look at this. . . . Whoaaa . . ."

"Stop it!" Jess was backing away. She had started to wheeze. "It's awful. Why did he do it, to make people fall? It's crazy."

Ellsworth scrambled back to his feet. "No. No, look. He didn't mean anybody to fall. I mean, it only goes up and down a little. Besides, that's why he wrote this and put it here. You know, to warn people. My grandmother, I don't know why, she just didn't see it or read it or something. I don't know what happened, but that's not what he wanted. He just wanted them to go up together. See, if two people go up at the same time, the stair won't move. Right? Like I said, it's a seesaw. You have somebody on each side, it all stays level. I want to try it. Come on."

Jess scrubbed at her face with her hands. "No way. I hate seesaws. When I was little, this big kid got me way up high, and then jumped off. . . ."

"I won't jump off," said Ellsworth. "Look, I'll stand here, like this. You stand there. I'll count, and on 'three' we'll both step up at the same time. You can hold on to the banister, even, okay?" He shone his light so he could see her face. Her eyes were huge, and she was chewing at her bottom lip.

"So?" she said finally. "What will you do if I don't? As if I had to ask. You'll go up alone, won't you?"

"I've got to. Come on, you know I do. The treasure's up there. That's what he says, right here. His last and his best is up there. I've got to go see what it is."

She took a big breath and let it back out. Then, very slowly, she came and stood beside him at the bottom of the stairs.

15

The Crack

Ellsworth let out his own breath. "Okay," he said. "Okay, then, you ready?" He could feel rather than see her nod. But that was all right. Things were easier when she wasn't talking. "Yeah, you better take the banister, just in case. Ready? One. Two. Three!"

They stepped up. The stair, for one scary second, rocked under their feet. Immediately and instinctively they shifted their weight for balance, and the stair stilled. Ellsworth found himself grinning, and flicking his light over, he saw that Jess, if not smiling, at least wasn't freaking out. "Yeah?" he said. She nodded.

"One. Two. Three." They took another careful step, and then another. Feeling more confident now, Ellsworth played his flashlight up to the landing, but they still weren't high enough to see anything but a kind of dusty dim light, as though a shutter had worked itself open. "Let's go, then. One. Two. Three."

This step was different. Ellsworth gave a grunt of surprise and heard Jess's sharp wheeze. They looked at each other, and each gave a tentative stomp. Ellsworth grinned again. This stair wasn't a seesaw. It was nailed solidly all the way across. So was the next one, and the next.

"So it was just the first three," said Ellsworth. "Once you get past those . . ."

"You don't *know*," said Jess. "Be careful." They were careful, but step after new step, the stairs felt as solid as the trees they'd come from.

It wasn't until they were almost at the top that Ellsworth looked up again. He squinted. This couldn't be right.

"What?" said Jess. "*What?*" Then she saw, too. "Oh!"

What should have been a second floor with rooms and a hall was nothing but a huge empty space. It soared up and up, all the way to the rafters, and its dim light came not from its big windows, still tightly shuttered, but from the small "attic" windows up under the roof. The air, imprisoned so long, was dry and hot and full of dust, but the space itself felt open and unhampered, free to be anything at all.

"Look at it," breathed Jess. "What's it for, like this? It's so big."

Ellsworth was already directing his flashlight beam carefully over the floor. "Yeah, but the floor looks just like the ones downstairs. Except, maybe—look, the pattern in the middle. It's bigger, see? A lot bigger. And there's something funny about the color. I need to—"

"No!" said Jess, but she was too late. He had stepped out onto the floor. He had taken three quick steps, actually, before it hit him. Downstairs, the only sound had been their breathing, their footsteps, their few whispered words. But up here . . . It was like the *floor* was breathing. It was sighing, and groaning, and creaking; strained, it was clear, to the limit. Ellsworth froze. "I'm going to go through, aren't I? I'm going to go through!"

"Yes! There's a crack! There's a *crack!*" The flashlight

swung wildly as Ellsworth leaped for his life. He landed precariously on the next-to-the-top step, bracing himself against the wall to keep from falling. His heart was beating wildly. If the floor collapsed, then the staircase would, too. He grabbed for Jess's hand.

"Come on! Come *on!*" They clattered down as fast as they could go, and when they reached the seesaw stairs, jumped from one to the next in perfect synchronization, as though it was a trick they'd been practicing for years. Then they half stumbled half ran until they reached the back door and the perfect, wonderful safety of the porch. They threw themselves down on the top step and breathed in, out, deeply, over and over again. Nothing had ever felt, smelled, tasted better to Ellsworth than the fresh soft early-morning air of the Square.

Slowly, he caught his breath and his head began to clear. Beside him, Jess was wheezing steadily, and he realized that he was still holding her hand. He shook free, slid down the rest of the steps, and stood up.

Logical. Think. Okay. What had happened? They'd figured out John Matthew's stairs. They'd climbed them. Yeah. And they weren't dead. Yeah, that was good. And they'd seen some stuff. They'd seen letters that might be initials and holes that weren't holes and a plaque with writing and a big weird space where John Matthew had maybe left a treasure. But mainly what they'd found was that if he *had* hidden something, they'd never be able to get it. The floor up there was rotten.

But was it? If it was rotten, wouldn't it have felt more . . . soggy? And what was there about the way it sounded that rang a familiar bell in his head? Ellsworth didn't know. He couldn't remember.

He turned and saw that Jess was finally breathing almost normally. She was also frowning. "What's that?" she said. "I just noticed it. What's that smell?"

He shook his head. "I don't smell anything."

"Something's burning," she said. "It smells like . . . it smells like a . . . cigarette." Her eyes narrowed, and then she pointed down at the sidewalk near his feet. "Look! You're practically standing right on it. Put it out!"

"Calm down," said Ellsworth. "It can't burn anything here." He took a step, though, and ground the cigarette out. He stared down at it, thinking. "Which one of them smokes, you know?"

She shuddered. "Dwight. Didn't you notice his fingers, how yellow they are? It's disgusting. But I think there's somebody else, too, because sometimes when I get up early for a run I'll see a couple of these stupid butts, still burning, just like this one. Dwight usually goes out later."

Could it be R.C.? Did he come out early every morning and walk around the Square? And today, had he followed him here to Richard's house? But why should he? If R.C. really wanted to see him, all he had to do was knock on Elizabeth's door.

But Ellsworth didn't want to think about R.C. right now. Right now the floor was more important. Maybe he should go see John. John was the wood guy, Dwight had said, so he might have some ideas. It might be good to take his dad's little box, to show him, and he could check in with Elizabeth at the same time. And try his dad again?

Probably. But it was funny. Much as he wanted to talk to Ben Robert, the Lake Breeze was beginning to feel very far away.

"Ellsworth? Wake up. Listen, I've got to go. Grandma will go nuts if I'm not there for breakfast. Not that I want anything to eat. I feel so weird, you know? It felt so funny in there. Like he really did leave something."

"Yeah, I guess," he said. "But how are we going to get it? You want to go see John, later? My dad said maybe he'll help, and he knows about wood and stuff like that. Maybe we could check out *his* floors, too. I want to see if that hole thing is anyplace else."

"I guess," she said. "Okay. Come get me. I'll just be cooking again. Today it's pies, Grandma says."

"Yeah?" said Ellsworth. "What kind?"

For the very first time, she grinned. It completely changed her face. It made her look like a little kid who'd just learned a joke she couldn't wait to tell. "Burned, probably. I never made a pie before."

She jogged off. Ellsworth turned the other way, his spirits lighter. She really wasn't so bad, sometimes. He decided to keep going on the south walk—he hadn't been that way before. The two big pine trees were to his right, and walking by them he saw that their trunks were so big around that he probably couldn't circle them with his arms. They went up and up and up, straight as arrows aimed at the sky. But they were dead, totally dead, as dead as trees could be and still stand, and the ground around them was a litter of branches and needles and long skinny cones.

The view to the left wasn't so hot, either. It was Thomas's house, the second treasure house, and it looked like after they'd found what John Matthew had hidden, they'd just plain given it up. Lots of the roof tiles were gone, and some of the bricks had loosened and fallen out, and two of the upper shutters were hanging by one hinge. And the porch steps were gone. Completely gone. It was a good thing, too, because the porch looked bad. It looked skewed and shaky. It looked, almost, like if you grabbed it in just the right place and yanked, it might collapse and then keep going, bringing the whole house tumbling down into a pile of dust.

16

Looking Back: 1932 and the Second Treasure

It is 1932 and the whole world is tumbling down. At least that's the way it feels to the Smiths and millions of their neighbors. The Depression, which arrived when the stock boom busted three years ago, shows no sign of going away. It's settled in comfortably and settled in hard.

Only two members of the original Smith family are still alive on the Square. Ionia, the "middle child," is seventy-nine now, still walks three miles every morning, still plays two Beethoven piano sonatas every afternoon, and has just put up her 1,249th jar of chili sauce, as well as her annual quota of canned peaches, pears, and every single vegetable known to the Western world. Ionia never married, but has, on her plump lap, dandled every Smith child born during the last sixty-five years. She's not planning on any of them going hungry.

Henry is glad of it. Henry, the "baby" of his family, is seventy-three and still likes to eat. He lives at Number Three West with his son, Rob, Rob's wife, Maud, and their two sons, Duncan, thirteen, and Bobby, ten. Duncan is a nice normal baseball-loving kid. Everybody likes Duncan. Bobby is the original kid from hell.

Well, that's not exactly fair. Bobby isn't bad. He's just . . . curious. Bobby is curious about everything, especially everything to do with Great-Grandpa John Matthew's treasures. He's always figured if there's three, there's probably more. Who knows what they might be? Who knows where? Almost as soon as he could walk, he's been rummaging through every attic, every cellar, and every other room in every house on the Square he can talk himself into. He's come up with lots of stuff *he* sure calls treasure, including a complete skunk family, stuffed, a real bayonet from the Great War, and a batch of pictures so dirty they make his eyes pop. Duncan's, too. They earn him two dollars on the open market, good money in 1932. But *real* treasure—well, that's still waiting.

That's why, when the word finally came down to open Number Three South, you would have guessed that Bobby was going to be right on the doorstep, ready to go. But you'd have been wrong. When the shutters of Number Three were fastened back that bright October day and the door ceremoniously opened, Bobby wasn't there. Both Bobby and Duncan were in bed, sick as dogs with chicken pox.

Truthfully, it probably hadn't occurred to the two Smiths who were there to invite him. Don't get the wrong idea. Charles (Samuel's son) and George, *his* son, maybe weren't the boys' favorite cousins, but they were family to be proud of. Charles was principal of Smiths Mills's high school, and at sixteen, George was the president of the student council and vice-president of the debating club. They were intelligent and responsible, and you could trust them with your lives and not regret it. It wasn't their fault that logic and treasure hardly ever go together.

They both knew immediately what they had to do first. They had to find the picture. Well, that was easy enough. They saw it the minute they came through the "kitchen" door. It was hanging right over where the stove would have been if there'd been one.

They looked at it for a long time. Then Charles cleared his throat. "Well, no mystery here, is there, son? Kind of what I thought all along."

"Sure, Dad," said George. "That's right. Me, too."

Charles chuckled. "But Grandma always had to make it fancy, didn't she? Just look at the leaves on that tree."

"Yeah, Dad, they're something," said George. "They're really something."

The whole tree was something. It was a big tree, a huge tree, an enormous tree. It was a *whole* tree, too, because half the picture showed it above the ground, against a blue, blue sky, and half showed it below, down in black, black dirt. But what drew the eye were those leaves. They were made of gold. Gold leaf, they found out later, which was a good joke, if you think about it.

"I always knew this treasure would be gold," said Charles. "So you're probably thinking, well, then, where is it? Well, George, those boys were twins. The chandelier in the first house had diamonds that looked like glass, didn't it? Well, I'll bet you anything that the one here will have gold that looks like brass. Why, it even rhymes, George, it even rhymes!"

"That's great, Dad. That's really great. But, Dad? Isn't there something wrong with those roots? Those tree roots? The way they're growing down so far? See, right down through all those layers of funny-looking rock under the dirt? That can't be right."

Charles laughed. "Grandma Betsy was a sweet lady, son, but

she sure didn't know much about science. Not about art, either. But no matter. Her picture did its job, and that's art enough for me. We'll just get that chandelier down, and then we'll have it."

They got the chandelier down, but, of course, they didn't have it at all. The brass, it turned out, was just brass and the glass, glass. It was a great rhyme and a beautiful chandelier, but treasure it wasn't. They searched the house high and low but didn't find anything else that looked like treasure either. Certainly nothing that looked like gold. . . .

They went back and had another look at the picture.

"What do you think, George? What do you think?"

"Well, Dad," said George. "It just came to me that this looks a lot like that big oak on the Sward. You know that one up at the north end, with the big gold leaves? And the picture here isn't just the tree. It's the underground part, too—roots and dirt and rocks. Do you think maybe Great-Grandpa buried the treasure under that tree?"

"George," said Charles. "You're a genius."

A lot of other family thought so, too. Much digging was done over the next few days. But except for a huge trench that had to be refilled and too many tree roots that never recovered, all that digging had no effect at all. Charles and George finally just had to give up. They brought the picture out of Number Three South, locked the house up, and went back to school, where they belonged.

Nobody else had much interest in trying their luck. If Charles and George couldn't do it, who could? Everybody just tightened their belts a little and opened another jar of Aunt Ionia's beets. All except Henry. Henry was tired of beets. And he'd been waiting his whole life to see what his father had squirreled away in that second house. He would have demanded a go at it if his gout hadn't just flared up again. Plaguey illness. All he could do was sit. So he sat and looked at the picture. Nobody else had wanted it, so it was hanging in his room.

A few days later, though, Maud finally let Duncan and Bobby out of bed. Duncan, a little scaly but his pitching arm intact, headed right for the ball field. Bobby's objective was much closer. Without so much as a knock, he barreled into Henry's room, right across the landing from his own.

"Where is it, Granddad? Where's the picture? Oh, boy, look at that. Are those leaves really gold? Those rocks are really neat, aren't they? All those different colors . . . Can rocks really be red, Granddad?"

Henry was rocking. "Some of them can, Bobbo. Some of them."

"There's blue ones, too, and green ones and lots and lots of black ones, and it looks like those roots are just sucking them up. See? You got to look close, but they're colored, too."

Henry looked close and stopped rocking.

"Oh, man, if I'd been digging I would have found something. Crummy old chicken pox! I know I would have, and now Mom says they've filled it all in. . . ."

"Doesn't matter, Bobbo. The treasure was never under that tree. Why do they all think my father built those houses, if he wasn't going to use them? No, don't worry, son. That treasure's still there, right where it was planted, and I think maybe you've given me an idea about where it might be. Call your ma for me, would you? I think you and me and Dunc need to mount an expedition."

Henry had to make a little fuss to get the house reopened, but he did. "Now, Maud," he said. "I want you to let those boys wheel me over there. Just for an hour, broad daylight, I won't let them come to any harm. I'm not going to fill their heads with crazy ideas. I just want them to have a look."

While they looked he waited for them out on the walk. He waited for a long, long time. He was almost ready to wheel off for help when Duncan finally came out the back door. "Dunc? Where's Bobby? You find anything?"

"Nothing, except some coal in the cellar."

"Of course," said Henry. "Of course. But which one? Which cellar?"

"Well, that's what's dumb, Granddad. If there's going to be coal, it should be in the coal cellar, in front, shouldn't it, where the delivery truck comes? But it's not. It's in the one under the kitchen. The root cellar. I say, so what? But Bobby says I have to go get shovels. He says we have to dig."

"Go on, then, Dunc. Get them! Get those shovels! And hurry!"

So Duncan got shovels, and while Henry cursed his gout and his immobility, the boys started to dig. The floor was packed dirt and tough going, but luckily they didn't have to dig long. Or far. Only a few inches down they hit a chain, a rusting iron chain that snaked around almost the whole cellar. At the end of it, down a few more inches, was a box. They dragged it out of the dirt, up the stairs, and plunked it chain and all in Henry's lap.

It was a small iron box lined with tin. At his first glance inside, Bobby scowled. It didn't look like treasure to him. It was just a pile of paper covered with seals and stamps. And a letter.

He needn't have worried. The papers were the deed to a small corner of western Pennsylvania, and the letter was from John Matthew explaining what it was. It was land that in an assay had been found to be some of the richest south of the Great Lakes. Gold? Forget gold. Think what can *become* gold, or as good as. Think iron, coal, limestone: minerals that in John Matthew's lifetime had become the most important in the world because of what you could make of them. Because what you could make of them was steel.

17

Matthew

Ellsworth wasn't thinking about any kind of treasure as he leaped up the three steps to Elizabeth's porch. All he was thinking about was food. Her back door was ajar, and as he pushed open the screen, he saw that she was sitting at the table, her bad leg on a chair. She wasn't alone. A man was standing at the stove, stirring something that smelled like breakfast. He turned and jerked his chin up in greeting.

"Ellsworth? We finally meet. I'm Matthew. If I shake your hand now, though, I'll burn these eggs. Plenty for all of us, so rustle up a plate if you want some."

"Uh, sure. Thanks. Hi. I just got up early and thought I'd have a . . . a look around."

Elizabeth smiled. "A good idea, before it gets too hot. Thanks for feeding the cats. They actually let me sleep a lovely half hour longer. All in all, I'm feeling very pampered this morning, I must say."

"I come over to meet you, and Liz puts me right to work," said Matthew. "Though she probably won't do it again after she tastes these eggs. . . . So what do you think? About the Square? It's beginning to feel real, isn't it? That's why I haul my students off to museums and battlegrounds every chance I get. *Places* are what make history live. Things. You walk a battlefield, you touch an old uniform with a bullet hole in it—*that's* when you know there was a real battle where real people got killed."

Ellsworth remembered yesterday, when he'd seen the Square for the first time. It *hadn't* felt real before. And he'd gotten a lot of things wrong, too. "Yeah. It's not like you think it'll be," he said, pulling up a chair. "Like those treasure houses, right? The way they look?"

Matthew rapidly chewed down a piece of toast "No, they don't look like much, do they? But when you think that John Matthew, that canny old Quaker, had the imagination to build them, to set the whole incredible scheme up—well, it just blows you away. How many people get a family history like this just handed to them on a plate? I was adopted, you know, so I'm doubly lucky—I was *chosen* to be part of all this. And, of course, we're still in the thick of it. There's something in that last house, I'm sure of it. And you know what, Ellsworth? We're going to find it."

Ellsworth's third bite of eggs went down the wrong throat.

"Honestly, Matthew," said Elizabeth. "Slow down. Are you all right, Ellsworth? Here, have some juice. Are you okay?"

"I guess," he croaked, finally. Matthew sure didn't waste any time. He was a lot older than Ben Robert, but he was solid and muscular in a way Ben Robert had never been, and his energy was like a force field. If you didn't get out of its way it could knock you down.

"Yep, we're definitely going to find it," Matthew repeated. He leaned closer. "I just need to do a little more research. I just need the answers to a few more questions.

The main one is why? *Why* did John Matthew build those last three houses and plant treasures in them? Sure, I know, Liz, you keep telling me: to provide for the family. But to go to such extremes? Why?"

"Is it so important, to know that?" said Elizabeth.

"Important?" Matthew had forgotten his eggs entirely. "You can't write good history without the 'why'! It tells you how your man's mind works. In this case, it's critical. How can we even begin to discover what John Matthew left us and how he left it if we don't know what he was thinking? And don't say 'the picture.' All that picture tells me is that there's something important, big time, about that pond. But does that tell me to go dig it up? I don't think so. Not after what happened with that oak tree in '32. Nope. So I'm stumped." His face went blank for a second and then lit up happily. "Yep," he said, "beleaf me, I'm stumped. I feel like such a sap, too, not knowing how to get to the root of things. Woodn't you know . . ."

Elizabeth was groaning. "He's terrible, Ellsworth. Terrible. He goes on like this all the time. Of course, I could tell him to branch out, and then maybe he'd twig to what's happening, but I don't want to encourage him. What do you say, Ellsworth?"

They both looked at him hopefully, but he shook his head. This was Ben Robert's kind of thing, not his, and suddenly, like yesterday, he felt a huge wave of longing for his father.

"I don't know," he said. "Listen, I think maybe I'll try my dad again, okay?" He shoved back his chair.

"Now there's a man I'd like to meet," said Matthew. "Liz

here says he knows pretty much all there is to know about the family—I'll bet he could answer every question I've got. You mind asking if I could call him sometime, get his take on John Matthew and that house? What do you think? Would he talk to me?"

"I don't know," said Ellsworth. "But I'll ask him."

"Say hello to him for me," said Elizabeth. "Give him my love."

But he couldn't do either. This time, at least, the machine picked up after a few rings, but he didn't want the machine. He wanted Ben Robert. He tried again, just in case, but after listening the second time to Mr. Rocco's impatient recorded voice, he finally blurted out a message. "Uh, Mr. Rocco? This is Ellsworth. Thanks for the thermos; Hugo did okay. Uh, could you ask my dad to call me today, as soon as he wakes up? Thanks."

What now? Maybe he should go back and tell Matthew and Elizabeth what he and Jess had found. If he did, though, Matthew would take over. He was a nice-enough guy, but he was a teacher—he just couldn't help it. Ellsworth wandered over to the picture and stared up. Funny. Yesterday, he'd hardly noticed the houses. But today they stood out just as clearly as the pond or the family dancing around it. They stood . . . behind everything.

He had to go find John.

He ran up the front stairs, grabbed Ben Robert's little wood box, and then hesitated. Front door or back? Front would be easier. No talk, no explanations . . . Yeah, well . . . With a sigh, he headed down the back stairs and into the kitchen.

Elizabeth was still at the table, but Matthew was gone, and it wasn't until he spoke that she noticed he was there. "Is it okay if I go see John?" he said. "I kind of met him yesterday, and I need to ask him something."

"Oh," said Elizabeth. "It's you, Ellsworth. What? Yes, of course, John. I was going to ask John something myself, wasn't I? Oh, yes, I remember. Could you see if he could give me a ride to Meeting tomorrow? My knee . . . Well, as you can see, my knee's still not in much shape for driving."

Her knee, still propped up on its chair, did look kind of puffy. And then he noticed that there was something wrong with her face, too. Something blotchy. "Uh, you need some water or something?"

She blew her nose. "What? No, no . . . But thank you. I'm fine. Matthew and I just had a bit of a . . . discussion, that's all. Part of an ongoing discussion, I'm afraid, but nothing to worry about, nothing to do with you. Just something we're trying to work out. No, you go talk to John. Some people think he's standoffish, but he's just shy. He'll be very glad to see you."

18

John Matthew's Box

It wasn't until he was nearly to John's house at the north end of the Square that Ellsworth remembered Jess. He'd told her he'd come and get her. But she was making pies or something. So he'd have to wait, and he didn't want to wait. He wanted to see John right now.

The little white dog was as friendly as ever. What had John called him yesterday? Woolman? He *was* kind of a woolly little guy, with perky ears and a stub of a tail that wagged like crazy as he led Ellsworth up the walk. There was no sound of carpentry coming from the shed, so Ellsworth walked up the steps onto the back porch and knocked.

John had to stoop to look out through his screen. He looked kind of scarecrowlike, loose and weathered, and what face you could see around his close white beard was lined and craggy. "Well, now," he said, looking down at Ellsworth. He pushed open the door. "Well, now, I saw you yesterday, didn't I? You must be Ellsworth. Come in."

His kitchen wasn't anything like Elizabeth's. Kitty's, either, at least not from the fast look Ellsworth had had at it yesterday. A big wooden table with two straight chairs sat squarely against one wall. An old gas range took up most of another, and on the third, a squat fridge with rounded shoulders sat next to a shallow sink. Over the few narrow countertops, white cabinets soared to the ceiling. The floor was wood. It was all about as empty and simple and clean as a kitchen could be.

John saw him looking. "Hasn't changed all that much since the thirties," he said. "A new fridge and stove some years back, but everything else is pretty much the same as when Ionia lived here. She and Emily both. Emily died of that flu after the first war. Don't know why Ionia didn't catch it, too, but she was a tough old girl, Ionia. I remember her pretty well. We didn't move in here until she died in '37, when I was nine, but before that she'd grab me whenever she could and put me to work. I dug a lot of dandelions for Ionia." He stopped and blinked and shook his head. "Sorry," he said. "Talking your ear off, aren't I? Guess I'm just putting off what I wanted to say. About Ben Robert. I was real relieved to hear he was okay. And I was always . . . real sorry about your mom."

Ellsworth nodded awkwardly and then opened his hand to show what he'd been clutching. "Dad sent this with me. He made it here, didn't he? I mean, you helped him?"

A slow smile spread over John's face. "Well, look at that. Ben Robert kept it, did he? Isn't that something? He was crazy to make a box like one of John Matthew's, and he worked like a dog on this little thing, and just look at it. It was hard enough for him to open one of those boxes, let alone make one."

"What boxes?" said Ellsworth.

"You never saw one? Well, no, maybe not. I gave him one for his sixteenth birthday, but he brought it back to me just before he went away. He asked me to keep it for him, keep it safe. You can come see it if you want, if you don't mind a bit of a climb. I put the whole kit and caboodle of them up on the third floor some years back. Didn't like watching them collect dust."

"The third floor," said Ellsworth. They were already moving down the hall and up the front stairs, and he was having to work to keep up. John's legs were long and he moved fast. "You mean the attic?"

"Well, part of it's attic," said John. He was on the landing now, pulling open a door. "But you have eleven kids, you need bedrooms. John Matthew put in four more when he rebuilt in '53. That's 1853, after the fire. So who's here now to use them all? One old man and a small white dog. Crazy, isn't it? Okay, here we are. All the little boys slept up here, with a nursemaid. Must have given her quite a time." He wiped his face with his sleeve. "Terrible heat up here, summers. Probably worse then, too, before the trees grew up. Now here, you'll be interested just like Ben Robert was, this room was Henry's. Henry, you know, your branch of the tree, your great-something grand-father. He shared with his twin, Tobias, but it was Henry who mainly put his mark on it. Look here, on the door. Probably got his backside warmed for that, don't you think?"

Ellsworth grinned. HENRY GEORGE SMITH I had been carved, deeply, into the wood with more *Henry*s, in every size and style, radiating out from it. He'd also included some dates and some attempts at animals that might have been horses or might have been dogs, and a house that was probably supposed to be this one.

"Not what you'd call art," said John. "But not bad lettering. Here now, though. Here's what I brought you to see."

Ellsworth turned. One whole wall of the small room had been fitted with shelves, and on the shelves, laid out evenly and precisely, were boxes. They were wooden boxes, every one different: some big, some small, some carved, some plain, some of dark wood, some so pale they shimmered in the dim light. What they shared was that they wanted to be touched. They almost cried out to be picked up and handled, to be turned over and over in hands, to have fingers sliding over them, working at them, opening them. Ellsworth started to reach out and then rubbed his palm hard down his jeans. He somehow didn't want to touch one with a sweaty hand.

"They all open different," said John. "Some easy, some so tricky it took me years to figure them out. Ben Robert's is on the hard side. Here it is now, right where he left it." He slid it off the shelf, a medium-size box made of small pieces of lighter and darker wood fitted together into patterns. He held it in his hands for a second and then bounced it gently up and down. "Huh," he said. "Wasn't like that when I gave it to him. He must have put something in. Well, that's what they're for, aren't they? Not too much point to an empty box."

Ellsworth was suddenly finding it hard to breathe. "Can I see it?"

"Well, now," said John. "Something *in* there kind of changes things. Might be something Ben Robert doesn't want anybody looking at. What do you think?"

"Well, he sent me this little box here," said Ellsworth. "And he told me to talk to you, that maybe you'd help. About the house . . ."

John peered down at him. "The house. Which house? You mean Number Two down there? What about it?"

"Well, you know. It's the last treasure house. And Dad thinks something's in there, and he said I could look, but he told me to ask you and Dwight . . ."

John had been shaking his head but now he stiffened. "Dwight. You talk to Dwight already, did you?"

"Just a little, yesterday. About the key. I thought I needed one, but . . ."

John's face was definitely harder now. So was his voice. "So Dwight's going to make you a key. What do you need from me, then?"

Ellsworth didn't know how he'd gotten into so much trouble so fast. "He's not. You, well, I thought . . . I mean, I need to know if it's safe. The house. The . . . floors. I mean, what if they creak, or something? Or . . . or bounce? Does that make them rotten? Dwight, he knows about clocks and keys and stuff. Not about wood."

John snorted. "You got that right." His face relaxed a little. "It's safe enough. I've had to let those other two houses go; they're bad, dangerous now, they should come down. But Richard's, well, I've kept it up, kept the roof solid, kept the water out. It takes a lot to kill an oak floor. Creaks, well, creaks aren't rot. You get creaks when you don't nail tight. But listen. You don't want to go in that house alone. I've got my reasons for knowing that, and I've got other ones for not telling. I made a promise to keep my mouth shut sixty years ago, and I'm not about to break it now, no matter what people at the other end of this Square might do."

He swabbed again at his face. "But we better get down from here now before our brains fry." He looked at the box in his hands. "If Ben Robert sent you to me, he probably wouldn't mind my giving this to you. So here you go. But listen. I meant what I said. I'm not sure I like the idea of you going in that house, anyway. But if you do, take somebody with you."

They clattered down the two flights of stairs quickly, not saying anything more. "You be careful now," John said as he pulled open the back door. "You hear me? And if you talk to your dad, you tell him hello for me. I've missed him all these years."

"Thanks," said Ellsworth. "Thanks a lot." He felt John's eyes on his back as he headed down the walk, but by the time he turned to close the gate gently in Woolman's face, the doorway was empty. There was no question about what he wanted to do next. He swerved off the sidewalk and around a clump of bushes to the big stump he'd found the day before; it looked like a good shady place to sit down. There was something in the box, because he could feel it shift as he walked, and he had to find out what it was.

It had been made, as he'd noticed earlier, by a lot of different-colored woods set into carefully arranged patterns. The one on the lid looked familiar, and it only took him a minute to remember why. It was the same pattern he and Jess had seen that morning in two of the rooms in Richard's house. Now he walked his fingers across the series of squares, stopping just before he got to the perfect dark circle in the middle. Here it didn't look like a hole you might fall through. It looked like an eye, a dark and powerful eye to protect any secrets the box might hold.

If it was, it was definitely doing its job. There was no sign of a latch, and the box didn't open any way at all that Ellsworth could see. He turned it and turned it again, and then started systematically pushing at pieces of wood. Once, a tiny triangle sank slightly under his finger, and he thought he had it. He was wrong. He found another spongy place, and then another, four in all, one on each vertical surface. They, more or less, even formed a straight line. But no matter how he pushed at them—hard, soft, in every kind of rhythm he could think of—the box stayed stubbornly closed.

It was time to go find Jess.

19

The Cemetery

He didn't have to do much looking. She was sitting on Kitty's back steps, dressed in shorts and a tank top, lacing up a pair of the whitest running shoes Ellsworth had ever seen.

"Where have you been?" she said. "I kept thinking you'd come. Don't ever make a pie. That pastry stuff is like glue, and then you're supposed to roll it? And then pick it up and put it a pan? I don't think so. Grandma went to lie down. I'm going for a run."

"A run?" said Ellsworth. "But look, John gave me this, I need you to . . ."

Jess yanked her second shoe's laces into a bow and stood up. She was giving off energy like a Fourth of July sparkler. She began bouncing gently up and down.

"Yeah, a run. You know, running? I go because, well, I feel cooped up in here sometimes, and then Grandma keeps making me eat about fourteen times a day, so I need to. I jog around the Square to warm up, and then there's this little door in Grandma's gate to the street. I've been going to that cemetery."

As usual, Ellsworth had to struggle to catch up. "Which cemetery?"

She sighed. "Are you asleep or something? You know, that one a couple of streets over where they're all buried.

Grandma made me go there right after I came because I—well, I couldn't sleep. I kept having those dreams. I thought she was just being mean, but I kind of see now why she did it. It sounds weird, but it's kind of nice. You want to come?"

"You mean where John Matthew is buried?" Ellsworth massaged the smooth wood in his hands while he tried to think. If he went with her, maybe he could get her to sit down when they got there and help him. Besides, this was a John Matthew box, wasn't it? So maybe seeing John Matthew's . . . grave would help, too. What a dumb idea. Except what else was there to do? He wasn't having any luck on his own, that was for sure.

Jess was looking impatient. "Of course. It's where everybody's buried. Listen, I've got to get going. You coming, or what?"

"I guess," he said. "But we don't have to go around the Square first, do we? Or, listen. Doesn't anybody around here have a bike? We could get there a lot faster on bikes."

She looked at him like he'd grown a second head. "You really don't have a clue, do you? And what's that box you're carrying? Leave it here. We'll go around once. Just try and keep up, okay?"

Even before he'd reached the south end of the Square, Ellsworth knew he was in trouble. Jess was loping along like one of those *National Geographic* animals on the plains of Africa, but he was already panting, his side was killing him, and his sneakers kept . . . sneaking around in front of where he wanted to put his feet. He tripped and almost fell, and then tripped again.

Jess was running in place now, waiting for him to catch up. "You brought that thing! You are really lame, you know that? Come on." She grabbed his free hand and began to jog more slowly, tugging him along with her. Ellsworth found that if he concentrated hard on his feet coming down, he could just manage to keep going. And keep up. They moved past house after house, yard after yard, and he couldn't shake the feeling that everybody was watching. Watching and what? Probably laughing their heads off. He pulled his hand free, gritted his teeth, and managed, somehow, to pick up some speed.

Finally they passed Kitty's house again and, swerving, went through the little door in her gate. They crossed the street and thumped their way down one block, two, lined with small, shabby houses closed tightly against the glaring heat. A little boy, dressed only in a pair of grubby underpants and wheeling a tricycle around a pitted driveway, immediately stopped, got off, and started jumping up and down. "Hi!" he shouted. "Hi, hi, hi, hi, hi!"

"Hi!" Jess shouted back to him. "Hi!" She turned to Ellsworth. "He's always out there, all by himself, poor little kid. Listen, there's the cemetery. They're all in the middle, John Matthew and all those guys, in front of those big pine trees, okay? I'll meet you there in a few minutes. I mean, we've hardly been moving. I've got to *run*." She didn't wait for an answer but took off flying.

Ellsworth immediately came to a stop. He was dripping with sweat. His legs were fifty pounds heavier, he hurt all over, and everything inside him was beating like a drum. He leaned over, trying to catch his breath. Who'd invented this running stuff, anyway? It was crazy. His breath finally slowing, he took a firmer grip on the box and plodded his way through the gate.

He'd always thought of cemeteries as quiet places, but this one was noisy with birds and squirrels, and the headstones glittered and winked at him as he wound his way through them. The pine trees, when he finally reached them, were towering over a wide pie-shaped expanse of grass, and he looked around, puzzled. If this was where the Smiths were, then where were they? If they were such a big deal, shouldn't there be something fancy here, something tall, made out of marble? An angel, maybe? All he could see were two urns in front of a half circle of bushes, filled with flowers.

The urns, and something glinting in the grass in front of them. As he walked toward it, he stepped on something that wasn't grass at all. It was a flat polished gray stone lying flush with the ground, and when he crouched down for a better look, he saw a name and two dates had been cut deeply into it. IONIA ANNE SMITH: 1853–1937. Looking around, he saw another small stone, and then another. TOBIAS IAN SMITH. HENRY GEORGE SMITH. Henry. He'd found Henry. He put the box down on Henry and began searching for more.

A lot of the names were only vaguely familiar, wives and husbands and children of Smiths, small print on Ben Robert's family tree. What he wanted were the big-print names, and one by one he found them: ROBERT, ALICE, and SARAH; MATTHEW and SAMUEL; ULYSSES and EMILY. Just in front of the trees, he hit the jackpot. RICHARD lay between ELLSWORTH and THOMAS, and above them, flanked by the urns, were the most familiar names of all. JOHN MATTHEW SMITH: 1820–1881. ELIZABETH SULLIVAN SMITH: 1825–1902. As Ellsworth crouched there looking at them, an ant started its way down the long curved valley of the *J*. Ellsworth flicked it away and put his hand down on the stone. It was warm.

Behind him, gravel crunched, and he spun around on his toes, almost toppling onto his face. But it was only Jess. She was breathing heavily now, her face was red, and she looked bigger, somehow, and softer, as though everything in her had relaxed and expanded. Starting across the grass, she stopped, reached down, and picked up Ellsworth's box. "What is this, anyway?" she said. "What's inside?"

"I don't know," said Ellsworth. "It's a John Matthew box. I mean, he made it, but John had it, and he gave it to my dad. And then Dad put something in it, because it's heavy, right, and then left it with him when he went. I mean, it could be something really good, but I can't get the box open. I'm usually okay with stuff like that, puzzles and things, but I just can't figure out how it works."

"So if it's a John Matthew box," said Jess, "maybe he'll help. You know? Don't look at me like that. Come on, put it on his stone, right there in the middle. Yeah, like that." She crouched beside him and then stared fixedly down at the box, as though willing it to whir and click, pop open, and reveal its secret. It didn't. It didn't do anything at all.

"Look," said Ellsworth. "There's even four pieces you

can push, these little triangles, see? I can even push them all at the same time if I use both hands. But that doesn't do anything either."

"Wait a minute," said Jess. She was down on her stomach now, her face so close to the box that Ellsworth could feel her hot breath on his hands. "Keep pushing, okay? Don't stop. There's a tiny, tiny little crack there now, all the way around. I think . . . I think it just needs . . . one other thing pushed. One other thing going down." She put out her finger, and hesitating only a second, pushed it down hard into the middle of the staring round eye. Then she took a breath that was almost a gasp. "Now you have to lift up!" she said. "Lift up! Now!"

Ellsworth lifted, his fingers quivering with strain, and the lid of the box came with them.

⚜ 20 ⚜

The Journal

Nestled inside the box, almost filling it, was a book. After staring at it for a second, he put a hand on it and turned the box over. The book slipped out. Gingerly, he picked it up. The cover felt thick and dense, like leather. The spine was rough and almost crumbling, but the front and the back were still intact and were a crazy quilt of dark brown and light, smooth patches and grainy.

Pulling the book gently open to the first splotchy page, Ellsworth found a name, written in ink. The ink was faded, but the name, written large, in bold strokes, was clear and unmistakable. JOHN MATTHEW SMITH.

"What is it?" said Jess. "What's it about?"

Ellsworth riffled through the first few pages and then a few more. "It's a journal. John Matthew's," he said. "The first date is . . . I can hardly read it . . . but it looks like 1843." He looked down at John Matthew's stone. "Okay. If he was born in 1820, here he'd be . . . twenty-three. Twenty-three. That's not so old."

"Eighteen forty-three," said Jess. She was sitting up very straight, her eyes intent. "So? So what happened in 1843? Read it."

Ellsworth squinted down. "'I begin this . . . account of my life,'" he started haltingly, "'on the day it . . . truly . . .

truly . . .'" He stopped and shook his head. "No. It's like the writing on the stairs. I can't get it. You try."

Jess was chewing on her lower lip. "Are you sure? The stair stuff was different; people were supposed to see that. Maybe he wouldn't want us reading this." She put her hand on John Matthew's stone. "Maybe he wouldn't like it."

Ellsworth thought about it for a minute. "Yeah, but my dad read it. I think it's okay." He reached over and plunked the book into Jess's lap. "Come on, just try. Okay?"

Finally she nodded, and gently pulled it open to the first page. She stared down at it, and then lifted the book up, bringing it closer to her face. Her eyes narrowed in concentration. "Okay. I hope you're right. Here goes. 'I begin this account of my life on the day it truly . . . commences. Today, May thirtieth, my beloved Betsy Sullivan and I exchanged our vows before God and the Meeting. Today, we entered into life's long journey together. May God ble—'" She stopped, frowning. "I guess it's 'bless.' One of those *s*'s is funny, it has a long tail on it . . . Okay. 'May God bless us and keep us both.'" She stopped again. "Married. They just got married."

"Yeah, well . . ." said Ellsworth. "Okay. So this is . . . what? About the family?"

Jess was slowly turning pages, looking ahead. "I think so. There's some stuff about the mills and designing a house. But then, here, look . . . It's 1844, and he says: 'It is with the most profound joy and thanksgiving that I record that today, April fifteenth, my beloved Betsy, after great trav . . . travail, was safely delivered of two healthy sons. Twins. The first we shall name Ellsworth James after my dear father; the second, Thomas David after hers.'" She looked up at him. "Doesn't that make you feel funny? I mean, your name, right there, so long ago?" Then something else struck her. "Hey, they didn't waste much time, did they? I mean, they were only married at the end of May. How old was she, anyway?" She ran a finger over Betsy Sullivan's stone. "Born 1825. So in 1844, she would have been . . . nineteen? Nineteen. Only five years older than I am now."

But Ellsworth was still five sentences back. She was right. It did make him feel funny, hearing his name from so long ago. Twins. One Ellsworth, one Thomas. And you knew. You knew what was going to happen to them, just a few years down the road. A few pages ahead . . . Hardly knowing what he was doing, he stood up. "I changed my mind. I don't want to read it now. Give it back, okay? Let's go."

Jess stared up at him. "What? We just started. Come on."

He shook his head and held out his hand. "*You* come on. Give it to me. It's mine. I want to put it back in the box."

She clutched it to her. "No," she said. "We can't stop now. It's not fair. It's John Matthew's. It doesn't just belong to you. They're my family, too, you know. Just as much as yours. They're my family, too."

We're the Smith family, his father had always said. *You and me, Zee. Just you and me.*

What if he was wrong?

"Yeah," said Ellsworth finally. "I guess . . ." Then he took a deep breath and let it out. "It's just, it's just . . . that there's a fire. And they're going to . . . die. You know?"

Jess shivered, and her eyes scrunched shut. "I know," she whispered. Then, after a long moment, her head came slowly up, and she looked somberly into Ellsworth's face. "But maybe if we find out what really happened, you know, the way *he* tells it, then it won't feel so bad."

Ellsworth looked away and then nodded abruptly. "Yeah. Okay." He threw himself back down. "Okay."

The journal quickly proved that Betsy and John Matthew hadn't wasted any time at all. During the six years after the birth of their first two sons, four more births were recorded: Richard in 1845, Emily and Ulysses in 1847, and Samuel in 1850. Jess stopped for a minute here, and pushed the hair away from her face, thinking. "Boy," she said. "How many is that? Six? I mean, think of all those diapers. They didn't have Pampers then, right? Or dryers?"

"No electricity," agreed Ellsworth. He closed his eyes for a minute, trying to figure out how many clotheslines you could set up on the Sward. Lots. He could almost see them, the miles of white cloth flapping in the breeze. And little kids rolling everywhere . . . Nice . . . Then he swallowed. It wasn't going to stay nice for long.

He was right. "Eighteen fifty-two," Jess was reading again, and her voice was suddenly unsteady. Ellsworth closed his eyes harder. The story was short and terrible. One summer night in 1852, eight-year-old Thomas, disobeying yet again his father's stern warning about books and candles, had sneaked up into his attic hideout for a late-night read. He must have stayed too long and fallen asleep. And the candle, instead of guttering out as it no doubt had countless times before, this time hadn't. No one would ever know how that small flame had turned into a stream of fire raging down the attic stairs. Or how his brother Ellsworth, minutes after being dragged out, had torn himself loose from a nursemaid's grasp and fought his way back into the house.

"'How?'" Jess read in a quavering voice. "'I saw him safe outside with the others. Except . . . not all of the others. I think we realized it at the same moment, that bravest of little boys and I, that his twin was still inside. The look he gave me that night, as the flames threw their monstrous shadows over the lawn, will remain seared into my brain until I die. It leaped from fear to anger to terrible resolve in the space of a second, and then he was gone. And then, both of them . . . Gone. Gone. Gone.'"

Ellsworth couldn't see Jess because his eyes were still tightly shut. But he heard her. The first sound was as though somebody had wrenched it out of her throat. And then she began to cry.

Shocks

She cried and cried. Ellsworth had never heard anybody cry like that. He knew he should do something, but he didn't know what. The only thing he could think of was to go get somebody, but how could he just leave? Finally, just when he was desperate enough to do it anyway, Jess's sobs began to slow. A few minutes later they'd dwindled to choked sighs and then to sniffles, and then she dug a Kleenex out of her pocket and blew her nose long and hard. Then she keeled over flat on her back and sighed.

"I feel better."

"You do?" said Ellsworth. She looked terrible. Cautiously he reached out a hand, snagged the journal, and slid it back into the box. No way she was reading any more of *that*. Not today.

"Yeah," she said, and sat back up. "Because, I don't know . . . Because it wasn't *me*." Her eyes teared up again. "I mean, that sounds terrible. But that's what hit me. Those kids, they . . . they burned to death. . . . And the house burned, too, right down. And us, we were able to save a lot of stuff, and none of us even got hurt. So I feel terrible for them, but, then, I feel better, too. You know?"

"I'm not sure," said Ellsworth. But he did. Because he'd been thinking, too, while she was reading. He couldn't help it. Because it was Thomas that started the fire, and it was Ellsworth who tried to save him, and he was glad it wasn't the other way around. And another thing. His own brother? His own brother, Thomas, who couldn't seem to get born after Ellsworth was, and so their mother died? He'd never said it before, even to himself. But he was glad it was that way, that way instead of . . . him. That it wasn't him who made her . . .

"I miss my mom," Jess said suddenly. "Because that was another reason I was crying? I miss her. I mean, we fight a lot, and I don't get why she married this guy; he's so phony . . . But . . . she's okay. She calls me every week, she says she misses me, too. The thing is, see, I know she'd never dump me. She'd never just . . . leave. That's what I can't get about my dad. When I was little? We did all this stuff together. I thought, well, you know . . . I thought he . . . loved me."

This was almost worse than crying. Then he didn't know what to do. Now he didn't know what to say. "I don't know," he finally said. "Maybe he just feels . . . Listen. I just thought. My dad, you know? My grandmother, she just died? And he wouldn't come back. For her funeral, even though they all wanted him to. It was like he couldn't. It was just too much, because of all that stuff, I don't even know what it was, but all the stuff that happened when I was born and my mother . . . died."

"Yeah," she said. "Yeah, maybe." She sighed. "Where is she?"

Ellsworth frowned. "Who?"

"Your mom. Is she here? With everybody else?"

He shivered. He'd never thought about it. Was she?

"How come you're looking so funny?" said Jess. "Didn't you ever wonder? Didn't you ever ask? I'll bet she is. Don't you want to look? Don't you want to find her?"

"Yeah," said Ellsworth hoarsely. "I guess. But where would she be? I mean, my dad's not here, or anything."

"Well, where's your grandmother? Maybe she's with her. Your grandmother would be new, right? So that should be easy. All the first guys, they're here, in the middle. So she'd probably be somewhere on the edge. Listen, you go over that way. I'll look over here."

Ellsworth crawled slowly to his feet. He felt stiff, as though he was a hundred years old. Was she really here? His mother? He was sweating, but he felt cold, too, and for a minute he wondered if he was going to be sick. He looked over at Jess. She was hunched over, moving rapidly from one recessed stone to another.

"No," she was saying. "None of these is right." Then she stopped. "Grandma showed me this one. It's my grandpa—David Smith-MacLeod. He died when my mom was little, see? Nineteen seventy-two." She stood there, blinking, and then reached up and scrubbed at her eyes. "It still makes me feel funny, you know? That she didn't have a dad either . . ."

"Listen," said Ellsworth. "I don't know. This is weird."

Jess turned on him fiercely. "No, it's not. Don't you get it? It's part of *us*. It's who we *are*. How can you not want to know?"

"Okay," said Ellsworth. "Okay! So where is she? *Where is she,* if you know so much?" They stared at each other for a long minute, and then Jess nodded.

"Okay. I'm sorry. But it's important. Look. My grandpa is here near where Ulysses is. So yours probably are, too. I mean, where your grand-whatever is. Who is it? Which Smith kid did you come from?"

Ellsworth closed his eyes and saw the door in John's house covered with carving. "Henry," he said. "Henry George. And I saw him. He's back there."

"Come on, then," she said. "I'll help you."

It didn't take long. Like Jess had said, his grandmother's stone was new. ISABELLE MARY LEWIS SMITH, it read. Someone had planted a careful row of flattish pink flowers around it, and around that, some kind of vine. It was Ellsworth who found the second marker. It wasn't far, but somehow, to Ellsworth, as he stared fixedly down at it, it *felt* far. It felt so far that it didn't quite belong with all the others. SARAH JANE CUTTER SMITH, it read. 1971–1990. And underneath: THOMAS ROBERT SMITH, 1990.

"Oh," said Jess. She looked at Ellsworth, her eyes very big, and reached out a hand. "Oh!"

He turned abruptly away. He didn't want to read anymore or see anymore or talk anymore. All he wanted to do was to get out of this place and get back to Elizabeth's and somehow reach his father. All he wanted to do was hear his father's voice.

He grabbed up the box and started walking as fast as he could. Jess stayed right behind him, but she kept her mouth shut until they got through the little door in the gate and back onto the Square. Even then her voice was subdued. "Grandma's car's gone. She's probably out shopping.

Listen, do you want something to eat? She made those pies, and there's still all this stuff left from yesterday, muffins and things. . . ."

He shook his head.

"Well, you'll come over later, won't you? Maybe we can go talk to more of those guys, find out more stuff. Okay?"

He half nodded, half shrugged. "I guess. Maybe."

"You really ran pretty good, you know. I mean, for the first time. So I mean, if you ever want to go again . . ."

He shook his head, but a kind of strangled laugh came up from somewhere, and he suddenly felt better. "Yeah, well . . . I don't think so. But, maybe, you know, I'll see you later. . . ."

"Okay, then." She sounded relieved. "Bye."

Back at Elizabeth's, Ellsworth found her in the library, hunched in an old swivel chair at her desk and staring intently at her monitor. He dropped the box on a chair behind a pile of books, but it wasn't until he stood beside her that she looked up. "Ellsworth. Hi. Look at all these e-mails, will you? I haven't decided yet if this machine is a blessing or a curse." Then she looked at him more closely. "Something's wrong, isn't it? What is it? What's happened?"

He shook his head. "I just want to try my dad again, okay? I still couldn't reach him earlier."

"Well, of course. I've already disconnected here, so the phone should be free. I'll just roll myself into the other room and—"

"That's okay." He didn't want her to leave. Somehow he felt if she was sitting there, that he'd finally get through, and finally connect with his dad, and the way he was feeling would just slip off him like a too-big, too-heavy jacket that somebody had given him by mistake.

He punched out the numbers, and after two rings it was picked up. His heart rose. "Mr. Rocco? It's Ellsworth again. Listen, I'm sorry to bother you, but could you go get my dad? He might still be asleep, but—"

"No, I couldn't go get your dad." Mr. Rocco's voice was the snarl he usually reserved for complaining guests. "You know why? He's gone. Just packed up and left. Quit. On a weekend. In the summer. After all I did for the both of you. So just don't bother calling again. Oh, yeah. And that thermos that worked so good? I want it back. I want it today." The receiver, slamming down, sounded like a gunshot in Ellsworth's head.

"What happened? What is it?" He turned. Elizabeth was looking at him as though he was sick. She was right. He was sick. His father had quit and left without telling him? Without calling him? What about his stuff? What about Trevor? Come back, Ben Robert had said. How could he go back if Ben Robert had gone?

He shook his head. He couldn't talk. Hardly knowing what he was doing, he walked stiffly over to the couch under the window and eased himself down next to a big mass of something that turned out to be Hodge. He saw dully that Elizabeth had come with him and was sitting now, just a few feet away, in her swivel chair. She sat quietly, her hands in her lap, and except for the hum of her computer, the room went still.

Sitting there in the warm sun next to the huge cat,

Ellsworth felt his muscles gradually unclench. But his mind was something else. It jumped this way and that, words and faces a jumble, fading in and then out. Then, slowly, they began to come together, finally settling into one face and one question. The face was his father's. But the question wasn't "Where is he?" It was "Who is he?"

"He's gone," he finally said. "My dad. Mr. Rocco said he just packed up and left. Where is he? Why didn't he call? And why didn't he ever tell me anything about *her*. About . . . my mom?" He stopped and swallowed. He found that his hand was on Hodge, had been for some time, had been petting him over and over, and that Hodge, against all expectation, was not only allowing it but purring. Elizabeth remained quiet, her head bowed, and Ellsworth finally got up the courage to go on. "Jess said her dad just . . . threw her away. And my dad . . . He left here and never came back, even though she was here, kind of, you know, under that stone, and my brother, too, he's there, too. And now my grandmother . . . But he never came back. So maybe now . . . maybe now . . . he's never coming back again. . . . Maybe he's . . . throwing me away, too."

There. He'd said it. And as soon as he'd said it, he knew it wasn't true. His father would never throw him away. If Ellsworth didn't know anything else in the world, he knew that. He shook his head hard, and then shook it again.

Elizabeth's voice was quiet. "No," she said. "Ben Robert would never throw you away, Ellsworth. And leaving here and never coming back? Well, I've always liked to think of it a different way. More like . . . running for his life. Twelve years ago he probably couldn't have done anything else."

She looked for a long minute over his head, gazing sightlessly out the window. Then she shook her head. "But your mother? That I can't understand. You can't be a whole person, Ellsworth, until somebody tells you about your mother. I hope Ben Robert will forgive me, but it looks like that somebody is going to be me."

Sally

Something hurt. Ellsworth looked down and saw his hands clamped over his knees, fingers digging hard even through thick denim. Beside him, Hodge purred and purred, and behind him, under the open windows, birds clicked and rustled through the fragrant summer bushes. Elizabeth's own hands, clasped lightly in her lap, were ugly in the bright morning light. They were square and blotchy, lumpy with veins and scored with countless small scars and scratches. They were ugly, but they looked as though if you grabbed onto them, they'd hold.

He sagged back, the breath whooshing out of him in a long sigh. "I don't know. I used to ask him about her when I was little, but he'd hardly say anything, except she was beautiful and she loved me. And he had one picture, but you couldn't see much, because she was holding a dog."

Elizabeth eyes softened. "Of course. Chevy. She called him Chevy. But you couldn't capture Sally with a picture, anyway. You had to see her eyes . . . hear her laugh . . . Sally was one of those people who'd just . . . light up a room. She made you feel good just being with her. She made you feel glad." She smiled herself now, remembering. "She certainly made your father glad. I don't think I ever saw Ben Robert happier than the day he brought her home from school a week or so after they'd met. He looked like he'd found a miracle."

She sighed. "Well, to Ben Robert, she *was* a miracle, I guess. She was his first real chance to be . . . normal. To live a normal life. I guess I'll have to back up a little if this is going to make any sense at all. You see, normal was the one thing his father couldn't let him be. I told you about the day Ben Robert was born. The happiest day in the world because R.C. finally had his son. But it was the only son he was going to get, so to R.C., he had to be perfect. The perfect son, the perfect replica. And nothing ever, ever, ever was going to hurt him."

She sighed again. "R.C. really thought he could do that. Mold him. Protect him. He could barely stand Ben Robert going to school, let alone joining the Boy Scouts or playing at sports. He might get hurt! He might get . . . contaminated! It used to drive Isabelle crazy. For a long time, though, it didn't much bother Ben Robert. He mostly lived in his head, anyway. In books. In the past. He loved all the family history and stories. He kept a big notebook, and he was always scribbling things down. For a long time, nothing else much mattered to him."

She shook her head. "Well, it couldn't last, could it? There must have been cracks before, but I think the real trouble started when he turned sixteen and they started talking about college. To R.C. there wasn't much to talk about. His alma mater, that's where Ben Robert was going. A good small business college, the next town over, where Ben Robert could study to be a banker just like his father.

He could live at home, and Isabelle could drive him to his classes, although maybe, maybe, in a couple of years, he could learn to drive himself, maybe. But no point rushing these things, is there? There's all the time in the world."

She gave a short laugh, and for the first time, her expression had faltered from its usual calm. Her mouth was tight, now, and her eyes clouded. "He was living in a dream. Ben Robert wanted to be a writer, and there wasn't much question about 'want.' Ben Robert *was* a writer. Business school? No. Absolutely not. No matter how much R.C. talked and argued and laid down the law, Ben Robert wouldn't budge. I just could never figure out why R.C. was so shocked. Stubborn? Of course Ben Robert was stubborn. He was his father's son.

"By the time Ben Robert started his senior year, then, things were different. He was different. He no longer was just . . . living in his head. He no longer could. And then, one day, walking to school, he saw a girl carrying what looked like her whole life from a car into one of those small houses over on the next street. He'd never paid much attention to girls, but even he could see that somebody that small might need a hand with a box that big. So he helped her. And bingo. He was gone. And so, well, and so was she. Sally told me they must have broken the world's speed record that day for falling in love."

But Ellsworth was already thinking ahead. "He didn't like her, did he? R.C. He hated her. He—"

"No," Elizabeth interrupted gently. "Hate is too strong. I don't think anybody could hate Sally. She was so . . . full of energy. So . . . alive. No, it was more complicated than that. She just scared R.C. to death, I think. She was such a threat to everything he wanted for Ben Robert. Among other things, and it hurts me to say it, there was . . . where she came from. Her mother, I gather, had left soon after she was born, and her father was alcoholic, became sick and then died. That's why she was here. She'd come to live with her aunt. She needed to live with somebody until she finished high school, and her aunt was the only relative she had. Her aunt, though, had her own problems. . . .

"All in all, not the kind of . . . background R.C. wanted for his son. And the thing is, it completely blinded him from seeing Sally herself. What she was like . . ."

"So," said Ellsworth hoarsely. "What *was* she like?" Sometimes, when he was younger, he'd had dreams about her. In them, she was always very far away, down a long hall or a long street, and all he could see of her were her arms, reaching out for him, and even though he would run and run he could never get to her. He'd been relieved, actually, when the dreams had finally stopped.

"What was she like?" repeated Elizabeth. She smiled. "Well, for one thing, she loved animals. She had two cats she'd brought with her. And Chevy, of course. He was the sweetest little thing, black and brown. Oh, and that was the other thing. She was crazy about cars. That must have scared R.C. right there. She said she'd always been crazy about them, just like her dad, and that he'd always let her hang around when he was tinkering. She even had one of her own that she somehow kept running. Of course, Ben Robert was hopeless about that kind of thing, and he just thought she was some kind of genius." Then her smile faded, and her shoulders came up in a gentle shrug. "Well, and maybe she was. But not, unfortunately, the kind of genius R.C. could value. The kind of genius he wanted on his Square."

Ellsworth was slumped over now, arms on knees, trying to take it all in. He liked how she sounded. Sally. His mother. She sounded nice. So how come R.C. couldn't like her? And then something else occurred to him. He sat up straight. "What about my grandmother? What did she think? Did she like my mother?"

Elizabeth leaned over, put a hand on Ellsworth's arm, and looked him straight in the eye. "Your grandmother loved your mother. Isabelle had the kindest heart in the world, and she loved Sally not only for herself but for what she'd come through. Most of all, though, she loved Sally for making Ben Robert so happy. And she loved you, too, Ellsworth. Always, always remember that. She loved you from the second you were born."

"Yeah," said Ellsworth slowly. "Okay. Then why . . . ? I mean, why couldn't she make R.C. be like that, too? And why . . . why did my dad just . . . stay away? I can see why he'd be mad at R.C. But why at her, too?"

Elizabeth sank back heavily into her chair and stared through the window for a long somber moment. Then she shook her head. "Well, Ellsworth. I can't tell you that. The answer to that is truly in Ben Robert's head, not mine. We'll just have to wait until he gets in touch." She leaned toward him again. "But when he does, you ask him. It's yours *to* ask. Okay?"

"I guess so," said Ellsworth. "Yeah. Okay. I hope he calls. I hope he calls soon. You know?"

"I'm sure he will," she said gently. Then she hauled herself slowly to her feet. "Ellsworth, I have to go out for a bit. One last commitment I made before I knew you were coming. I promised some friends I'd sit in their garden for an hour and talk to them about moving some plants, and they'll be coming to pick me up soon. But the answering machine will be on. So you don't have to sit by the phone. Will you be all right for a while on your own?"

"I guess so," he repeated.

"Look," she said. "Come see one thing, anyway, before I go. It's out in the front hall. You remember, I told you? About another little sign my friend put up? My favorite, because it's in such a good spot? Why don't you grab that chair there and come and have a look."

Ellsworth felt that if he stuffed one more thing into his brain, it would jam and never start again. But he picked up the chair obediently and followed her as she found her cane and made her way into the hall. He hadn't really looked at the hall before. Like in Richard's house, it was dark, with heavy woodwork and paneling halfway up the walls. But here, above the paneling, there was wallpaper covered with roses, climbing roses of pale yellow. They were climbing up trellises that led the eye up, too, up and up and up.

The crack in the ceiling was all too clear. It was wide, and after a straight run of about six feet, zigzagged crazily until it disappeared into the molding. For one second, Ellsworth was back at the Lake Breeze, seeing *his* crack of a few days earlier, the one that Trevor would have been right about, the one that had been an omen. This crack, though, was just a sign of yet another thing in Elizabeth's house that needed fixing. Actually, it was a sign that if it wasn't fixed soon, the whole hall ceiling was going to come crashing down.

Elizabeth had followed his gaze up. "Pretty scary, isn't it?" She didn't sound scared, though. She sounded almost cheerful again, and settling herself down on a stair, she gestured with her cane. "The sign, though. You see it? Tacked up there right next to the widest part of the crack? The sign makes you look at it a completely different way. Very useful, having to do that, don't you think? Turn on the chandelier, give yourself some light. Is that chair high enough? Can you read it?"

The chair was just barely high enough. The ceiling and sign were still almost six feet above him. But the chandelier was bright, and the letters, as usual, were very bold and written in very black ink. Cranking his neck back as far as it would go, Ellsworth read the six short words. LET LIGHT AND LIFE BREAK THROUGH.

Let light and life break through. He read it again, but it still didn't make much sense. Break through? From where? From the room above? Elizabeth's bedroom, maybe? But if something broke through here, it wouldn't be light and life. It would be plaster and boards and then, probably, her bed and her chest of drawers. He clambered back down off the chair, and Elizabeth must have seen from the expression on his face—that if there was a joke there, he didn't get it.

She laughed softly. "Yes, I know. Silly. But just tuck it into the back of your mind for the times when life seems, well, seems to be falling apart. That's the best time for . . . things to open up. For all kinds of unexpected things to make their way through. Not just bad ones. Good ones, too." She stopped abruptly and then was silent for a long minute. When she finally spoke again, it wasn't to Ellsworth anymore. It was to herself. "There's only one catch, though, isn't there?" She nodded and then nodded again. "Yes. Just like it says. You have to let them."

23

Exploring

A few minutes later, she was gone. Ellsworth carried the chair back into the library and then just stood there staring at the phone. He hurt all over. His legs were stiff from the run, and his stomach felt like a giant was squeezing it, hard, with both hands. Mostly, though, he just felt like big pieces had been chopped off him. His mother was real now, the cemetery and Elizabeth had made her real, so now she was dead in a way she'd never been dead before. And his father had disappeared.

Hodge had left the couch and was racked out just in front of it, in a last little pool of morning sun. Ellsworth hunched down and gave him a scratch under the chin. He didn't stir, except to raise his head so Ellsworth could scratch more easily, but he immediately started to purr again, just like he had earlier. Ellsworth's stomach unclenched, just a little. Hodge was so big and so warm and had finally, for some reason, decided to trust him. His mother'd liked cats, Elizabeth said. She'd had two of them. Ellsworth's hand stilled. What had happened to them? Cats can live a long time, can't they? Would . . . would his father have given them to Elizabeth when he'd gone away? Was one of them still left?

"Hodge?" he whispered. Hodge didn't answer. He only opened one eye, yawned widely, stretched out his front legs, and went back to sleep. Ellsworth laid both hands for a minute on his broad side, feeling the steady rise and fall, up and down, move into and join the beat of his own body. "Hodge," he whispered again. Yes. Maybe. He stood up and stretched, too, feeling better.

Except he didn't know what to do. Get some lunch, maybe. Then he could always check out one of Elizabeth's broken clocks, or the old TV, or even the plug on her mixer. He'd noticed it after supper last night—it was practically falling off. Or he could read the rest of John Matthew's journal. No. Not that. Not now. The thing was, he didn't really feel like doing much of anything except being there in case his father called. There was an answering machine, but Ben Robert hated answering machines and usually just hung up when he heard one. It was better to be around.

He got himself something to eat and wandered out into the hall and into the front room. It wasn't any more exciting than it had been yesterday when he'd passed through. It was just a living room full of fat chairs and couches and almost as many books as the library without quite as much clutter. This time, though, he noticed a photograph, a brownish one standing on a shelf, of five women in old-fashioned dresses. He went for a closer look.

1900, it read. *Betsy Sullivan and "The Girls": Emily, Ionia, Sarah, and Alice.* He didn't know anything about Alice or Sarah, and John had only just mentioned Emily and Ionia earlier. But Betsy Sullivan . . . He knew about her. She'd been married to John Matthew and had had all those kids and painted all those pictures. She didn't look much like an artist *or* an old lady. Sitting in a chair that was too big for her, she looked more like a kid herself. She was short and plump and smiley, and her feet, hanging out from under her long dark dress, didn't quite touch the floor. The "girls" seemed older, somehow. They were tall and serious, except for the second one, who just looked like she wanted to get away from there and get busy doing something else. Maybe that was Ionia. She looked like somebody who'd like to dig dandelions.

Dig. There was something about "dig" he'd been going to do. Holes, that was it. He'd been going to check the rooms for patterns in the floors that looked like holes. This was a good place to start, because it was a front room, and that's where they'd found one of the patterned floors at Richard's. He turned and looked around. One, two, three, four rugs, instead of the one big one in the library. They didn't look very heavy. He dropped down on his knees and rolled them up, one after the other. The only thing under them was fine grit and two pennies and some scraps of paper and cat hair. No pattern, no hole. This floor was plain.

He stood up, kicked the rugs out flat again, and went across the hall. He pushed open the big sliding door into the dining room and immediately forgot about floors. In the middle of the room, under a smaller version of the chandelier in the hall, was a pool table. It was a big, beautiful pool table made of some kind of dark wood, heavily carved, and held up by a giant pedestal. An elaborate rack, holding cues, balls, and a lot of stuff he didn't recognize, hung on the south wall above a narrow sideboard. That was all, except for twelve chairs, he counted them, standing in a neat row against the walls. They looked solid enough, but their seats were covered with some kind of thin red mate-rial that was splitting into thin strips that were splitting into threads.

But why any kind of chairs, if the room was for pool? Then he got it. There must be a way to eat at that table, too. There must be a cover someplace that fit over it. It didn't take him long to find it. It was in a little room between the dining room and kitchen filled with cupboards right up to the ceiling. What he was looking for was behind the door, although it took him a minute to recognize it. It wasn't one big piece of wood, but eight smaller ones, all of them heavy as lead. So you could carry them out one at a time, and then—he looked at them more closely—you could peg them together to make one big tabletop. Neat.

He wandered back and ran his hand over the shabby green felt. He'd never seen a pool table before in a house. He'd never seen one at all except on TV. They'd been play-ing some kind of tournament—billiards, they'd called it— and it'd been less boring than he thought it would be, the way they had to aim the ball sometimes so it would bounce once or twice and then hit the second ball into the pocket. They couldn't be off even the littlest bit—they had to be just exactly right. He'd never played sports, much, but pool might be fun. Yeah. He'd ask Elizabeth about it when she got back.

He remembered the floor. But this one, like the library, was covered by a huge flowered rug, and under it was a pad, and the two of them wouldn't budge. After the front room, though, he bet he wouldn't find anything anyway. He was more and more getting the feeling that the only house with "holes" in the floors was Richard's, because it was there that they were a clue to the treasure. The treasure that must be upstairs, connected to that big "hole" in that big empty room where the floor sounded rotten . . .

Except John seemed to think it wasn't. John had said that floors that sounded like that just needed nails. Yeah. Yeah! That's what he'd been trying to remember this morning, just after he and Jess had come back outside. He knew he'd heard that sound before. It was in an apartment he and his dad had lived in once where the floors creaked so bad it drove them both nuts, and when they'd finally tracked down the landlord, he'd said one of these days he'd be over and drive some more nails into the subfloor. He'd never come, of course, and they'd finally just packed up and moved.

So the sound, then, maybe didn't mean so much. But what about that crack? He'd seen it, and Jess'd seen it, too. Maybe, though, it didn't mean so much, either. Maybe it wasn't so dangerous. Ellsworth walked back into the hall and looked up. This crack here didn't seem to bother Elizabeth much. She even liked it. Maybe John Matthew had *put* that crack in Richard's floor. But could you do something like that? And why would you, even if you could?

It didn't make any sense. Nothing made any sense. Where had his dad gone? Why didn't he call? Those were the *real* questions, and as they echoed in his head, Ellsworth found himself wandering back into the library and flopping down on the couch. He needed to think. Think. He looked up drowsily at the picture. His dad had liked that picture. He'd looked at it all the time. And it hadn't changed. There they all were, the houses, the pond, the family, dancing around and around and around. He liked it, too. His father should come back and look at it again. That's what his father should do. He should come . . . Ellsworth's eyes were closing, words receding. They were just drifting now, up and up, like soap bubbles in the wind. That's what his father should do. His father, Ben Robert, should come here, come back here to the Square.

24

The Picture

The phone was ringing. In one groggy motion, Ellsworth sat up and rolled to his feet. The phone! His dad! His dad was calling! Then he saw that Elizabeth was already speaking quietly into the receiver. She hung up, turned, and saw him, too.

"Oh," she said. "It woke you. I'm sorry. It was just Kitty, asking us to supper. I told her I was busy tonight but that you might come. Jess seems to have something she's anxious to tell you. Kitty said they were out most of the afternoon, which makes me feel doubly guilty for leaving you on your own." As she'd been talking, she'd turned the desk chair with her cane and now eased herself down. "You were all right by yourself? You found something to do?"

Ellsworth sat down, too, and tried to wake up. He must have slept for a long time. Everything was sticking to him; he felt like he'd been through a car wash. "Yeah," he said. "It was okay. I looked at your pool table, and stuff. Listen, though. I was thinking. About my dad leaving the motel. Do you think maybe . . . I mean, do you think he'd come *here*? Except, no. He hardly let *me* come. So that's nuts."

"I don't think it's nuts," said Elizabeth. "It feels right to me, Ellsworth. It feels right." She leaned toward him. "Because listen. Something's changed here. Before, there wasn't anything here he thought he needed. Now there is. You."

"Yeah?" It took a second for this to percolate through his brain. Then he took a deep breath and let it out again. "I guess. The thing is, if he's coming here, he probably wouldn't phone. He hates phones. He'd probably just come." He shook his head. "Except our car's a wreck. I hope he makes it."

"If he doesn't, we'll hear," said Elizabeth. "I'm sure we will."

"Yeah," said Ellsworth. He stood up. "Listen. Maybe I will go to Kitty's. Is that okay? I need to talk to Jess."

"Of course it's okay. Could I ask a favor, though? Could you stop at Matthew's en route and tell him I'm still expecting him? We usually play Scrabble on Saturday nights."

"Okay," said Ellsworth. His eyes slid to the chair where he'd dropped the box. Should he take it with him and show it to Matthew? Maybe not. But something was nagging at him. "I was supposed to tell John something, too. I think I forgot."

"My ride to Meeting," said Elizabeth. "That's all right. I'll call him. I'll call Kitty, too, if you'd like, while you're getting ready. Maybe when you get back, you and Matthew and I can sit out for a bit like the two of us did last night. I enjoyed that. Talking, and getting a little breeze. . . . I don't even mind looking at the Sward so much after the sun goes down."

She shook her head. "It looks so terrible. I couldn't prune this year, because of my knee. And then came the drought. And now, worst of all, our wonderful white pines have to come down. A blister rust hit them a few years ago, hit millions of pines and killed them all. I kept hoping the experts would come up with something to save them that we could afford to use." She sighed. "But they didn't. Poor pines. They'll upset Ben Robert, I'm afraid. They were his favorite climbing trees—he said from the top of them he could see the whole world."

"Do *you* think something's in that house?" Ellsworth said. The question just popped out. "You know, a real treasure, something that'd be worth something if we found it?"

Elizabeth thought for a minute and then nodded. "Yes," she said. "I do. John Matthew said there were three treasures, and I believe him. I'm just afraid that whatever it is might disappoint some of us. The picture's so different from the first two. It's . . . so personal this time. It just doesn't seem to point to something we could *sell*. Maybe Abner's seen something I've missed. Probably somebody should ask him—he's the art expert. We hardly ever see him anymore, him or Josie—they have another home, another life, really, in Vermont, although I think they're here right now for a few days. But I'm almost thinking that this last treasure might be more . . . symbolic. Not diamonds or coal mines this time but something John Matthew wanted to tell us. Something about the family."

Then she smiled. "I can see you don't like that idea any better than Matthew does. So that's another reason to stop by his house. If the two of you put your heads together, you'll probably be able to prove me wrong." She heaved herself to her feet. "Well, you go get cleaned up, and I'll give Kitty a call. She'll be happy to see you there."

Kitty did seem happy to see him there. More than once, as they were eating in her cool bright kitchen with its flowered wallpaper and soft chair cushions, she put down her fork, looked from Jess to Ellsworth and back again, and said, "Oh, what a treat this is! To have the two of you here, at my table. Ellsworth, have some more ham. Jess, you like Jell-O, you said you liked Jell-O, now you finish that salad right up, and there'll be peach pie for dessert. Oh, this just makes me so, so happy."

Ellsworth was feeling pretty good himself. His dad didn't make pies, and fresh peach pie wasn't something that came up much in school cafeterias. He ate two pieces. And Elizabeth seemed to think he was right about Ben Robert, that if he'd left the motel he was probably coming here. And she thought there was treasure. She didn't know what it was, but she thought it was there.

The only thing that made him a little nervous all the time they were eating and clearing the table and stacking the dishwasher was that Jess hardly said anything at all. Of course, it wasn't too easy for anybody to say much of anything when Kitty got going, but Jess wouldn't even look at him. Was she mad about something? Except she didn't look mad. She looked jumpy. It wasn't until they were finally outside, sitting on the back steps, that she told him what was wrong.

"Grandma took me to this craft show this afternoon, out at the fairgrounds. Well, it wasn't just crafts. It was an art show, too, a big deal with prizes and everything, and Grandma wanted me to go because one of the judges was that guy? Abner, you know, on the other side of the Square?

Josie, his wife, she was there, too. Grandma wanted me to meet them, because they're hardly ever here—they have a gallery, or something, in Vermont, and they're always going places to buy stuff. I guess they're only around now for a couple of days.

"Anyway, so I met them, and then Josie started going on about the picture. You know, *the* picture, the one at Elizabeth's. Josie said that the picture *is* the treasure. She said that John Matthew wrote something on the back of it, about how happy it made him to see all of them, you know, dancing around together. And then Abner, *he* said—"

"Wait a minute," said Ellsworth. His mind was churning. "So John Matthew liked the picture. So what? Why does that mean that there isn't something else? I mean, what about that stuff he wrote on the stair?"

"Do you mind? Can I finish?" Now Jess *was* looking . . . not mad exactly, but close enough. Ellsworth shut up.

"Okay. So then *Abner* said he thought the same thing as Josie. He said he knew they were right because of the frame. He said the other pictures had these plain wood frames that John Matthew probably made himself, but this last one had an antique thing that cost all this money. So that shows that the picture was *it*."

Now Ellsworth was up and pacing. "No. I mean, listen, this guy Abner, he's an art dealer, right? So that kind of thing, frames and stuff, *would* be a big deal to him. But there's *got* to be something else. John Matthew . . . He was . . . He liked . . . " Now he was struggling, because he knew what he meant, but he didn't know how to say it. "I'm not saying the picture isn't important. It is. But it's hers, you know? Betsy's. John Matthew did stuff other ways. He built stuff. Those boxes. And toys—Dwight said he built toys, mechanical ones. So this last treasure, well, it would be something . . . something you could get your *hands* on." He nodded hard, finally satisfied. He was right. *That* was right. He knew it was.

Jess actually looked impressed. "Yeah, well, okay. I hope you're right. You should have heard them, it was like they knew everything, and who was I, even? So I really hope they're wrong. I really want there to be something and for us to find it."

"Yeah," said Ellsworth. "Yeah."

"Did you find out anything more? About the floor?"

"Not really. The creaks probably don't mean anything, and I looked in Elizabeth's front room, and her floor's just plain. But I'm still not sure about that crack. Listen, though. I've got to go over and tell Matthew something. I tried before dinner, but he didn't answer."

"He's gone."

"What do you mean, gone?"

"Grandma and I saw him when we were leaving for the craft show, and he had a backpack, and he said he was going away for a day or so. He looked kind of upset. But when she asked him what was wrong, he told her to mind her own business. Grandma thinks it's probably Elizabeth. She says they probably had some kind of fight."

"What do you mean, some kind of fight?" said Ellsworth. Then he remembered Elizabeth's face that morning. "So if he went away, how come he didn't call her? She thinks he's coming over tonight."

"Well, he wouldn't call her if he was mad. Do you think they're . . . you know?"

"What?"

"You know. In love."

Where did she come up with these things? "What do you mean? They're cousins."

"They're *distant* cousins. Besides, he's adopted; Grandma told me. So that makes it okay."

"I don't know what you're talking about. They're friends, okay? But forget that. If Matthew isn't home, then I know what I want to do."

"Go back in the house."

"Yeah, sure. But not yet. There's still some things we've got to find out. So let's go talk to Abner. I want to ask him about the picture."

25

Abner

Without saying anything more, they crossed onto the Sward. It was beginning to feel familiar; he gave the big stump a whack as they passed it and automatically skirted a clump of parched-looking flowers he'd almost tripped over the day before. Even though it was still daylight, the light under the trees felt weak and flat, like the kind you get from a forty-watt bulb. It made everything look even deader than it was.

"Why don't they water it?" Jess said. "We don't get any rain all summer at home, but we don't let things get like this."

"Water would cost millions on something this big. Mr. Rocco, at our motel? He used to complain all the time, how people wasted it, how much it cost him. Besides, who'd do it? Elizabeth does that kind of stuff, and she can't now." He stopped. "Shhh. Get down. Behind the bench. There's John, and I don't want to talk to him right now. He'll ask about the box, and I don't want to tell him what's in it. Not yet."

Jess hunched down beside him, and they peered through the narrow slats. "There's Dwight, too. Look. Look what they're doing. I told you, didn't I? See, they're almost running into each other. Listen to the dogs, they're going nuts, so now they'll just turn around and . . ."

But they didn't. "They're not going," she whispered. "They're just standing there. They never did that before."

"Yeah." She was right. They were just standing and staring at each other. Then Dwight gave a massive sneeze.

"Gesundheit," said John. It seemed to startle them both.

"Thanks," said Dwight. He hauled out his wad of Kleenexes and blew his nose hard. Each stared into the other's face for another moment and then both turned at the same time, hauled on their dogs, and walked away.

When they were out of sight, Ellsworth stood up. "How come they hate each other, anyway?" Jess was brushing off the twigs and stones that had stuck to her bare knees.

"Grandma said—" she began, and then stopped.

"What?"

"I don't know. Something to do with your dad. Something about when he and your mom got married."

"Why should they care about that?"

"I don't know. That's just what she said."

Ellsworth shrugged. "Well, I don't get it. But let's go."

Abner's porch was unswept, the back door was tightly closed, and the uncurtained windows looked blank and lifeless.

"You knock," Ellsworth said. Jess gave him a look.

"Okay, okay," he said. It didn't matter, though, because nobody answered. He knocked again, and they were just about ready to turn away when the door opened, and Abner stood there, looking out.

"I'm sorry," he said. "It took me a minute to realize somebody was here. We don't get many visitors from the Square. How nice. Come in." He was almost as tall as John, but clean-shaven. He was wearing an expensive-looking shirt and perfectly creased slacks, and although his white hair looked a little tousled, his eyes were shrewd and bright above the heavy glasses perched on his nose. As soon as they were through the door, he looked from Jess to Ellsworth and back again, and smiled.

"Amazing," he said. "Now, I met this young lady this afternoon, and as the two of you are so very obviously related, you must be Ellsworth. Am I right? Of course I am. Come in. My wife, Josie, will be desolate that she's missed you, but she came home from the fairgrounds with a bad headache and is already in bed."

Jess was turning around in a slow circle. "Wow," she said. "I've never seen a kitchen like this. Cool."

"Thank you," said Abner, obviously pleased. "We had it done a couple of years ago, with Josie, of course, doing most of the design. Simple and elegant, I think. If you like it, though, come see the living room."

The living room was even more of a shock. The wall between the library and the front room was gone, and the remaining walls were covered with pictures. The huge space practically vibrated with color.

"We change them from time to time," Abner said, motioning his guests down onto a big gray couch, "depending on what we've just bought, or our mood, or the season. We sell them, too, of course, if we tire of them or if an artist begins to get a following."

"Like there?" said Ellsworth pointing. "That empty space there?"

"Very good," said Abner, peering at him more closely.

"You know, it's really amazing, the two of you, you can't be closer than fifth or sixth cousins, and yet there you are. Genes are like artists, I've always thought, the way they combine so little basic material into such an enormous variety of style and subject. At the same time, echoes, there are always echoes, a twentieth-century painter unconsciously using a motif from the seventeenth—"

"Listen," said Ellsworth. "I'm sorry, but we need to ask you something."

Abner blinked and pulled off his glasses and sat back in his chair. "Of course," he said. "Please. Go ahead."

"It's about the picture. *The* picture, you know, the one that's hanging at Elizabeth's that you want to sell."

"But I don't want to sell that picture." Abner shook his head. "The family voted to sell it. You asked about that empty space on the wall. That space is always empty when it's not our turn to hang it. It will break my heart when that picture is sold."

Ellsworth and Jess both stared at him. "Oh," said Jess. "We thought—"

"Listen, then," Ellsworth interrupted. "Jess and I, we want to find that treasure. I know you don't think there is one, but we do, and if we can find it, well, the picture stays here. On the Square. But we need a clue, and we think it's probably there, in the picture, like it always was before. But we don't know what it is. So we thought, maybe, you saw something we didn't. Could you come look at it?"

"Oh, I don't need to look at it," said Abner. He tapped his head. "Every brush stroke of that painting is right here. Right here. But have I noticed something that you haven't?

I don't know. I could tell you, though, the most magical thing about it. To me, personally, anyway, the thing that makes my breath catch in my throat when I see it or even think of it. I don't know if it will help, but do you want to know?"

Ellsworth glanced at Jess. Her eyes were wide, and he had a feeling his were, too. They both nodded.

He leaned toward them, his hands grasping his knees. "They're dancing," he said. "Aren't they? They're dancing, they're floating around that pond. But their feet are absolutely, solidly, flat on the ground. You go look. And then you tell me. How did she do it? Is it a clue? I don't know. I only know it's a miracle."

Half an hour later, Ellsworth opened the screen into Elizabeth's kitchen and was just closing it when TigerLily zipped through and then sat abruptly down and began washing each other. "Hi, guys," he said. "Where've you been? Where's Elizabeth?" They were too busy to answer. Coming in farther, he saw that a note had been propped on the table. *Ellsworth,* it read. *I phoned Matthew and got his machine. It looks like he's gone battlefield hunting. So no Scrabble for me. Can we leave more talk for another evening? I'm suddenly feeling tired, so I think I'll call it a night. Let's plan on pancakes for breakfast, though. Love, Elizabeth. P.S. Could you lock up, please? Thanks.*

It was a cheerful enough note, but left him feeling restless. It was only nine o'clock. Why was everybody going to bed? He'd slept so much that afternoon he hardly felt tired at all. And after hearing Abner, he wanted to look at the picture again to see if the family really was floating with their feet solidly on the ground. Abner had mentioned another thing, too. He'd said that Betsy Sullivan had somehow managed to make the pond look big even though it couldn't be. Fifteen people were dancing around it holding hands, and fifteen people weren't very many.

But what about the real pond? How many people would it take to dance around *that* holding hands? Not too many now that most of it had dried up. Maybe there were even enough people here on the Square. Maybe . . . maybe that's what John Matthew had wanted to happen all along, and it was only this year, the year of the drought, that it could.

Ellsworth climbed the stairs to his room. And maybe the answer was in the journal, in the part they hadn't read yet. But the journal, like the picture, was in the library, where Elizabeth was sleeping. He'd left it behind those books on that chair. Right. Ellsworth fed Hugo, got into his pajamas, and pulled a big padded rocking chair next to the window. Dusk was finally falling over the Sward, fireflies beginning to flicker out of the tall grass. Then something else moved, and a man was suddenly standing at the end of Elizabeth's walk. He was short and gaunt, and although his face was in shadow, his hair, an untidy mass of tight white curls, shone in the dim light.

Ellsworth sat very still, hardly breathing. Any movement, he knew, and the man would be gone. R.C. His grandfather. Except that standing there, staring up at Elizabeth's house, he hardly looked like a man at all.

He looked like a ghost.

26

Dwight's Story

It took Ellsworth a long time to get to sleep, so it wasn't until he heard Elizabeth calling him the next morning that he woke up and rolled out of bed.

"I'm sorry," she said as he appeared at the bottom of the stairs. She was propped against the stove, flipping pancakes. "I hated to wake you, but I wanted to make good on my promise of a hot breakfast before John picked me up for Meeting."

Ellsworth held the platter while she filled it, and carried it to the table. "What kind of meeting is it?"

"Meeting for Worship," she said. She smiled at him and pushed over a bottle of maple syrup. "Quaker talk for church service. John Matthew and Betsy started the Meeting here, so it's very old. It's still a good-sized group, too, but John and I are about the only Smiths who've stayed active. Come have a look some time. You might like it."

"Yeah," said Ellsworth cautiously. "Maybe. Sometime. What do you do?"

Elizabeth chewed pancake for a minute, thinking. "Sit quietly and listen. Wait. Pray. And sometimes, when God speaks clearly to us, we share the message." She caught the expression on his face and laughed. "Sounds spooky, I guess. But it's not. It's peaceful, mostly. Refreshing. Often very moving. Speaking of which, I'd better get if I'm going to be ready in time. I'll be back in a couple of hours. Do you have any plans for the day?"

"Not really," said Ellsworth. Last night he and Jess hadn't made any because when they'd come out of Abner's, Kitty had been calling her, and she'd had to run right off. "Do you think maybe my dad might get here today? How long do you think it takes, driving?"

"Ellsworth, I just don't know. The only thing I'm sure of is that he must be coming as fast as he can."

Ellsworth nodded. "And one other thing I was wondering. R.C., you know? My grandfather? Do you think he's . . . okay?"

Elizabeth sat back down. "Why do you ask?"

"I saw him last night. Out here, in back of the house. He didn't look so good. He looked kind of like you could . . . see right through him."

She shook her head. "We've got to do something. We've tried to visit him, John and Kitty and I . . . We've left food and notes. But he won't answer the door. Or the phone. If you saw him outside, that's good. But it's not good enough. John and I will go after Meeting, and we won't leave until he lets us in. He has to see people. He has to talk. He has to start *living* again." She stood up again and sighed. "Well, I'll hold him in the Light this morning. All the rest of us, too. We certainly need every bit of it we can get."

Elizabeth didn't seem to like doing dishes any more than Ben Robert did. Ellsworth washed up the pile in the sink— it had always been his job, anyway—and then, hearing the front door close behind her, went to retrieve John Matthew's box. He hefted it gently. Good. The journal was still there. The picture was still there, too, and looking up at it, he saw what Abner had meant. They *were* all dancing with their feet flat on the ground. And the pond did look big even though it wasn't. So that's what he'd do. He'd go have a closer look at the pond, and then he'd go find Jess.

Was it ever going to cool off? Stepping outside was like walking into an oven. The bees in Elizabeth's flowers were still bumbling, but in slow motion, as though even *their* energy was finally drying up. The pond looked unchanged, flat and dank and scummy. No big hand thrust up out of it, waving treasure. No. If it held any secrets, they were deep down in the mud. And John Matthew wouldn't do mud.

Just then he heard a soft plop, and then another and another. Small bodies were disappearing into the water, and he caught one goggling at him as it went down. There *were* frogs. And as he squatted down to watch for more, the gentle ripples smoothed out, and he smelled a rich stew of green things growing and rotting, and saw bugs skittering over the surface. So it wasn't completely dead. It was just a little dry around the edges. All it needed was some rain.

Passing Dwight's house, he saw the black cocker spaniel splayed out under the biggest sundial, a water bowl close by her head. She looked up at him, tongue hanging, tail vibrating, but made no move to get up. She was old and fat, but her eyes smiled when he reached down to pet her, and her ears felt like silk. Just like it had yesterday, Dwight's voice came from behind the screen door. "Her name's Tara. She's about a year younger than you—I got her to replace your mom's dog, Chevy. Got Chevy from your dad, just before he left, but she never settled. Just kind of pined away. Nice little dog. I missed her. Tara's a good dog, too, but she's getting old now, just like the rest of us. Except that girl, now, and you. I was kind of hoping you'd stop over again. You want to come in?"

"Okay," said Ellsworth. He guessed Jess and the house could wait a little longer. "Sure."

All he could think when he saw Dwight's kitchen was that Elizabeth would feel right at home. Dwight didn't have plants and knitting and fruit and cats, but he had clocks. Also watches. Also door locks and window locks and lockboxes and alarms. The only clear space in the whole room was the table, where he obviously worked at taking most of these things apart and putting them back together again.

"Want to know what your mom had to say the first time she walked in here?" Dwight hauled a large mantel clock off a chair and motioned Ellsworth to sit down. "Sure you do. She said, 'Dwight, I think I've died and gone to heaven.' And you should have seen her with those toys of John Matthew's. She'd play with them by the hour, trying to figure out how they worked. Not rough, you know. She had the touch—John Matthew would have been tickled to see her. So that's why I couldn't resist her when she asked to see the house. That's why I got into so much trouble."

"The house," said Ellsworth. He sat up straighter. "You mean Richard's house? My mom and my dad went in?"

Dwight settled himself more comfortably in his chair. "Treasure, now. There's something about treasure, isn't there? It tugs at you. Sally sure wanted a go at it. See, she and Ben Robert, they were crazy about each other. Just crazy, I never saw anything like it. But R.C., well, he thought lots of things, but part of it was he just thought Ben Robert was too young. He was only just eighteen, and Sally was his first girl, and R.C. thought, well, he thought . . ."

"Yeah," said Ellsworth. "Elizabeth told me. He didn't like her."

Dwight looked relieved. "That's right. He didn't like her. And Sally figured okay, okay, you don't like me. But what if I . . . figured out how it worked? What if I was able to get my hands on what John Matthew left? Wouldn't that make me a hero? Wouldn't you like me then? And she could have done it, you know. I'll go to my grave thinking she could have done it."

"Wait a minute. What do you mean, figured out how it worked. What . . . ?"

"No, you interrupt me now, I'll never get it straight. Now, Ben Robert should have known better. *I* should have known better. I was here on the Square when your grandma got hurt in that house, and I watched R.C. throw that key into the pond. Sally just had us bewitched, that's all, that's what I think. Whatever it was, I made another key, and the three of us went over there one fine night to try our luck. And just the second we had that door open, just the second before we would have been inside and home free, who comes walking along? Who?"

Ellsworth could hardly breathe. "What happened?"

"What do you think happened? I think R.C. actually lost his mind, at least for a minute there. Just plain went crazy. He said things, well, I think afterward he must have felt ashamed, but by then it was too late. He said things I don't think any of us ever forgot, and I know Ben Robert never forgave. And a week later to the day, Ben Robert and Sally ran away in Sally's old car, and when they came back, they were married."

Ellsworth shut his eyes tight, trying to push out of his mind everything R.C. must have said *then*. It all seemed to be colored in red, like an explosion. Like blood. But his grandmother. What about her? "What about my grandmother? What did she do?"

"Izzy? Izzy, well, we all loved Izzy, a sweet, sweet lady, Izzy. And she loved Ben Robert, for sure, and had a soft spot in her heart for Sally, too. But the thing was with Izzy, that when R.C. said jump, the only thing she ever knew to say was 'how high?' No, Izzy couldn't help. So Elizabeth took them in, and then you got started, you and . . ."

Ellsworth shoved back his chair and stood up. Thomas. But Thomas was dead. And so was his mother. And so was his grandmother, now, and he'd never get to know any of them. None of them at all. "I've got to go."

Dwight stood up, too. "Now wait a minute. Wait a minute. I got off on the wrong track. I didn't mean to remind you of all that. I was just going to tell you how handy your mom was, and how I think she could have figured out what John and I couldn't, all those years back. How maybe you and that girl can do it now. Because, you know, you can't go alone. You got to promise me that, now. And take some good lights, you'll need some lights. Because here's the key. Ellsworth, listen here now. I changed my mind. I made one for you, after all. I made you a key."

But Ellsworth didn't care. He didn't care about the key, and he didn't care about Dwight and John and Richard's house all those years back. He was yanking open the screen door and letting it slam behind him. He was leaving.

27

Looking Back: 1942 and the Wrong Smiths

All those years back . . . It is 1942. The country is at war, and the family is divided. Bobby and George have enlisted. Duncan has not and might soon be in prison. Conscientious objectors are not popular in 1942. Duncan doesn't care. As a Quaker, a birthright Quaker, he will serve, but he will not kill. Is he a hero or a coward? It depends on who you ask around the Square. And what about Bobby? George? There is not so much division there. Everyone is worried for them, and they should be. A lot of soldiers soon off to battle won't ever be back.

John and Dwight, cousins and best friends, are fourteen now, and edgy. Jumpy. They're too young to fight, but they're more than old enough to read papers and listen to news and begin to keep maps of campaigns with pins stuck in them for battles. They think Bobby and George are lucky, *lucky,* they're crazy to join them, but although they never mention it, they're scared for them, too. They never talk about Duncan at all. Duncan plays the best ball they've ever seen, and coaches them, too. Duncan might have turned pro. But now? John, especially, is torn. He's a Quaker, too, at least he guesses he is. But could he make Duncan's choice? He doesn't know.

So John and Dwight are restless. They're more than restless, they have to *do* something, they have to do something daring, that could get them into trouble or cover them with glory.

Richard's house sits there, at the bottom of the Square, dark and locked and waiting. There really isn't any question about whether they'll go in and see if they can find out what's there. It's just a question of when and how.

The how isn't hard. Neither of them much likes school except for shop. John has already discovered woodworking. Dwight has already found that anything he can take apart he can put back together again, better. He knows that a little oil and the right skeleton key will open that house in a minute; John knows that if the floors are oak, they're probably okay.

As to when, they wait for a dark night, a little cool, a little rainy, the kind of night when adults head thankfully for living rooms and chairs and newspapers and fires. They have a history project, they say. They're going to a friend's house to work on it. They'll try not to be late.

They have no trouble getting in. They shine their flashlights up at the picture and around at the initials and down at the circles in the floors. They read the words on the bottom stair and cautiously make their way up. The upstairs floor stops them, but not for long. It creaks and breathes and sighs, but it holds them. It allows them to walk over to what, undoubtedly, is a crack in the floor.

And then what? They see where treasure might be, must be, but they fail. Why? Is it a failure of observation? Of ingenuity? Of expertise? Or does something frighten them up there because it isn't time, it isn't the right time or they aren't the right Smiths, frighten them so thoroughly that they never go up those stairs again, never even talk about going?

They fail and leave and promise never to tell anybody, ever, about what happened, never even to tell about the picture or the circles or the initials or the stairs. They never tell anybody about the stairs and the trick for going up them.

They never tell anybody about the stairs.

28

Back in the House

"Where's Jess?"

"Ellsworth!" said Kitty. "Come in! Why, you're all out of breath! Now you just sit down here for a minute. Jess is running around somewhere, too, she seems to do it every day, although how she can in this heat, I just don't know. She only just left, I'm afraid, so she might be a while."

Ellsworth sank down into a chair. He didn't know why what Dwight had just told him had bothered him so much. But it had. For the first time, Kitty's bustling and bubbling didn't seem silly. It seemed nice, like his being a little kid somebody cared about. He gulped down the glass of milk she put in front of him and let her words wash over him in a comforting wave. What was she saying?

"I've been wanting to tell you," she was saying, "how wonderful it is having you here. You're just the nicest boy. And what it's meant to Jess! It's been night and day since you came, the way she's been the last two days, sleeping, eating, why she even laughed yesterday! I can't begin to tell you . . . " She leaned over and planted a kiss on his cheek. And then another. "There. One from me. And one from Izzy." Tears came to her eyes. "I miss her so much. And she would have been so, so proud of you."

It should have been embarrassing. But it wasn't. He swallowed a couple of times and finally managed to get the word out. "Thanks." Then he got awkwardly to his feet. "Listen. I better go. Could you tell Jess to come over? No. I'll just go find her. And, you know, thanks for dinner last night, too. It was good."

"Anytime, Ellsworth. You're just welcome here anytime at all."

Ellsworth made his way down the steps and across her yard, and when he rounded the side of the house, there was Jess, jogging slowly through the little door in the gate. Her face was red and she was breathing hard and her T-shirt looked like water would run out of it if you touched it.

"Hi," she said. "I gave up. It's too hot."

"Listen," he said. "Can you come? I don't want to wait anymore. I want to go back in that house."

"What happened?" she said. "Did something happen? Did you finish the journal? Did you figure something out?"

"No," he said. "Not really. It's just Dwight. He told me that my mom almost went in there. And my dad. And I think *he* really did go in, him and John, a long time ago, and almost found something. So I'll bet I can do it." He nodded, half to himself. "Then I'll show him."

"Who?" she said. "Now? I need a shower, and—"

"No," he said. "If you go in, your grandmother will have someplace she wants to take you or something. I don't want to wait."

"Well," she said. "But don't we need those keys? They're upstairs."

"Oh." Then it came to him. "I didn't lock it again yesterday. I forgot. So it'll be open. Please?"

Jess pulled up the bottom of her T-shirt and wiped her face. "Yeah, okay. I guess so. Okay."

The Square was deserted, but as Ellsworth climbed the steps of Number Two South, he saw that the porch was no longer empty. A plastic bag had been plunked down right in front of the door. Inside the bag were two big flashlights, a can of WD-40, and a key. Also a Post-it note with a few scrawled words from Dwight. "Sorry if I was out of line. Maybe you can use this stuff. Don't do anything dumb."

"Oil?" said Jess. "Why oil? I don't like oil."

"It's not really oil. It's just squirty stuff, for locks and things. We don't even need it, the door's already open. But I'd forgotten about flashlights. The flashlights are good. Here."

He shoved one at her, turned the knob, and pushed the door open. The minute they were in, with the door shut behind him, he took a deep breath. It was okay now. They were in, and Dwight's flashlights were what flashlights ought to be, and today they weren't just wandering around, a little nervous about every step they took. They knew where they were going.

In the front hall, though, Jess stopped abruptly and pointed her flashlight up to the elaborate *R* carved into the woodwork over the big door. "I know now. You didn't answer me. About the journal. Did you read the rest? Was there anything about the letters? If they're all here, they've got to mean something, right? I've been kind of fiddling with them, even, trying to turn them into words. I was always good at that when we did it in school. You know, the teacher writes 'Happy New Year' on the board and you have to make as many words as you can with the letters. Like 'pay' and 'pen' and . . ."

She wound down, finally, swung her light around, and then, from out of the blue, she exploded. "Stop it! Stop looking like that! First you say, 'Come, come, please, Jess, you've got to come.' And then I do something or have some kind of idea and you have a fit. 'I'll bet *I* can do it,' you said. 'Then *I'll* show him.' See? You don't really want me here, do you? You wish you could do it alone, because that's how you like to do stuff, alone, and you're just mad because for once you can't. Well, guess what? I've been saying it and saying it. It doesn't just belong to you. It belongs to me, too, and if I want to do something, I'll do it, and if I want to say something, I'll say it. You got that?"

She was standing practically chin to chin with him now and glaring into his eyes. "You got that?" she repeated. "Because if you don't, I'm just—"

"Okay."

"What?"

"Okay. I'm sorry. It's just, I want to get going. Because maybe somebody'll come and stop us. Or it'll be hard to find. Or it'll be hard to figure out. But I didn't mean . . . Look, okay, maybe I didn't really want you here at first. Like yesterday. It was more that my dad said I shouldn't come alone. But now . . . " Ellsworth hardly knew what he was saying. He sure didn't know what he was going to say next.

And now, of course, when he wouldn't have minded her talking, she wouldn't say a word. She just stood there looking at him, her mouth tightly closed, her chin up, her hair so wild it was practically giving off sparks. He struggled on. "But now . . . Look. Now I want you here. I'm glad you're here. Okay?" Silence. *"Okay?"*

She sighed suddenly, a long deep sigh, and shook her head. "I guess so. I guess you mean it. You're so weird you probably wouldn't know how to lie. Just don't ever look at me again like that, okay?" She turned and walked over to the bottom of the stairs. "Come on, then. Let's go." But then, as he stepped into place next to her, she sighed one more time. "I wish your name wasn't Ellsworth. Don't you have a nickname?"

"Nickname?" he said. Now that she was going to come, his mind was already following his flashlight up the stairs. "Yeah, sure. My dad's the only one who uses it, but maybe it's okay if you do, too. My dad calls me Zee."

29

The Right Kids

No matter how much Ellsworth wanted to believe in the floor at the top of the stairs as he and Jess stepped out onto it, he felt like the Wright brothers must have felt just before that first airplane lifted that first inch off the ground. It should stay up. But if it didn't, they were probably going to die.

One step. Two. Three. Ellsworth took a tighter grip on his flashlight with both slippery hands and willed his stomach to stay where it belonged. The floor was holding firm, if *firm* was the right word; it felt more like it was bouncing just very slightly under their feet, and along with the bounce went the same kinds of sounds that had scared them so much the day before. It sighed and creaked and groaned, as though what they were walking on wasn't a floor at all but the back of a giant, an old sick giant with aching bones who was shifting painfully at being disturbed. Shifting, but not breaking; not rotting in some kind of disgusting way to suck them down. So far, then, so good.

Ellsworth took three more steps and then stopped. "You there?" he whispered hoarsely.

He felt Jess edge up beside him and then heard her let out her breath in a wobbly kind of sigh. "I guess," she said. Then her flashlight swung down, and her next words were a gasp. "It's that crack!"

"It's okay," he said rapidly. "I see it. But it's okay. Look. See?" He moved his light to show her. It was a gap, all right, but it wasn't jagged and splintery. It was uniform, about two inches wide, and it was smooth, and it was curved. "It couldn't just've happened like that. He must have made it. John Matthew. Yeah. Because look! Oh, man. Look what's in the middle!"

What was in the middle was a huge oval, that, no doubt about it now, had been cut out of the floor. Surrounded by its two inches of empty space, it seemed to hang, suspended in air. In another way, too, it was separated from the planks around it. Instead of unvarnished oak, the wood of the oval was painted. It was painted blue, uncountable different shades of blue. Dotted over its surface were painted lily pads, and sitting on the lily pads were frogs.

Ellsworth felt like a big bucket of cold water had just been poured down his back. "It's the picture. See? Those frogs? Sitting there? It's the pond!"

Jess's flashlight was swinging excitedly. "Yeah, okay! But not just the pond! See?" She was turning now, like a big top. "Don't you see? On the walls. Look! She painted the houses, too. There's three and three and three and one, just like on the Square."

With a wrench, Ellsworth shifted his eyes and his light from the floor to see what she meant. She was right. They looked like the picture, too. "Yeah. But the floor's more important. This pond, here, I don't get how he did it. I mean, it can't just be hanging there." He crouched down, probing down into the crack with his light. Then, with a grunt, he lay down flat and carefully slid his free fingers along the edge. There had to be something holding the oval up. Then he grunted again. "Yeah. There's something here. Listen, I need more light, okay? Take mine, too, okay, and shine them both down here."

But the light didn't do much good. The crack was too narrow. He'd have to do it just by feel, except even that was hard in such a small space. But what he was touching was metal, he knew that, and it was thin, like a rod, except for here—he felt upward—this part that was attached to the floor. That was a solid plate of some kind, with screws. He slid his finger down along the rod again, as far as it would go, reaching, reaching, and suddenly his heart began to pound. There. It wasn't one piece of metal. It was two. It was two of them, hinged together.

He yanked out his fingers and sat up. "I need the bag," he said.

Jess shone the light down into his face. "What? What did you find? What bag?"

Ellsworth, blinded, pushed her arm away. "The bag with the oil. I left it at the top of the stairs. There's a hinge down there." Now his mind was racing. "And there's got to be more, right? One arm, that's not going to hold up that whole pond. Get the bag, okay, while I . . ." Still speaking, he flopped back onto his stomach, pushed himself a couple of feet to the left, and stuck his fingers back down into the crack. "Yeah, okay. There's another one." He slid and felt again, and then again. Then he lay there for a minute, breathing dust and trying to think, and then he was sneezing and sneezing and sneezing again. He clambered jerkily to his feet. "You got it?" he said when he could finally speak.

One of the flashlights Jess was holding was pointed at the pond, but the other one was directed straight down, so he couldn't see her face.

"Look," she said, and stopped.

Ellsworth sighed. He'd forgotten about Jess and oil. "Okay, so I'll get it. But how come you're so scared? Nobody ever started a fire with WD—"

"Look," she said louder, pushed the second flashlight into his hand and then shoved his arm down so it was pointing the same way as hers. "Down there. There's something carved in the floor."

"Yeah?" said Ellsworth, and looked. "What, there? No. That's just a knothole. I think. Isn't it?" He didn't want to look at things carved in the floor. He wanted to oil those hinges. Because they were the key to everything, because hinges make things move, and if he could get all of them working . . .

But now Jess was kneeling down and dragging him down with her. "It's not a hole." She put down her flashlight and dug a fingernail down into whatever she was seeing. "It's just filled up with dust, right? I just need to get it . . . I just need to . . . Okay! Come on! Look! It's a letter! It's an initial! It's—what is it?—it's an *E*! An *E* like downstairs . . ."

Ellsworth peered down halfheartedly. What was it about Jess and initials, anyway? "Yeah. Well, maybe. Maybe it's an *E*. But so what?"

"So what?" Their faces were close enough to the light that this time he could see her face. She had a big streak of dirt down one cheek, and her eyes were blazing with a combination of excitement and disbelief. "So what? So if *E* is here, the other ones are. So we've got to look for them. They've got to mean something."

"Yeah, yeah. Okay." She probably was right. "Listen. You look, okay? I got to work on those hinges . . ."

Jess wasn't listening. She was already crawling around, pushing her flashlight with one hand and feeling floorboards with the other. The other thing she was doing was stirring up dust, and Ellsworth sneezed again. Then he realized she wasn't. "I thought you were allergic," he said.

"What?" she said. "Oh. I took a pill before I ran. Look! Here's some more. A *T.* An *R.* But look! Here's the other *E.* One *E*'s for Ellsworth, right? Then this one's for Emily." She sat up and swung around to face him. "That's my middle name, did I tell you? So don't you see? It's us. It's like it's saying we really are both supposed to be here."

Ellsworth, now cradling the bag in his hands, stared back at her, slowly taking in what she'd said. *E* for Ellsworth. *E* for Emily. Suddenly he saw her face light up and realized he was grinning. She was right! This *was* right, the right time, and they *were* right, the right kids . . . Crazy as it sounded, it was like John Matthew had planned it this way. It was like John Matthew, finally, was going to let it all happen. He was going to let them find the last Smith family treasure.

But an hour later, a long, hot, dusty, heartbreaking hour later, it was clear that he wasn't going to let them do it alone.

❧ 30 ❧

Richard's Story

"It was supposed to be easy." Ellsworth was pacing back and forth in front of the bench by the pond. "That's how he meant it to be. They were supposed to read that sign on the stairs and go up together and look at that painted pond and know."

"I guess," said Jess. She was slumped down on the bench, her legs sticking straight out. She was even more sweaty now and streaked with dust and frowning. "But so what? We read the sign and went up together and looked. And maybe we know. But so what? We still can't do it."

"Yeah," said Ellsworth. "Yeah. We need more people. Lots more people. How many of us are there, anyway?"

Jess counted off on her fingers. "Grandma and me, two. Matthew, three. Dwight, four. Abner and Josie, six. Then there's you and Elizabeth and what's-his-name . . . John. Oh, yeah, and—"

"Forget him," said Ellsworth. "Okay, that's nine. Ten, when my dad gets here. Yeah, but maybe by the time he comes, Abner and Josie'll be gone. And Matthew's not back yet, is he? So there'll probably never be enough. And even if there were, we'd never get them up there. I mean, Dwight and John hate each other, and Matthew, he's mad at Elizabeth, or something. I just don't get why John Matthew set it up that way, having to have so many . . ."

He stopped pacing. "Why" reminded him of what Matthew had said. That *why* John Matthew built the treasure houses was the big question. Ellsworth had almost forgotten again that he and Jess had something that might give the answer.

"What?" said Jess, jerking herself upright. "What?"

"The journal. We've got to finish it."

"Well, I've only been trying to tell you that for about a million years," said Jess. "Okay, look. Grandma's going to be having a fit, wondering where I am. And I've got to get a shower. So let's meet back here in an hour and read it."

"Well, okay. But not here. There's too many people here."

"Well, where then? The cemetery?"

He hesitated. He didn't know if he was ready for the cemetery again. But where else was there? He nodded.

"Okay," said Jess. "I'll tell Grandma we're doing some kind of family history project. Well, we are, aren't we? She'll love it."

Elizabeth was back from Meeting and mixing tuna fish for sandwiches when Ellsworth walked in. She sounded pleased with the idea, too. "I'm glad the two of you are finding something cool to do in this heat. Give my regards to Matthew, please." She frowned briefly. "Not Matthew across the Square. Matthew Duncan, 1858 to 1928, my great-grandfather. My mother said that her earliest memory was of him teaching her how to do somersaults across the Sward. Definitely a Smith it would have been fun to know."

The cemetery wasn't as empty as it had been the day before, but the Smith plot was big and spread out and sheltered by pine trees, so that when Ellsworth and Jess were finally settled, one against each urn, they couldn't hear much except the occasional car crunching along gravel and the odd dim voice in the distance. They opened the box quickly this time, and Jess turned out the journal and began looking for where they'd left off the day before. "I've got to be more careful," she said. "These corners keep breaking off. Look. He didn't write in all of it, it's only half full. Except that then he skips a lot of pages and then he writes one more. That one, let's see, it's 1864."

"That's almost twenty years before he died, isn't it? Yeah, look. He died in 1881. So what happened in 1864?"

"I don't know. But look what happened earlier. Here. Look here. It's all messy, his writing at the end, like he just kind of scribbled it down. And look, at the bottom of the page, here. It's all blotchy, like it got wet." She looked at him, wide-eyed. "Like somebody had been . . . crying. It gives me the shivers. Did somebody die then, or something?"

Eighteen sixty-four. When was that? That was the Civil War. And somebody did die in the Civil War. Ellsworth rolled over onto his knees and found the marker between the twins. Yes. There it was. RICHARD SULLIVAN: 1845–1864.

"Richard," he said. "Richard got killed. And it's Richard's house we're looking in. So this is important. This might give us the clue. Listen. Go back, okay? To where Richard starts. Start reading there."

"Okay. Okay. Hold on. This isn't so easy, you know. I've got to get used to it again, how he writes things. Okay.

Well, there's lot of stuff earlier about all the kids, and Richard's in that, a little bit. But, let's see. Here. This one starts out with him, right off, with his name."

"Okay. Read that."

"Eighteen fifty-seven," started Jess. "Okay. Here goes. 'Richard is nearly thirteen years old, and it grieves me to admit that I'm worried about the boy. I have nothing against books—what could be more important than learning? But it isn't his schoolbooks that he lavishes every spare second on, not his Virgil or his mathematics or his French grammar. No, what he can't seem to get his fill of is rubbish. Oh, he calls it poetry and saga and romance, and it is, according to his tutor, good-enough specimens of its kind. But it's rubbish all the same, full of dangerous nonsense about knights and dragons and glorious battles. Unreal battles, without smells or sights to sicken and kill. Dangerous battles. Rubbish.'"

Ellsworth's head came up, and he gazed blankly over the dying expanse of grass. R.C. Somehow that last part sounded just how he bet R.C. would sound. "Richard is *my* story," Ben Robert had always said. Ellsworth crossed his arms hard against his chest. Did he really want to know how this was going to turn out? He had to. For one thing, Jess was still reading.

"'Eighteen fifty-eight,'" she was saying. "He's still going on about Richard. 'What am I to do with this boy, this beloved boy of mine? I try to be patient, but Uly and little Sam show more sense. The Treasures, for example, which I found with such excitement in that dusty shop in London more than fifteen years ago—'"

"Treasures?" said Ellsworth. "What about treasures?"

"Yeah, well that's coming next, okay? Don't make me lose my place. Here. Okay. 'All the children love them, of course. Who would not? But they look and touch, hear their stories, line them up this way and that, and then are content to see them locked back away. But with Richard, they have become something more. He keeps them by him constantly. I fear that they speak to him, call to him, encourage him to turn his back even further on the sensible and practical, encourage him to dream of quests, Holy Grails, righting the wrongs of the world. These voices I cannot call rubbish—how can I?—but for that very reason they represent, in these troubled times, a danger that turns a parent's heart cold in his breast.'"

Ellsworth was sweating. So close to the pine trees there wasn't any breeze. It was beginning to be hard to concentrate, to get the gist of what Jess was reading.

She was reading about 1859 . . . 1860. Troubled times were growing anguished as the terrible wrong of slavery was becoming more and more impossible for anyone, let alone Quakers, to ignore. Richard was fifteen now, immersed no longer in poetry but in the antislavery literature that was pouring from an ever larger number of powerful pens.

"'I share his conviction,'" Ellsworth heard Jess say. "'Our Society abhors the very thought of slavery. Haven't I myself written of the importance of keeping our newer states free? Haven't I opened my purse to those Friends dedicated to helping as many of those brave people as possible escape to freedom? But Richard's conclusions . . .

How have I failed him if he believes, against all I and our Society have taught him, that war could be an answer? That killing could be a solution? Despite all my attempts, he refuses to listen when I try to tell him of the unutterable horror that war always, always, unleashes.' "

Jess was reading faster now. Eighteen sixty-one. Richard's sixteenth birthday. Fort Sumter. War. John Matthew's increasingly frantic efforts to prevent Richard, tall for his age, fully grown, from enlisting. " 'Insanity. Insanity. Even with my consent, which of course I refuse to give, they'd no doubt turn him away, and rightly so. But he doesn't eat. He doesn't sleep. When he talks to me at all, it is to rail against me for refusing to supply the Union with cloth from our mills, cloth for uniforms for the Union troops. He has no care, I see, for *my* conviction, the testimony of my whole life.' "

Then it was 1862. It was Richard's seventeenth birthday, and three days later, the horrors of Shiloh. Twenty-four thousand men. Twenty-four *thousand* in two days, on both sides, gone. And then, like a great bell tolling the year down: Bull Run. Antietam. Fredricksburg. Ellsworth saw that Jess's hands were trembling so much now that she could hardly turn the pages. Because she knew what was going to happen in 1863 when Richard turned eighteen and when his father wouldn't be able to hold him back. Ellsworth knew, too.

No one was able to hold him back. " 'I scarcely have words,' " Jess read in a voice she couldn't keep steady, " 'hardly the will, even, to describe this birthday. Betsy beyond tears, the little ones clinging to her. Ionia, Richard's special pet, understanding only that he was leaving, and questioning over and over: "Richy? Richy? Why do you have to go?"

"'And I . . . I knowing he didn't have to, that even the new conscription couldn't, at eighteen, touch him . . . I, tormented by the memory of my poor lost boys, overwhelmed by terror and rage at the thought that yet another of my sons might be snatched from us forever, and this an even more senseless slaughter, this a wicked slaughter . . . I . . . I cannot go on. . . .'"

Jess stopped, too. She threw the book onto the grass and put her hands over her face. She wasn't crying like she had yesterday, but she was shuddering, as though she was cold instead of boiling hot.

"Isn't there more?" Ellsworth finally said. "You said there was one more page, later."

"You read it," she said, her voice muffled behind her hands. "I can't. I can't read any more."

His stomach clenching, he picked up the journal. Fumbling through it, he finally found what he was looking for. It was three or four pages ahead of where she had stopped, and the paper was smooth again instead of wrinkled with tears. It was just two short paragraphs written in dark ink, the handwriting controlled but cramped.

Ellsworth studied it for a long minute. The o's and a's were hardest, because they looked almost the same. "Okay," he finally said. "'Eighteen sixty-four.' That's how he starts, like you said. Now." His finger followed the words, one at a time. "'My wife forgives me. She says it was no curse, what I said to him, to Richard, to my son as he left to die. But she is wrong. I know what I said. "Go," I said. "But if you do, it's with no blessing of mine or of our Society or of God. You go alone."

"'He went alone. He wrote to his mother, but we never saw him again. He survived a year of war, and then, on June third, 1864, was killed in Grant's great bloodbath at Cold Harbor, Virginia.'" Then Ellsworth took a long breath and another and finished. The last words were written so forcefully that the pen had broken through the paper. "'No child of mine shall ever be alone again.'"

☆ 31 ☆

The Plan

Ellsworth couldn't sleep. The heat had finally seeped through the solid brick of Elizabeth's house, and his room, even with the two other windows forced open, was stifling. The old bed sagged, and thoughts scurried around and around in his head like rats. Why didn't his father come? He hadn't called. Maybe he really wasn't coming, maybe he really had headed off someplace without him. Maybe, like Richard, he was . . . No. But then why wasn't he here?

And then, what about R.C.? He didn't really care about R.C., why should he, but Elizabeth did, and she'd said at supper that though he'd finally answered the door that afternoon to her and John, he'd said hardly anything and hadn't invited them in. She'd looked sad and tired, and Ellsworth had kept hoping that Matthew would come over to cheer her up, but he hadn't. Maybe he wasn't home yet. Maybe she'd hoped that *he*, Ellsworth, could cheer her up, but he couldn't. He couldn't even fix her mixer, though he'd tried—it needed a new plug, and he didn't have one. She was probably beginning to wonder why she'd even asked him to come at all.

And how were they going to find what John Matthew had hidden? The journal hadn't really given them a clue after all. It sure hadn't told them how they were going to get everybody to help them. His mind plodded again and

191

again and again around the Square, counting faces and houses and numbers. Finally, gradually, they all dimmed, drifted together, and pulled him down into sleep.

When he woke up the next morning, it felt late. It was still hot, but padding over to look out, he saw that the sky had changed. The white glare had flattened to dull blue garnished with clouds. Elizabeth had said that the radio had forecast thunderstorms later today or tonight. Maybe.

Something else had changed, too. He had a plan. It had come to him in his sleep. They didn't *need* thirteen people. John Matthew couldn't have counted on that many, not exactly. What he'd counted on was a group. So it was simple. All he and Jess had to do was just ask the family, one at a time, on their own, to meet them at the house sometime today. And they just wouldn't tell them that anybody else was coming that they might be mad at. He'd ask Elizabeth and Dwight and John, and Matthew if he got back. Jess could ask Kitty and Josie and Abner. Once they had everybody there, and explained what they'd found and how John Matthew had planned it all, people would be so excited they'd forget about everything else. They'd have to.

It suddenly felt important to ask Elizabeth first. Now. He zipped in and out of the bathroom and into his clothes and five minutes later was heading down the back stairs to the kitchen. It wasn't until he was almost at the bottom that he realized that if he was going to talk to Elizabeth alone he'd have to wait. Matthew was back and was here and was sounding serious. "Listen to me, Liz," he was saying. "Just listen to me."

"Hi," said Ellsworth, clattering down the last couple of stairs, and they both jerked around to face him.

"Ellsworth," said Matthew. "Good. I have a question for you."

"Please, Matthew," said Elizabeth. "No."

"It's okay, Liz," said Matthew. "I just really want to know. Ellsworth, what do you think? How old are we?"

Ellsworth thought maybe he should just turn around and go back to bed. Matthew snorted.

"Okay," he said. "I'll make it easier for you. Which one of us do you think is older? Don't worry—no penalty if you're wrong. Nobody gets hurt. Liz or me? Me or Liz? What do you say?"

Ellsworth looked reluctantly from one to the other. Then he saw that it *was* easy. He knew exactly what to say, because it was true. "I don't know. You both look pretty old to me."

Matthew grinned, and Elizabeth's face relaxed. "Thank you, Ellsworth," she said, pushing herself to her feet. "That was definitely speaking truth to power. Because you're right. We both are pretty old." Her attention swung back to Matthew. "It's just that I'm older," she said. Her words were crisp. "And I've been living alone for a long time, and I'm a lousy housekeeper and a terrible cook, and when I feel like it, which is often, I read until two A.M. *And*, as I've told you again and again, my name is Elizabeth. Not Liz. It's important to me, Matthew. If you don't understand that, you don't understand anything."

"*And*," said Matthew, slapping his hand on the table and

then standing up to face her, "you're refusing to admit the *only* important thing. You know what it is. You *feel* what it is, the same as I do. Please. We can't just throw it away."

"At the moment," said Elizabeth quietly, "the only thing I know is that we're making Ellsworth uncomfortable. Leave it, Matthew. Now."

"All right," said Matthew. "I'll leave it. But do one thing for me, will you? While I was away, I made something for you. It's a sign to add to your collection. You'll have some idea how long it took me to find it, knowing how little I've ever read the Quaker worthies. But this is from William Penn. And from me. So read it please, later, when you're not upset. And Li—Elizabeth? Think about it. Give it a chance. That's all I'm asking." And then, not waiting for her reply, he turned and took Ellsworth by the arm. "Come out for a minute, okay? We need to talk."

"Yeah, well, okay," said Ellsworth. "But there's something I want to ask Elizabeth."

"It'll just take a minute." Matthew steered Ellsworth out, and then sat down with a big *whoosh* on the porch steps. "Don't wait until your forties to fall in love, Ellsworth. That's my advice to you."

"Yeah, well," said Ellsworth. "Okay, thanks. But, listen, can I ask you something?"

"Ask away. Then I've got a question for you."

Ellsworth dove in. "The thing is we found something in the house. Richard's house? Jess and me? But we need you to help us get it."

Matthew's eyes suddenly narrowed. "Richard's house?

What do you mean you found something? I don't have a key yet to Richard's house."

Ellsworth mentally bonked himself on the head. He'd forgotten about that. How had he forgotten about that? "Yeah, well, see, I do. Or kind of. I mean Jess had these skeleton keys. And then Dwight— "

"Are you telling me," said Matthew, and now he looked completely like the teacher he was, "that you went into that house alone?"

"No," said Ellsworth. "No, look, I know you wanted to go, too, but you were away, and Jess and me, we were talking, so we—"

"So you went in there, the two of you, without an adult, knowing full well that it could be dangerous. . . ." Matthew looked dangerous now. His face was turning red and he was rising slowly to his feet.

"Look," said Ellsworth. This wasn't working. This wasn't working at all. "Why are you so mad? You won't even let me explain."

"I came over here," said Matthew, "partly to talk to Elizabeth and partly to ask you if you wanted to start exploring. Well, I guess I shouldn't have bothered. It doesn't look like either of you needs much of anything I have to offer, does it?"

"No," said Ellsworth. "That's not true. I mean, we do need you. Jess and me. This afternoon, I thought, if you could just come . . ."

"Jess and I," said Matthew in a level voice. "It's Jess and I. And I don't think so, Ellsworth. What I think is that I'm going home now to think seriously about what could possibly have been in my head when I came to live on this Square. Maybe I'll see you again, and maybe I won't. Don't bother to see me out." And with that, he strode down Elizabeth's walk, whacking flowers out of his way with his hands as he went. Reaching the end, he just escaped crashing into John and Woolman.

"Sorry," said John. Matthew grunted and kept going.

"He doesn't seem too happy, does he?" said John. "Can't say you do either. So I'll keep it short. I've been thinking. A couple of days ago you were asking questions. About the house, Richard's house, like you wanted a look. Well, okay. Maybe it's not such a bad idea after all. But you'll need some light. You'll need those shutters back. So how would you like to go down to my place now and help me get a ladder, and then I'll give you a hand. What would you say to that?"

Ellsworth thought for a minute. Why not? Elizabeth probably wasn't in the mood to listen right now, so why not talk to John instead?

"Sure," he said. "Let's go."

Another Quarrel

Halfway down the Square, John stopped and dropped his end of the ladder. Above his close-cropped beard his face was flushed and sweaty. "Sorry," he said. "Got to catch my breath." He wiped his face and looked up. "Funny sky, isn't it? Clouds, sun, a little of everything. Saw some heat lightning in the west last night, so maybe we'll get lucky. We'd better. If we don't get some rain soon, this whole place will dry up and blow away."

"Yeah," said Ellsworth. "Except there isn't any wind. I mean, there is up there. Those clouds are moving. But not down here."

"Guess that's why it feels so close. I'm going to let you do the climbing, down there, if that's okay with you. Not afraid of heights, are you?"

"I don't think so," said Ellsworth. "I mean, I've never been on a ladder before."

"Well, it's high time, then. Keeping a house going takes a lot of ladder work. Shutters, gutters, roofs, chimneys . . . Every bit of it important."

They started off again, moving steadily until they got to the south walk, where John stopped so abruptly that Ellsworth almost lost his grip. "Now what's he doing there?" The old man stooped down to get a better look.

"He's always got some harebrained scheme going, doesn't he? What's it now?"

Ellsworth didn't have to see the stout figure turning onto the walk to Richard's house to know that it was Dwight. John's voice had told him that. Dwight was carrying a big cardboard box. It looked heavy, and Tara wasn't exactly helping him out. She kept taking a step and stopping, and taking a step and stopping, and Dwight kept bumping into her. His box was sliding lower and lower. Ellsworth glanced at John's face and then away. The next step Dwight took he got tangled up in Tara's leash and almost fell, and Ellsworth put down his end of the ladder. "Maybe I should give him a hand."

John's breath came out in a snort. "Yeah. Yeah, I guess maybe you'd better, before he kills himself. Then you tell him we have business there and don't need him getting in the way."

It was too hot to run, but Ellsworth ran anyway, and managed to grab Dwight's box just before it hit the ground. Dwight staggered a few steps farther, lowered himself onto the stairs, and sat wheezing, trying to catch his breath. As Ellsworth eased the box down, Tara stuck her nose into it. Ellsworth peered in, too. It was full of hardware: screwdriver sets and socket sets and at least two more cans of lubricant and another, bigger flashlight, and two Coleman lanterns. Dwight had stopped wheezing and lit a cigarette and was shaking his head.

"I was upstairs and spotted you two coming and almost lost my breakfast. No sense, that's what some people have, no sense . . . Dragging ladders around in this heat . . .

Probably thinking about climbing them, too, and getting himself killed. He wants to open those shutters, doesn't he? Oh, yeah, I know how his mind works, all right. He thinks it's the nineteenth century; he thinks you need daylight. Listen to me now, you need more light, I brought you more. Leave those shutters be." Then his gaze shifted out and up and his chin came up, too. "Oh, it's you, is it?" he said. "Well, you heard me. Stop acting like you know more than anybody else."

Ellsworth hunkered down. Woolman was there now, too, and he and Tara were companionably sniffing at each other and at him, and he petted them and ducked their wet tongues and hoped Dwight and John would forget he was there. But he didn't have to worry. They weren't interested in him.

"You always did like sticking your nose in where it had no place being," John said. "Well, some of us got work to do here, so the thing for you is just to go on home and let us get on with it. Go on now, and take that cigarette with you. You want to kill yourself, Ellsworth here doesn't need to watch."

Ellsworth heard the porch steps creak and knew that Dwight was getting to his feet. There was a long moment of complete silence, and Ellsworth finally looked up. Above him, the two men were staring at each other like they had on the sidewalk the day before. The white of John's beard was a startling contrast to the red of Dwight's face, now getting redder.

"You always did think you knew better, didn't you? You always did like to point fingers. Fourteen years ago, you were right behind R.C., weren't you, blaming me for what happened with Ben Robert. I didn't have to put up with that, not from you. You were just jealous because it was me he trusted, me he came to—"

"Yeah, and look where it got him. Just because you had to stick your nose in where it didn't belong."

Ellsworth was on his feet. What was the matter with them? Why were they still fighting over this stuff? What good did it do?

"Cut it out," he said. He couldn't stop himself. "Just cut it out, okay? Since I got up this morning, everybody's been fighting. I'm sick of it. And leave my dad out of it. Maybe I know what he meant now, about if there's something here in this house, nobody's going to find it. John Matthew, he wanted it to be easy for us, you know? But it's not, because you guys, everybody, you won't let it be. So could you just go? Both of you. I'm sorry, okay? But just go."

They looked at him for a minute, mouths open, and then John, his eyes suddenly sick, turned, growled a word at Woolman, and started down the walk. Dwight waited just long enough to see that he was turning west, dropped his cigarette, and ground it slowly out. He reached down with a grunt and gathered up Tara's leash, and only then did he look at Ellsworth. "Sorry," he said.

Ellsworth sank down on the bottom step and closed his eyes. It was all crazy. They were all crazy. Did they *like* to fight? Well, he didn't. He wasn't used to it. It was stupid. They were supposed to be his family, but they were all so dumb. Even Elizabeth, a little, this thing with Matthew, and he didn't want Elizabeth to be dumb. He'd thought it would be so easy, getting them all down to help. A plan? Forget it.

The step beside him creaked. Now what? But when he opened his eyes, it was only Jess. She was dressed in a blue shirt and white shorts, and as he shifted over to give her more room, she folded up her long brown legs and plunked her head down on them. Her voice, when she spoke, was muffled. "Well, at least they went away when you told them to."

"Yeah, but did you hear them? Now we'll never get them up there."

She raised her head and nodded. "Grandma either. I came down here because we had a fight, and I wanted to think, and then I saw Dwight coming and hid. See, I had this great idea, last night, you know? About how we could make it work, if we just asked them . . ."

Ellsworth straightened. "Yeah? Me, too. But—"

"But I did it wrong. I told her how we'd been in here, and you should have heard her. 'I told you not to go in there! It's so dangerous! It's so irresponsible! You could have been killed!' She acted like I was five years old."

"Matthew did the same thing," said Ellsworth. He sat up straighter, suddenly feeling a little better. "I figured that out, too. Ten of them, you know, that'd have to—"

"No," interrupted Jess. She had straightened, too. "Nine. R.C. doesn't come out. But nine might be enough."

"Ten," said Ellsworth. "My dad's coming. I know he is."

"Yeah?" said Jess. Then she slumped back down. "Yeah, but what's the point? I mean, these guys wouldn't go up there together. And Grandma sure wouldn't, and Abner and Josie, they're leaving tonight. So that just leaves Matthew, right, if he's back, and Elizabeth. . . ."

But Ellsworth was already shaking his head. "They had a fight, too." He stood up, though, and started kicking gently at the step, thinking. He and Jess had both had the same idea. That had to mean something. That had to mean it could work. He didn't have any idea how, but maybe if they *did* something, anything, it might get things going.

"Yeah," he said. "Okay. Listen. What do you know about ladders?"

✠ 33 ✠

The Storm

Ellsworth and Jess stood on the slate walk in back of Number Two South, looking up. Jess's shorts weren't white anymore, and Ellsworth's T-shirt was black, and their faces looked like they'd just been plucked, dripping, out of a pot of boiling water. But they felt just fine. They had gotten all the shutters on Richard's house opened and fastened back, and they hadn't gotten killed doing it.

"It looks better," said Jess. "It doesn't look, you know, dead anymore." Ellsworth nodded. The windows made all the difference. Even dirty, they opened the house up. The inside would look different, too. He couldn't wait to see the pond with real light on it. Light. He blinked. It had changed again. While they'd been working, the sky had narrowed to glittering, shifting slivers of blue. There weren't just more clouds. They were bigger, too, and rimmed with black, and he was glad he was no longer at the top of a ladder, because the wind had come up. Random gusts touched down here and there, ruffling the grass at their feet. Higher up, though, it was steadier and the tops of the trees had begun to sway.

"ELLSWORTH . . . !" The voice sounded, in the charged air, as though it were coming from miles away instead of halfway across the Square. "ELLSWORTH . . . ! WHERE ARE YOU? COME HOME, PLEASE!"

"That's Elizabeth," said Jess. "Listen. Do you think I could come, too? I don't want to go back to Grandma's yet—she's probably still mad. Besides, I don't know. The sky . . . I don't like it. It's weird."

"Weird?" said Ellsworth. "It's just a storm coming. But, okay. COMING," he bellowed. "WE'RE COMING!" He gave the house one last satisfied glance and then turned and took the walk in two fast leaps. "Let's go."

What they had to figure out, he thought as they skirted the pond, was what to say to people. Maybe they'd just have to come right out, spell it out for them. Beg them, maybe. He wasn't quite sure how you went about begging people, but maybe Jess—

But Jess had suddenly stopped.

"Ow," he said. "Hey. Watch it, okay?"

She wasn't listening. "Who's that?" she said.

"Who's what?"

"That. There. Standing on the porch."

Ellsworth looked, and everything else faded. "It's my dad!" Five seconds later he and Ben Robert were both at the end of Elizabeth's walk, and Ben Robert was holding him so tightly he could hardly breathe.

"Zee," he was saying. "Zee." Then he stepped back, his hands still on Ellsworth's shoulders, and peered down into his face. "You're okay? You're still in one piece? They haven't eaten you alive?"

"You got here," Ellsworth said. He was trembling, but it felt good. Everything felt good. "You *were* coming here. Elizabeth said you were, but Mr. Rocco sounded so mad, and then the car, I figured the car . . ."

Ben Robert gave Ellsworth's shoulders one last squeeze and shook his head. "You never did give that car credit. You keep it under forty, all it needs is a quart of oil every hour or so. Oh, Zee. Of course I was coming. I knew about two seconds after your bus left that I was crazy letting you come here alone, and then I went even crazier trying to get away. Mr. Rocco was at his finest, of course. Not so much about me leaving—he doesn't really need a night clerk, and he knows it. No, it was you, you maybe not coming back. 'What am I supposed to do without the kid?' he kept saying. 'I need the kid.'" He nodded. "I knew exactly how he felt. Man, but it's good to see you, Zee."

"Me, too," said Ellsworth. "I mean, you, too. I've got all this stuff to tell you. And ask you. And oh, yeah. This is Jess."

"Jess. Hi. Hey. Should I know you? You definitely look like somebody I should know."

Jess didn't answer. Turning to see why, Ellsworth noticed that she was trembling. "What's wrong?" he said.

She shook her head. Her face looked bleached. Her hand came up, pointing at something down the walk. She stepped back and then back again.

Ellsworth and Ben Robert both turned, and then Ellsworth felt a sharp pain and looked down to see his father's fingers digging into his arm. R.C., still as a statue, was standing at the end of his walk. Ellsworth tried to swallow, and couldn't. He'd wanted to see R.C., at least he thought he had, but not now. Not when his father had just come and had looked so happy, and now, instead, looked like he'd just been fed into a big machine and cranked out the other end. Then Ellsworth heard the thunk of a screen door closing and saw Elizabeth limping as fast as she could across the back porch.

The air suddenly felt darker, thicker, hard to breathe. From far away, thunder growled, and then again, and on the Sward the wind stirred up leaves, dead leaves and branches, like a hand stirring papers on a desk and suddenly, impatiently, tossing them into the air.

Elizabeth paid no attention. "Ben Robert," she said. "Listen. Please. He's changed. You have to understand that he's changed." She was speaking slowly, like she might to a child, on a roof, too near the edge. "He's grieving. He's wasting away. Look at him, Ben Robert. Look at him closely. Have some pity on him. Ask him . . ."

"Ask him what?" Ben Robert had come back to some kind of life, but his voice was as bitter as his face. "Ask him to forgive me? For wanting a life of my own? For loving someone in a way he knows nothing about? For not understanding how my mother, my mother, could just . . . give me up?" His words now were beginning to crack. He gripped Ellsworth's arm harder and stared over his head at the old man, who was still standing frozen at the edge of his yard. "My mother, who couldn't disobey him. Who wouldn't even talk to me after my wedding. And later, when something was wrong, wrong with Sally, when I swallowed my pride and went to her, to ask for help, because we didn't have insurance, how could we have insurance, she said no. She wanted to help, she said, but she couldn't. And you know why. Sure you do. We all do. But nobody knows better than him." The last word was spit into the air and hung there like poison. The words that followed were no better. "I'd never ask him for anything."

But he couldn't turn away, either. He stood staring at R.C., staring just like R.C. was staring back, unmoving, and it seemed suddenly to Ellsworth that the air between them was vibrating, humming, as though a switch had been flipped and a thousand volts of electricity hurled along the walk. And then there was a tremendous bang, and Ellsworth heard Jess cry out and felt every hair on his body stand on end and then every *cell* in his body reverberate with the flicker of something that he saw only out of the corner of his eye. It was a flicker of absolute energy. His senses, all of them, exploded, and then the two tall pines at the edge of the pond exploded, too, and burst into flame.

34

Fire

Jess screamed. Something fell smoking and sparking onto the walk next to her, and then it was raining fire and she and Ellsworth were swung around and squashed together against Ben Robert's chest. Ben Robert yelped and the next moment let go of them, grabbed the bottom of his T-shirt, and dragged it over his head.

He probed at his back. "Ouch. Ellsworth? You okay? Jess? What hit you?"

Jess, her eyes enormous, pointed shakily at a smoking pinecone at her feet. "It just bounced. It just hit me like somebody threw it, and then it bounced." She took a long shuddering breath. "Is it out? Is it over?"

But Ellsworth, turning slowly around and around, saw that it was far from over. The south end of the Square looked like a battlefield. It was littered with branches and cones and bunches of pine needles, and most of them were burning. The ones on the walk only smoldered, but on the Sward, the tall grass, much of it dead after two months of drought and swaying now in the wind, was already beginning to catch. The thunder was closer now, the racing clouds darker, but there was no rain. You could almost choke on the air, it still felt so dry, because there was no rain at all, and if they didn't do something fast, the whole end of the Square could go up in flames.

As Ellsworth started to run, he felt, along with a huge surge of energy, a rush of relief. Because he wasn't alone. The Square was exploding again, but this time with Smiths, a whole kaleidoscope of them. Behind him, he heard his father and Jess stopping, stamping, running again. Out of the corner of his eye he saw Elizabeth awkwardly dragging the hose from her flower bed, and across the Sward, Dwight wrestling with one of his own. A moment later Matthew crashed through bushes, looked around, and crashed back out again. In only minutes he had returned, a fire extinguisher in hand and Kitty close behind. And finally, now, moving steadily down the Sward, came John. He was armed with a dripping blanket. He threw it down on a smoking branch, stomped on it, grabbed it up again, and kept on coming.

Dripping. Wet. Yes. Get something wet. Get it wet from the pond, thwap some fire out, get it wet again. His T-shirt maybe? Yes! Hauling it off, Ellsworth swung toward the pond and then jerked to a stop, his eyes burning. The pond wasn't a pond anymore, but a sea of flames.

It was his dream. It was his dream from the Lake Breeze. But no. Not quite. What was burning wasn't water. It was pine branches. They had burst from the trees overhead, slammed into the pond's muddy bottom, and were waving now like fiery flags.

Then Jess was beside him, her face black with soot and her eyes urgent. "We're getting it out here. But, Zee, the porch! Look!" He swung around again to follow where she was pointing through a gap in the bushes. What looked like almost the whole top of a tree had been propelled to

Richard's back steps. It was mostly charred black but was smoking gently. What if underneath, against the old, old wood of the steps, it was burning?

He threw his T-shirt into the water, dragged it out again, and began to stumble his way through debris. It felt like he was hardly moving at all and that he'd never reach it, and the house and whatever was inside would burn, burn to the ground. As he reached the slate sidewalk, he saw two things at once. One was a tiny flicker of flame eating away at the corner of the bottom step. The second was Abner. He didn't look anything like the Abner of two days ago. His face was bright red, and his pale trousers were streaked with black. He was brandishing a rake and moving fast, and in what seemed like only seconds he'd dragged the smoldering mass down onto the sidewalk and was pulling it apart. He was breathing hard, but he nodded approvingly as Ellsworth twacked his wet T-shirt onto the step and then stomped on it.

"That's the way," he said. "I think we're going to be all right. The roof, you see? It wasn't touched. We were fortunate with the wind—it sent most of the sparks the other way. But look! There! Lightning again! We shouldn't be out here. We should be inside, all of us. And where's the rain, you know? Where's the rain?"

Lightning but no rain. Lightning but no rain. It sparked something in Ellsworth's memory: Colorado, the year they'd lived there, dry lightning and forest fires out of control. But more important were Abner's other words. "All of us . . ." he'd said. And he was right. All the Smiths were there, on the Sward, on the Square, this minute. The fires were almost out, and in another minute, every one of them would start running for cover. What if, *what if,* WHAT IF he could get all of them running here?

"Listen," he said. He jumped over the pile of brittle, blackened pine and looked up into Abner's face. Despite his calm words, Abner looked tired now, old and tired and ready to quit. Ellsworth knew that whatever he said had to be fast and had to be right. "Listen. There's something I've got to tell you. Something important. Remember I said that Jess and I thought it was here? The treasure? Well, it is. Jess and me, we've found it, we've almost found it, but the only way we can get it is if everybody gets it. Everybody, see? So we've got to get them here. All of them, now, we've got to get them here. Can you help me? Please?"

For a second Abner just looked blank. Then he blinked a couple of times, and a slow smile crept over his face. "This is one of the strangest days of my life. But yes. I can help." He turned and put his hands to his mouth. "Josie? Josie! Come here, would you? We need to get inside, and this young man has something to tell us. So please, come now, quickly!"

The strangest day of his life. Yes. That's what Ellsworth thought as he ran back out onto the Sward. It was the strangest day of his life, and as the thunder rumbled closer, it was getting stranger. Jess, as though she'd read his mind, was running to meet him, and she wasn't alone. Her grandmother was trotting behind her, trying to keep up, trying not to trip, and she wasn't alone either. Matthew was on one side of her, and Dwight on the other. Dwight had dropped his hose, but Matthew still had his extinguisher.

The sight of it, so sturdy and dependable and red and shin-ing, galvanized Ellsworth with energy.

"Yes!" he shouted. "Yes! Get them on the porch and keep them there. I'm getting my dad!"

He didn't have to go far. He rounded the pond, where the branches were slowly burning out, and saw Ben Robert and Elizabeth and John all at once. They were moving slowly toward Elizabeth's house, she leaning heavily on both of them. Ellsworth dodged the bench and skidded to a stop. "Can you come? Please? Down to Richard's house. I know it sounds dumb. But it's not."

Could they come? He thought for one terrible second that they couldn't. Elizabeth's eyes were dull with pain, Ben Robert's with exhaustion. Even John's tall sturdy frame drooped.

"Richard's house?" said Ben Robert. Then his head came up, and a spark of life came back into his face. "Richard's house? You mean, you got in there, Zee? You . . . ?"

Ellsworth nodded. "We found it. Me and Jess. But we can't get it. Not without you. Not without everybody. Okay, Dad? Okay?"

Elizabeth was looking from one of them to the other and then back again. Her face was streaked with dirt, but her eyes were bright again, too, and she didn't waste a second. "Ben Robert? John? Can you turn me around? Can you help me get there? Of course, okay. We're on our way."

35

Together

They ended up just about carrying her, but they did it sur-
prisingly quickly. As they jockeyed their way up the porch
steps, Ellsworth could see that everybody else had gone
inside. It was a good idea. Lightning stabbed again from the
west, and even Richard's house, "jinxed" as it was, seemed
a hundred percent safer than being outside. He grabbed his
T-shirt on the way past, wrung it out, and pulled it over his
head. It was clammy and filthy, but he felt better having
something on.

For a moment there was a surge of chatter, a surge of
excitement. Elizabeth was propped as comfortably as possible against a windowsill. Ben Robert, looking dazed, was
shaking hands, enduring hugs, trying to find something to
say to people he hadn't talked to for almost thirteen years.
But where was Jess? Ellsworth panicked for a second, but
then saw her head poking around the doorway from the
hall. She was a mess. But then, everybody was a mess. They
smelled, too. The whole room smelled like the only time
Ellsworth had gone to camp and it had rained and they'd
spent every minute they could shivering and coughing
around smoky fires.

Jess gestured to him. "Come here. What's the matter?"

"I don't know," said Ellsworth. "But what if we can't
explain? What if we're wrong? What if it doesn't work?"

"It's got to work," she said. "Listen. All those fires? All over the Square? That was my dream! They were the fires I was scared of. But I didn't start them. Are you listening? I helped put them *out*!" She was a mess, but she looked, too, like she'd just run a big race and won. She looked like she'd just won the big race of her life.

"Yeah," said Ellsworth slowly. "The fires . . . You're right. We did put them out. And everybody's okay, too. And we got them here. . . ." His courage was coming back, just in time. Even Kitty was dwindling down into silence, and people were drifting away from Ben Robert and, suddenly, awkwardly, away from each other. Dwight from John. Matthew from Elizabeth. Abner and Josie from all of them. The only "all of them" who wasn't there was R.C.

But his father was. And Elizabeth. They were standing next to each other now, Ben Robert holding her arm, but Elizabeth wasn't looking at Ben Robert. She was looking intently, instead, at him. "It's okay, Ellsworth," she seemed to be saying. "It's time now. It's time for you to tell us what we're waiting to hear."

Ellsworth took a deep breath and said the first dumb thing that came into his head. "Hi," he said. Luckily, it didn't seem to matter. Everbody was listening. The only sounds were the wind rattling the windows and the steady rumble of thunder. He took another deep breath and kept going. "This is weird. Everything. This whole day. Since I got here, really. But it's just like, it was time. Jess and me being here, and her skeleton key working, and then the journal. Finding the journal in Dad's old box and reading it. So it was like we were supposed to. Supposed to find out where John Matthew hid it. The treasure, I mean. It wasn't hard. Because that's all he wanted, wasn't it? Like he said in the journal. He just didn't want any of his kids to be alone."

If the room could get quieter, it got quieter now. Ellsworth swallowed. "So. You'll see. When you come. We have to go upstairs. The stairs are a little tricky. But it's okay—we just have to go two at a time. And the floor up there sounds funny. Scary. But it's okay, too. John, he said it was, and he was right. And Dwight gave us some oil. So I think we can do it. I think it'll work. So, well, I guess, I guess what you all need to do is just . . . come." He stopped. He didn't know what else he was supposed to say, except that obviously it hadn't been enough. Everybody was just still standing there, looking at him. Looking confused. Waiting for more. Then, to his great relief, Ben Robert finally spoke.

"Sorry, Zee. Shell shock, I guess. We all got a little blasted out there. But what you're talking about is . . . Richard's treasure? It's really here?"

Several people nodded, and then Elizabeth spoke up, too. "Here, and upstairs, except it needs all of us to get it. Isn't that right, Ellsworth? Jess? Then I say, if everyone agrees, lead the way!"

She and Ben Robert had made it all right. Everybody had started talking again, quietly, but they were moving, too. As he went through the door with Jess, he turned to look. They were moving slowly, they were straggling, they were limping, but they were coming.

There was a murmur of surprise at the stairs, at John

Matthew's careful engraved words and the slight seesaw movement of the first three steps. Kitty's eyes, looking at them, were suddenly filled with tears. "This is what 'moved,' isn't it? This is why she fell. Oh, Izzy. Why did he have to make it like this? Why did he have to make it so somebody could get hurt?"

It was Matthew who answered her, his voice rough. "Because treasure hunting's always risky. People *can* get hurt. But then, if they're lucky, they find treasure, too. You know, I only knew Izzy for a few years, but I think she would have gotten that. If you don't take chances and risk things, there's too much you'll never have. So I'll bet she would have forgiven John Matthew. I'll bet she was that kind of woman."

There was a moment of silence, and then Ben Robert spoke. His voice wasn't quite steady. "Do you think so?" he said. "Was she?"

It was Elizabeth who spoke up after another beat of silence to answer him. "Oh, yes," she said, leaning toward him. "Oh, yes, Ben Robert. And I don't just *think* your mother was that kind of woman. I know." She gave the merest flick of a glance toward Matthew and then looked away.

"Listen," said Ellsworth. Everything was getting too complicated, and he was beginning to feel a little desperate. "Listen, we need to get going, okay? The thing is, can you do it? Two at a time? Like me and Jess just did? Can you come?"

To his great relief, he saw that Abner and Josie were making their way steadily past the others to stand in position at the bottom of the stairs. "Of course we can," said Abner. "This all just gets more and more amazing. Josie, my dear? Shall we lead the way?" Josie smiled at him. She was a tall thin upright old woman with a swirl of white hair, and she somehow managed to look better than anybody else there.

She and Abner didn't even have to count. With perfect coordination, they stepped up onto the first stair, the second, and then the third, and then, squeezing past Jess with triumphant smiles, gestured Ellsworth on. As he climbed, he looked back and saw that Jess was encouraging her grandmother and Matthew to give it a go. Behind them stood Ben Robert and Elizabeth, and behind them, looking grim and uneasy, the two old men who had been such enemies for such a long time. He had a sudden inspiration. "Uh, you guys? John? Dwight? Would you mind, I mean, could you come up next? John, you know, maybe you could have a look at this floor again before everybody else gets up here. And Dwight, well, your oil is here. But I don't know if I used enough. So could you come?"

They didn't look like doing anything together ever would be okay, but they came. In fact, a small smile even flickered over both their faces as they finally stood silently, shoulder to shoulder, staring down at the first trick stair. It was as though they were remembering what it had felt like sixty years before to be standing, just maybe, on the brink of solving the mystery of the last family treasure. They steadied themselves against the banister and wall and then, with the barest of nods, took the first step up. They stepped again and then again, and then kept on coming.

Ellsworth felt a surge of elation. He ran up the last few stairs and stepped out onto the floor of the enormous room. Just as it had done the night before, it creaked alarmingly under his feet. But this time he hardly noticed. He hardly even noticed the murmurs and exclamations behind him as one by one, the rest of the family stepped out to join him.

The room, now, with its shutters back, was filled with light. But it was no ordinary light. Dim one second, flashing the next, it was a magical light, and it turned the huge bare hot room into a place where you could believe, instantly, that anything could happen. It was so different from the room where he and Jess, the night before, had crawled and sweated and sneezed that for a moment he could hardly remember why they were there.

Then Kitty broke the spell. Her voice was awestruck, and it reflected the expression on the face of every person in the room. "It's the pond. Why, it is, isn't it? It's the pond."

36

Almost Theirs

Ellsworth almost, almost, could have kissed her. She'd gotten it. "Yeah! See, John Matthew built it, and then Betsy Sullivan painted it. She painted it just like the picture, with the pond and all the houses. Like I said, it wasn't supposed to be hard. This time, John Matthew, he just wanted the family to walk up the stairs and see all this stuff and know . . . know where to find it."

Elizabeth's eyes were huge. "It's the picture come to life, isn't it? With us all here, it's come to life! And there's really more? There's really a treasure?"

"There's got to be. It's got to be under the pond," Ellsworth said. "You guys? John? Dwight? You've been here. So you think I'm right? That it's got to be in the space between here"—he stamped gently—"and the floor he built underneath? Two floors, that's why it feels so bouncy and makes all those sounds. But then, you've got to figure out how to get it up, right? How to make the pond come up? There's kind of two parts to that; at least we think there is. See, yesterday, I found the arms and Jess found the initials and—"

"Whoaaaa," said Matthew. "Slow down a little, okay? History teachers are at a big disadvantage here. I think I understand the two floors. But arms? Initials? Where?"

"Okay," said Ellsworth. "Arms." He squatted down and

slid his hand down the crack. "You can't see them, right? You have to feel them. But there's a whole bunch of little hinged metal arms, all the way around, and they go from the floor here to, I'm pretty sure, the middle of the pond. Like the spokes on a wheel, right? And if you could make them work, the pond would come up. They're real old, but Dwight, he gave me some oil, so I oiled them real good. And they loosened okay, the hinges wiggled. But I couldn't get them to work. I couldn't get them to unfold." For a minute, it all came back to him, the day before, the frustration, the darkness illuminated only by the huge flashlight Jess shone down on them, the oil mixed with sweat and dust on his face. And then . . .

"And then, Jess, well, she found the initials." He turned to her. "You tell them, okay?"

"Well, see, they're here. You've got to come close. See? They're in the floor. Real little and carved real deep, so you've really got to look. Here's an *E,* for Emily, that's my middle name—"

Matthew broke in softly. "And for Elizabeth. Definitely *E* for Elizabeth."

Elizabeth didn't say anything, but her mouth twitched toward a smile.

"Yeah, okay, sure," said Jess. "But the thing is, they're all here. I mean, there's thirteen of them, one for each of the kids. John Matthew's kids, and Betsy's, just like in the picture? And Zee, Ellsworth, right? He didn't tell you, but there's thirteen of those little arms, too. So we think this is how it works. Look, okay? I'm going to step on the *E,* and Zee is going to step on the next one, that's *U.* And . . . "

She gestured broadly, like a magician doffing his tall black hat. And as she and Ellsworth both stepped firmly down on an initial, the section of pond right in front of them started to rise.

But it didn't rise far. It only rose an inch before it ground and screeched to a stop. "Watch out!" John said, but they'd both already stepped back.

"Yeah," Ellsworth said to him. "I know. Too much on one or two places, and the whole thing might crack. But he didn't want it to be just one or two places. See, what he *wanted*, I think, is to have the *whole* picture up here. The houses, and then the pond, and then, well, everybody, like Elizabeth said, around it. Maybe they couldn't dance, like in the picture. But . . . " He turned to Abner. "You remember what you said, how Betsy made it look like they were dancing even when their feet were on the ground?"

Abner nodded, smiled, and also doffed an imaginary hat. "Excellent," he said.

"Thanks," said Ellsworth. "So I think what he wanted was for everybody to just stand on all the right places, where the initials were, and then the whole thing would just come up. And what would be under there, I mean, what *is* under there, it's got to be, is the treasure."

It was then that Josie lifted a hand to speak. Her voice was clear and sharp. "Abner? How can this work? There aren't thirteen of us. If there is something down there, it might be priceless. Shouldn't we get it out as quickly as we can? Shouldn't we just saw through that pond and just lift it up and . . . ?"

The next moment became, to Ellsworth, one of his

clearest memories of that day. In all their years on the Square, nobody in that room had lifted any kind of real finger to find the most important thing John Matthew had left. And yet now, as if one body, the whole family turned and stared at Josie in utter disbelief. Then Abner smiled gently and shook his head. "Don't worry, my dear. We're in good hands here, and the treasure is, too." Then he turned to Ellsworth. "But there *are* only ten of us. Will that be enough?"

"I'm not sure," said Ellsworth. "But we've got to try. If we could just get it up high enough to *see* . . ."

"Well, of course we have to try, Ellsworth. Of course we do." Kitty looked about ready to explode with excitement. "And now, I know this might sound silly, but I want to stand right over there on that *U, U* for Ulysses, my great-grandfather, you know. Why, he died only ten years before I was born!"

"Oh," said Ellsworth blankly. He hadn't thought about people maybe wanting a specific initial. But who should get which one, and what if two people wanted the same one? Then he saw, with great relief, that Matthew had taken charge. He was nudging them into place like students on their first day of school: John to *S* for Sarah, Dwight to *A* for Alice, Abner to *R* for Robert, and Josie to *T* for Tobias.

"He was Robert's favorite brother," he told her. "All right? Good. Now. Who's left?"

"I am," said Elizabeth. Her voice, as usual, was quiet, but her eyes were smiling at him. "And I'm *M*, aren't I? *M* for Matthew. That's where I belong, isn't it? What did William Penn say? When you looked him up? 'Let us try what love can do,' that's what he said. And he was right, I think, and you are, too. So I'll try." Looking steadily at him, she took a couple of slow painful steps and positioned herself firmly on her initial.

"Will you, Elizabeth?" said Matthew huskily. "Will you, really?"

She nodded. The thunder was finally quieting, the flashes receding. The light in the room was steadier now: dim and gray and flat, and most of it, at that moment, seemed to gather in her face. "Yes," she said. "Yes, Matthew, I will."

"Well, now." It was Ben Robert. He was looking from Elizabeth to Matthew and then back again, a small smile playing over his tired face. "Well, now. I think I can manage the rest. I'm *H* for Henry, and you, Zee, surprise, are *E* for Ellsworth. Jess is *E* for Emily, and Matthew . . . Matthew? You listening? You're *S* for Samuel. Yeah, that should do it." Then he swayed back. "Hey! *Hey!*"

Over the last few minutes as they'd moved to take their places, the floor's steady protest had cranked up to rasping groans. Under their feet, old metal had begun to scrape against old metal; old hinges, newly oiled, had begun to move. Now the suspended "pond" that had begun, slowly, to creep up, began to rise with a vengeance. One inch, two inches, three inches . . . Ellsworth, dragging his eyes for an instant away from the steadily widening crack, saw that everybody was standing exactly the same way as he was: solidly, a little stooped, as though concentrating every atom of weight onto the mechanism below their feet.

The metal rods propelling the central oval steadily higher could now be seen. Then, so suddenly Ellsworth's heart lurched, there was something else as well. Underneath the pond, right under its center, was a small wooden platform. The angle was too steep to see what, if anything, was on it, but Ellsworth felt a tingling in his hands. Something was there, all right. And it was theirs. It was almost theirs. And then, with a sickening squeal, the whole of John Matthew's wonderful mechanism ground to a halt.

"No!" Ellsworth's anguished protest echoed around the circle. "No! Please! No!" He looked wildly over at Jess. "What? We've got to do something! What?"

Jess shook her head. But she was staring at the floor, at the two initials that stood between Ellsworth and her in the circle. Now she pointed. "I don't know. But look. There. That's where it's wrong."

"What do you mean?" But he knew what she meant. So her answer, when it came, was no surprise at all.

"We need somebody else," she said. "Somebody to stand there. Right there," she said, and pointed at the *R* for Richard.

37

R. C.

Ellsworth could never remember afterward how he got down the stairs. He must have jumped. He couldn't remember, either, walking down the hall and through the kitchen and out the back door onto the porch. It was only when he stepped down onto the walk that he woke up to find himself gazing down at the blackened remains of the top of the old pine tree, and shivering. The wind had changed. It was steadier now, and cooler, and raising his face to it, he noticed, blankly, that the clouds had finally smothered the last bit of sky. They *were* the sky now. They were heavy and dark and low, and under them, everything on the Square looked dirty.

Jess told him later that she'd asked to come with him, but that he'd just shaken his head and headed for the stairs. Like a zombie, she said. He'd looked like a zombie. Now he shook his head again, to clear it, and made his way slowly down the walk. At the end of it, he took as deep a breath as he could, squared his shoulders, and turned left. He knew where he had to go.

But it was slow going. This piece of the walk had been hit the hardest when the lightning cracked down out of nowhere to zap the pines with fire. The debris was everywhere—shards of limbs and hunks of ragged bark and tangles of scorched branches. And then, suddenly, there in front of him was what was left of the two old trees. They were no longer just dead. They were gone. Ellsworth stared at the jagged, smoldering, ugly stumps and suddenly, standing there, felt absolutely and completely alone.

"Zee!" He turned, almost blindly. "Zee, wait!" It was his father who was calling, and his father who was zigzagging toward him down the ravaged walk, half running, half falling, finally reaching him. Just as he had done earlier, he grabbed Ellsworth to him, and for a long minute they just stood there, holding on to each other as hard as they could. Finally, simultaneously, they stepped apart.

"You just left, Zee," said Ben Robert. "I was just standing there, feeling bad because I couldn't help, and then Jess said something, but I didn't really catch what it was, and then you were gone. I'd never have let you go on your own if I'd known where you were heading. Not again, Zee. You've got to know that. You've got to know that's true."

Ellsworth nodded. "Yeah," he said. "It's okay, Dad. I know. But . . ." He sighed. Saying things right was so hard. It would be so much easier if words were like puzzle pieces and you could just click them together to make the picture. He took another deep breath and tried again. "See, the thing is, you hate him. So I guess I thought, I don't know, that there wasn't any point. Because I want him to come. If he comes, it might work. You know? But you said . . ."

"Yeah," said Ben Robert. "I know what I said." He shook his head and gazed wearily down. "Look at them. Poor old pines. They were so great, once. When I was a kid, I'd climb up as far as I could go and sit and look out over the whole world. The river's down there, you know. The

Hudson . . . I always wished I could tell him. Tell my father. Because he loved that river. When I was little, he'd take me to the port and show me the ships. They were from everywhere, filled with everything, bananas and oil and sugar . . ."

"So why didn't you? How come you didn't?"

Ben Robert shook his head again, his voice sad. "Because if I'd told him, he would have chopped them down. For my own good. So I wouldn't fall out of them and break my neck. Zee, if I hope anything in the world for you at all, it's that you'll never, never, never be on the receiving end of that kind of love."

He was silent for a long minute and then his chin came up and he forced a smile and he reached over and touched Ellsworth's arm. "Well. So. No point dwelling on that now. If we're going, we'd better go."

But his smile didn't last. When he saw the leaf-choked shambles of his mother's garden, his face twisted, and it was only very slowly that he followed Ellsworth down the walk, stepping with great care over each weed-filled crack. Ellsworth wasn't moving very fast either as he climbed the steps to the porch. Even with his father, he wasn't quite sure he could do it. He didn't know if he could actually make his hand come up and knock. And when the door opened? Would he actually be able to look into R.C.'s face for the very first time and say what he had to say?

He had to. He pulled open the screen door and tried the knob. It was locked. He rattled it, rattled it again, and then, his heart suddenly pounding, he knocked. He knocked and knocked, harder and harder, as hard as he could.

"Cool it, Zee." Ben Robert was tugging at him gently, his

other hand digging down into a pocket of his jeans. "Try this." He held up a key. "I've been lugging it around for a lot of years," he said huskily, "but it should still work. If the lock's like it always was, you'll need to wiggle it a bit to the right. Okay?"

Ellsworth stared down at it. Then he pushed it in slowly, wiggled it a little to the right, and turned it. The door slid open.

It didn't slide far. Ellsworth pushed, and then pushed again. There was something in the way. "What is it, Zee? What's the matter?" Ben Robert's voice was still hoarse, but now, under it, was an edge of fear.

"Don't know," said Ellsworth. He shoved harder and finally, with a clutch of relief, saw what he was pushing. It was a big cardboard box. "Box," he said. With a grunt, he got it out of the way and slid through the opening, his father right behind.

The kitchen was full of boxes. Some of them were small, and some of them were big. Most of them were carefully taped shut, but one, the smallest, was gaping. Overhead came the sound of something scraping over the floor, and then the steady *thump, thump, thump* of yet another box coming down the back stairs. When it got to the bottom, it overturned, and a pile of books spilled out. There was a clatter of footsteps on the stairs, and then R.C. was standing there, looking even thinner than Ellsworth had remembered, and almost as dirty as they were.

He gave them only the briefest of looks. "How did you get in here? Get out." But his words were irritated rather than angry, as though he was talking to strangers who were taking up his valuable time. "You'll get your things soon enough. I'm working as fast as I can. Now get out of here and leave me alone."

Ellsworth shot a look at his father, but Ben Robert's face was white and clenched and still. "What do you mean?" said Ellsworth. "What are you doing?"

"What does it look like I'm doing?" said R.C. "I'm getting this stuff out of here. I can't believe I let this nonsense go on all these years. Those rooms . . . She wouldn't let me touch them, you know. His, just like he left it, all those books, every one of his books. And then that little room and that crib, and then that little bed, because the baby, that baby kept growing. We didn't know where he was . . ." Now R.C. stopped, and when he spoke again his voice sounded almost strangled. "We didn't know where he was, you know, of course you know, but we knew he was growing. . . ."

Ellsworth felt like he was in the middle of a nightmare. "He? Who? What are you talking about?"

"You know what I'm talking about. I'm talking about this." R.C. grabbed the smallest box, the one that was open, and shook something out. He held it up. It was a small knitted sweater, blue, with a little hood. He dropped it into Ellsworth's hands and then rummaged deeper into the box. "And this." This was bigger, a pair of bright red overalls, a yellow horse embroidered on the bib.

"Baby clothes," said Ellsworth helplessly. "Dad? I don't get it. Are they yours? From when you were little?" Ben Robert shook his head again, but now his eyes were closed and his face a mask of pain. "Then . . . Then . . ." And then Ellsworth finally got it. "These are mine? These were for me?"

R.C. deflated right before his eyes. He fumbled for a chair and slumped down. And now his words came slowly, as though being dragged by a big hook. "Of course they are. She started the day he left. Making things. For a while, that seemed to be enough. I think that's what kept her sane then, knitting and sewing, cutting things out and stitching them up. But then, after a while, she wanted you to have them. Wear them. But we didn't know where you were. Elizabeth knew. Izzy begged her. But she said she'd promised him that she'd never tell us. He hated us so much. Izzy could never understand how he could hate us so much. And she could never believe that you'd never, ever come back."

And now Ben Robert finally spoke. "It was never her. I never hated her. Tell him, Zee. It was in what I wrote for you. . . ."

But now R.C. was back on his feet. "What did you say? What did you call him?"

For a moment Ben Robert looked blank, and then he nodded. "Yeah," he said. "You remember. I wouldn't have thought you'd remember." He looked over at Ellsworth. "Zee was what I called my mother when I was little. Her name was Isabelle, but everybody called her Izzy. Izzy . . . Zee . . . So when I shortened Ellsworth to Ellsie, the Zee just jumped out. It felt good calling you that. It felt good." He turned again to his father. "I never hated her," he repeated.

"You didn't even come back for her funeral," said R.C.

"Nothing would have hurt her more than that," said Ben Robert. "You know that. My coming then. *Then,* when she couldn't . . ." His face twisted, but he held his father's gaze. Finally, the old man gave a grudging nod.

"If you'd come then, I would have killed you." They stared at each other, and then, strangely, slowly, almost all of the tension drained out of Ben Robert's face, and he, too, gave a nod.

"Yeah," he said. "Or I would have killed you. That was the other reason. But I'm here now, aren't I? And Zee, he's here, too. What do you say to that?"

"I don't know," said R.C. "How can you ask me something like that? How can I know something like that? I don't."

"Listen," said Ellsworth. He knew if he didn't say something now it would be too late. Maybe it already was. "Listen. If you don't know, can you come? That's why we're here. We need you. We've found Richard's treasure. But we can't get it without you. So can you come, before they all leave? They're all waiting for you, everybody's waiting. Listen, see, I know you don't like that house. But . . ." And then, as though she was talking to him, whispering right in his ear, he heard Elizabeth's voice, telling him what to say. "But Isabelle? My grandmother? I think she'd say okay. I think she'd want us to. Because it would be the three of us, right? You and me and my dad? It would be the three of us doing it together."

He didn't wait for an answer. He couldn't. He pushed open the screen door and walked out onto the porch and down the steps. His heart was pounding again, even harder.

Behind him, the door creaked back open, and then he could hear footsteps, one set of footsteps moving across the porch. One. He tried to swallow and couldn't. He was on the sidewalk now, and the weeds in the cracks suddenly seemed impossibly high, ready to tangle around his feet and pull him down and wrap him up and eat him. And then the door behind him opened again. It whooshed slowly shut, and a third person started to make his way across the porch.

Something cold and wet plopped down on Ellsworth's head, and then again, and again. He looked up. It had finally started to rain.

38

Under the Pond

Jess was on the porch, pacing. When she saw them, her face lit up like a rocket. "You're here. You're all here! Are you okay? You're wet!"

Ellsworth took the steps in two leaps. "Well, sure we're wet. It's raining. But yeah. We're here." He looked over at R.C., who was standing, in a dazed kind of way, staring at the door. "Listen, can you go up with my dad, and tell them we're coming? R.C. and me? We'll be there in a minute."

Actually, he thought, he didn't have a clue how long they'd be. R.C. was there, all right, but just. He was stepping into the house now, but cautiously, as though he wasn't quite sure it was real. The light from the old windows, gleaming now with rain, rippled over his wet face, and he turned and blinked and turned again. He saw Ellsworth and stared at him, puzzled. "You're different, close up. Like . . . him, but like somebody else, too. You remind me of somebody else. Who?"

Ellsworth shook his head. "I don't know."

"No," said R.C. He ran his hands over his dripping head. Then he sighed deeply. "We needed rain," he said. His voice choked. "She always loved the rain. She loved it when her birdbath filled . . . Overflowed . . . And then the birds would come. She always loved that."

Ellsworth cleared his throat, not sure exactly what was

going to come out. He really wished he'd known her. Izzy. Isabelle. His grandmother. He really wished he had. "Maybe she'd be kind of happy, then, you know? Because there hasn't been any rain? And now there is?"

R.C.'s head came up. "You think so?" he said. He slowly nodded. Then he looked over Ellsworth's head at the door into the hall. "It's upstairs, isn't it? That's where you want me to go." He turned to look right into Ellsworth's eyes. "I don't know if I can."

"Yeah, but see, I'll show you," said Ellsworth, eager now. They'd gotten so far. They only had to go a little farther. "You just need two, you just have to do it two at a time. Elizabeth, she even did it. And Kitty. She got up okay, too."

R.C. swallowed, his mouth working. "Kitty. No sense at all, Kitty, but Izzy always loved her. I never understood it, but Izzy always loved her, and now she keeps leaving food, I don't understand it, I don't want it, but there it is, so I eat it. . . . No sense at all."

"Come on," said Ellsworth. He'd baby-sat once, and that was what this felt like, like nudging some little kid along. "It'll be okay. They're waiting. You know, it's just through this door here, and down the hall. Then we just have to do it together. Just the first three steps, and then it's okay. You ready?"

But R.C., finally standing at the bottom of the stairs, shook his head. He was staring down at them like he'd been seeing them in nightmares for forty years. "No," he said hoarsely. "I can't." He stepped back.

"Hey," said Ellsworth. "Come on. Really. It's okay."

Instinctively, he held out his hand. For a minute, R.C. didn't respond. Then, still staring down, he reached slowly out and took it.

Ellsworth took a deep breath and let it back out. "Okay," he said. He tightened his grip. "You ready, then? Come on. Come on now. One, two, three, up."

Halfway up the stairs, R.C. stopped. He turned and looked down at the hall. He looked for what felt like a long time, and then he turned back, gave Ellsworth's hand a light shake and dropped it. He gazed down at his grandson, and for the first time his eyes weren't confused or puzzled or angry. They were tired but calm. He laid his hand flat on Ellsworth's head and held it there for a long moment. Then he nodded. "I know now. It's Duncan. My father. That's who you remind me of." He raised his hand and looked up. "And you were right. There they all are."

There they all were. They were clustered right at the top of the stairs, and as R.C. came up the last step, they reached for him, one after another, to shake his hand, some gracefully, some awkwardly, but all of them obviously relieved to see him after his five-month exile. "R.C.," said Kitty, her eyes bright with tears. "Oh, R.C."

"Don't get excited now, Kitty," he said. "I'm all right."

"Well, I guess we are, too," said Dwight. "Now you're here, and we can get this thing going." He gave a brief grin. "Been thinking, though. John Matthew wanted us all here, Ellsworth says. Wonder what he'd say if he could see us. This crew probably wasn't exactly what he had in mind when he went to all that trouble to hide whatever's under this floor."

John answered him. His voice was testy, but there was a glint in his eyes that said he'd been thinking more or less the same thing. "So what?" he said. "We're what he's got. Let's get to it."

Ellsworth caught Jess's eye. She grinned, and he grinned back. He suddenly felt like flying. They'd done it. Everybody was here. The huge room, which before had been still and somber and sweltering, had changed. Somebody had opened some windows, so it was cooler now, and the light coming in, though still subdued, felt alive. It was strange and watery and mysterious, filtered by the raindrops that slid this way and that down the old glass. High overhead, more rain thrummed down on the roof. He saw John's fast satisfied glance upward and nodded. John had been right. The roof was tight.

Everybody was moving now toward the middle of the room and the pond. Ben Robert was slumped with weariness and Elizabeth was limping badly and Abner and Josie were holding tightly to each other's hands. But they were all moving, and as one after another of them took their places, the floor's groans gave way again to the rasp of metal.

"R.C.?" said Ellsworth. "Grandpa? You're here. On that *R* there, between me and Jess. Okay?" It was okay. They were all in their places now. They were all where they were supposed to be, and the oval panel in the middle of the floor was slowly rising, up and up, higher than before. But then, just before it rose quite high enough, it ground again to a stop.

"No," said Ellsworth. "No, please. Keep going. Keep going!"

"It's okay," said Jess breathlessly. "It's okay. We just have to hold hands. We have to hold hands, like in the picture. Hold hands and squeeze as hard as we can. That's all we have to do. That's all. . . ."

And all of them, without a question, obeyed. Like wings rising, their arms floated up, their hands joined, and Ellsworth, holding on to his father on one side and stretching for his grandfather on the other, saw everyone else's face startle into what he was feeling, too: energy, energy flowing from one of them into the next like a current in a wire. They could, almost, have been dancing.

Smoothly now, one last mechanism clicked into place, and in a continuous motion, the oval around which they were all standing rose a final foot, so it was just about level with Ellsworth's waist. It stopped cleanly, with a second final-sounding click, and Ellsworth, releasing first R.C.'s hand and then his father's, squatted down to look. The feeling of being charged was still strong, so strong that for a moment he couldn't move farther. He could only stare. Under the panel was the platform he'd glimpsed earlier, and on it was a wooden box about eight inches square. Ellsworth leaned forward as far as he could, grasped the box, lifted it, and pulled it from its resting place of one hundred and twenty years.

39

Inside the Box

By means of the heavy interlocking leaves, Elizabeth's huge table had been transformed from green felt to dark mahogany. It had been covered with a wrinkled but white cloth Jess had found in a drawer in the pantry. Sitting in the middle of it now, in lonely splendor, was the box.

Jess dragged the last of the big dining chairs from its place against the wall and placed it at the head. "That's twelve," she said. "That's one too many."

"Yeah," said Ellsworth. "But listen. I've been thinking. Let's put the picture there. You know, right there at the end, propped up so everybody can see it. And, well, I don't know, it sounds dumb, but so *he* can see *us,* too. John Matthew. See we did it."

Her eyes widened. "That's good. That's really good. You know," she continued, trotting after him, "I'll bet you wouldn't have thought of that before."

"Before what?" said Ellsworth. He was concentrating on getting a good grip on the picture so he wouldn't drop it when it came off the wall.

"Before you came here."

"Yeah, well. Maybe. Give me a hand with this, okay? It's heavier than it looks."

But it wasn't just that it was heavy. It was the way he felt, the way his hands wouldn't stop shaking. It was like

Christmas morning when Ben Robert had to have his coffee and then make a special big breakfast and then expect Ellsworth to eat it before he could see what was under the tree. Everybody had just taken it for granted, *taken it for granted* that they couldn't open the box until they were clean and dry and had had a little rest and something to eat. Something to eat, okay, but the rest was crazy. Crazy!

"What time is it?" he said to Jess. "Why aren't they here?"

"How should I know?" she said. "I'm here, aren't I? And I can hear Elizabeth and your father—they're in the kitchen. Okay, okay, listen. Wasn't that the back door? Yeah, that's Grandma, all right. And Matthew, I hear him, too. Come on. Let's go get them."

"You go," said Ellsworth. "I want to stay here. But tell them to hurry, okay? If I don't get to see pretty soon . . ."

The door swung shut behind her. He pulled out one of the middle chairs and sat down. He put his chin down on his hands and stared at the box. It wasn't, in any way, a "wonderful" John Matthew box. Its dark fine-grained wood was nice, but there weren't any carvings on it, or inlay, and it looked like you could get it open just by lifting a metal latch.

He even had a pretty good idea what was inside. This was the last treasure. This was Richard's treasure. And there was something that Richard had loved, that all the kids had loved, some *things* that John Matthew had found and bought in London. "The Treasures," he'd called them. The Treasures.

But what were they? They weren't very heavy. What if they were just . . . pretty little things? Junk? What if Abner or Josie just picked them up and shook their heads and . . .

"Zee?" Ellsworth raised his head to see that while he'd been worrying, they'd come. They were there. Ben Robert was pulling out the chair next to him, and Kitty and Dwight and R.C. were settling down across the table. In another minute Abner and Josie had joined them, and now Jess was beside him and John beside Ben Robert, and Matthew was helping Elizabeth drag out the big armchair at the end. She sat down carefully and gave him a nod of thanks as he took the last empty seat. Then she looked down to the other end of the table and smiled.

"The picture," she said. "You know, when we were there earlier, living the picture, *in* it, I kept thinking about what's on the back of it. What John Matthew wrote . . . You remember, Ben Robert. I'm sure you do."

" 'Thou hast turned for me my mourning into dancing,' " Ben Robert said quietly. "Psalms 30:11, and when I was a kid, I didn't have the faintest idea what he was talking about." He was silent for a moment, looking down at his hands. "Then, for years, it just seemed incredible. That she could paint that picture. That he could write those words and mean them. Now? I don't know. Maybe I'm beginning to see it might happen."

"Incredible," Elizabeth echoed gently. "Almost as incredible as us. All of us. Here." She smoothed a wrinkle out of the cloth in front of her and then looked up. "I know none of you will be very surprised if I ask you something. John Matthew, there, would be surprised if I didn't. A lot's happened today, and there's more to come. I think what we need now is silence."

Something between a sigh and a murmur drifted around the table, and she followed it, looking quietly at each of them in turn. Ellsworth didn't know what she saw, but it was obviously okay, because she placed her hands back in her lap and shut her eyes. Ellsworth glanced at his father. Ben Robert gave him a faint smile, and then, as though it was the most natural thing in the world, crossed his legs, folded his hands, and closed his own eyes as well.

There was a rustle of bodies rearranging themselves. A few chairs squeaked. Then, slowly, the room became still. It was as though everything that had happened that day was dropping, settling, leaving a great quiet space above it that was clear and light and calm. Ellsworth felt it, he couldn't help but feel it, and there was a funny look on Jess's face that said that maybe she felt it, too. The space and the silence went on, and deepened, and then Elizabeth broke it with the simplest possible words. "Thank you," she said.

Then she turned to the right-hand side of the table. "Ellsworth? Jess? You found it. I don't think most of us can quite believe it, but you did. So what's there? What did John Matthew leave for us in his last house and his last box?"

Ellsworth looked at Jess. "You do it," she said. "I wouldn't even have gone in there if you hadn't, well, you know . . . You do it."

"Yeah?" said Ellsworth. He swallowed.

"Yeah," she said.

Ellsworth took a deep breath, for courage. "Okay," he said. He leaned over and pulled the wooden box carefully toward him. It really was light. Was it too light? Was it . . . empty?

It couldn't be. It couldn't be, and as he pulled up the little metal latch and raised the lid, he saw that it wasn't. Lying inside, tightly enough that he had to struggle to get it out, was a second box, a mottled blackened box made not of wood but of . . .

"Silver." It was Dwight who spoke. "That's silver. But there's something inside, isn't there. There's got to be something inside."

It took Ellsworth a minute to figure out how it opened, because this latch was trickier. It was set in an elaborately scrolled frieze, and first he had to find it, and then he had to push it exactly right. When he finally did, the box, in one beautifully controlled movement, swung smoothly open. Another sigh echoed around the table.

"What is it?" said Jess. She had pulled her chair closer and was breathing down his neck. "What's there?"

What was there was an envelope, not of paper, but of cloth. It had been closed by ribbons tied into knots. Now, as soon as Ellsworth touched them, the ribbons flaked to threads. Willing his hands to stop shaking, he pushed them aside and unfolded first one and then two heavy layers. Lying underneath were what John Matthew had left them, and it only took one look to see why he and all his children had loved them so much. Beside him, already, Jess was reaching out a hand to touch them. They were something anybody would want to touch, to handle, to play with. To polish. To arrange and rearrange and line up in rows.

"The Treasures" were a perfect set of glowing, silver spoons.

⊰ 40 ⊱

The Treasures

They were the strangest-looking spoons Ellsworth had ever seen. He picked up one to look at it more closely. It was about six inches long. Its bowl was huge—much bigger and flatter than normal—and was attached to a slender stem. At the stem's end stood a tiny figure, wearing a flat hat and holding something in its arms.

From across the table came a strangled sound. "Good Lord." It was Abner. He cleared his throat. "May I?" Ellsworth slid the spoon over to him, and he picked it up carefully and then turned it around and around in his hands. "Silver isn't one of our specialties," he said, "although I have the standard references, of course, which I'll go and get in just a minute. But this is an apostle spoon, don't you think, Josie? And unless I miss my guess, it's very, very old."

"Let me see that," said Dwight. Abner passed it down to him reluctantly, obviously hating to let it go. He then peered eagerly over to where Jess had spread out the rest of the spoons in a careful row. Each one had its own little figure at the top, and all of them were different.

"Wait a minute," said Abner. "I can hardly believe what I'm seeing. How many spoons do you have there?"

"Nine, ten, eleven, twelve," counted Jess. "Well, twelve here, but then he's got one over there, so that makes thirteen. And that's so cool because it's just like the initials, right? Just like the kids!"

But Abner was shaking his head. "There can't be thirteen. I'm getting my books right this minute, but I know enough about apostle spoons to know that a full set, a very rare full set, is twelve. I'm going to go out the front, if you don't mind, Elizabeth. It's faster." He made his way quickly out of the room.

"Can we see the rest of them, Jess? Can you pass them around?" Elizabeth's voice broke the spell, and suddenly everybody was talking at once, passing the spoons eagerly from one hand to the next, examining and trying to identify all the little figures.

"Now, one of the apostles is John, of course," Kitty was saying. "Who's got John? And there'll be a Matthew, too, and a Thomas, they're all in the family, but then Peter, I don't think we ever had a Peter . . ."

Dwight's voice broke in louder. "Hey," he was saying. "Listen up, everybody. Look. This is a funny one. This one here. It's different. The silver's different, and the way it's made. It's later. And look here now, that's engraving. A date and some words. I can almost . . . but no, I can't. I need my lens."

"Here," said Abner. He had reappeared, one large book under his arm, another closed on a finger that was keeping his place. "I brought mine." There was a tremor in his usually calm voice. "Josie. This is incredible. Look here. Sixteenth century, almost certainly. Elizabethan. Do you know how little silver has survived from that period? And an entire set? Almost unbelievable. I can name five museums right off the top of my head that would go into a bidding frenzy this minute if they knew. Where in God's name did John Matthew find them? And I was right. There can't be thirteen. The set is always the twelve disciples, minus Judas, of course, because nobody includes Judas, and then Saint Paul—"

"Listen now," Dwight interrupted. "We're both right. There's thirteen, all right, but this spoon here sure wasn't made in any sixteenth century. Look at this: 1880, it says, clear as a bell. John Matthew had this baby made to match the other ones, that's what he did. . . ."

Ben Robert spoke for the first time. "Eighteen-eighty. That was just before he died. You said there were words, too, Dwight. What? What are they?" He was leaning forward, and his fingers were beating a rapid tattoo against the edge of the table. There was a look on his face that Ellsworth knew well, that absolutely concentrated look he got when he was writing.

"Well, now," said Dwight. "Let me see." He peered carefully through the small lens and, turning the spoon in his big hands, read the rest of the engraving, slow word by slow word. "'This is my beloved Son in whom I am well pleased.' That's what he wrote."

There was a moment of complete silence. Ben Robert's fingers had frozen in mid-beat. Across the table from him, R.C. sat like carved stone. Only Dwight seemed to be oblivious to the effect he had just made. "Well, now," he said. "That's the Bible, isn't it? That's Jesus. Well, sure it is. See, here, this little guy here, he's carrying a cross, you see that, R.C.? So there's your thirteenth, Abner. Thirteen, just like Jess there said, because that was John Matthew's number, wasn't it? And Jesus, to go with the disciples or apostles or whatever, well, it just makes sense." He suddenly noticed that everybody was just sitting there, silent. "Well, that's right, isn't it? What's the matter?"

"Nothing's the matter," said Elizabeth quietly. "And, of course, you're right, Dwight. About Jesus. But what we're all thinking, I think, is that John Matthew meant more than that. This treasure was Richard's treasure, Richard who went away without his father's blessing and never came back. I think this was John Matthew's way of finally . . . coming to terms with . . . what he had done. What Richard had done. And to say, just simply, that he . . . loved him."

It was still raining, but only faintly now, the gentle patter against the windows filtered, as was the light, by the soft drape of the old lace curtains. Ben Robert's movements, too, were gentle as he pushed back his chair and stood up. He was smiling, just a little. "You never give up, Elizabeth, do you?"

"No, Ben Robert," she said, looking at him steadily. "I never give up."

He nodded. Then he reached over and touched Ellsworth's shoulder. "Sorry, Zee," he said. "Don't worry. But I'm just too tired now to take this all in." He made a vague gesture of apology and then walked clumsily out of the room.

"Dad!" said Ellsworth, and shoved his own chair back.

"Don't." It was R.C. from across the table. He, too, was up now, and he, too, looked so tired he could hardly stand. "Let him be. You always had to let Ben Robert be when he was upset. You always had to . . . wait, and let him be, and let him come back on his own, when he was ready." He looked toward the door, his eyes bleak. "But Izzy was right, wasn't she? This time I waited too long."

"No!" said Ellsworth. "Look! I mean, it's not too long. He did come back. He's here!" His father wasn't like Richard, he thought stubbornly. He wasn't! He stared at his grandfather, and the room remained absolutely silent as R.C. stared back at him. Then the old man nodded.

"Yes. You do remind me of him. Of Duncan. My father." He nodded again. "He never ran away from anything." Then he, too, made his unsteady way out of the room.

A long sigh ran around the table. Kitty swabbed at her face, and Dwight and John shifted in their seats. Elizabeth closed her eyes and reached toward Matthew. He took her hand and grasped it hard. Then Ellsworth felt something, too. Jess was poking him on the arm. He let go of the box he'd been gripping and sank back in his chair.

"Well, now," said Abner. "Well, now. If I can get back to those spoons? All right? The thirteenth one, now. The thirteenth one's a replica, that seems clear enough. But the other twelve . . . We'll have to have them carefully examined and authenticated, of course, but if they *are* original and all one set, well, they're just simply . . . priceless. Ellsworth. Is there anything more in that box? Anything John Matthew might have included to tell us where he got that set and who made the Christ figure? Provenance, you know. We need provenance."

"Yeah," said Ellsworth. "Okay. I don't know." He didn't know what provenance was, but it was good to be doing something. He picked up the cloth the spoons had been wrapped in and gave it a shake. Two small sheets of paper fell out, and he pushed them over.

"Ah," said Abner. "Yes. Look here, Josie. London, 1843, a bill of sale. And then Boston, yes, 1880. Incredible."

"Okay," said Ellsworth. "Here's something else. On this box? The silver one? The inside isn't as dirty as the outside, and there's writing here, too."

"Yes," said Josie. She had one of Abner's books open in front of her. "I've been wondering about that box. Abner, look at the style of it. The filigree, that frieze around the middle. Now look here, at this picture. Similar, wouldn't you say? Almost identical. That's American silver, I'm almost sure of it. Eighteenth-century, pre-Revolutionary silver. What was it you just said, Abner? Boston? Isn't that where your family came from originally? Before they moved here?"

"Oh, yes," breathed Abner. "Boston, indeed." He looked from Josie's face to the picture, and then over to the box. "Well, if it's who you're thinking, who *I'm* thinking, we'll know as soon as we get it cleaned. The maker's mark will be on it. The famous silversmiths always left their mark."

"Abner, now, you just stop it," said Kitty. "You're trying to act like you're smarter than everybody else. What are you saying? Who are you talking about?"

"Well, Kitty," said Abner. "I'll tell you. If these pictures here are any clue, then who I'm talking about is Paul Revere."

Ellsworth hardly heard the babble of voices. A chill slid over him. Paul Revere. He didn't know anything about apostle spoons and Elizabethan silver, but everybody knew about Paul Revere. He peered down again at the writing. "Jess," he whispered. "Look at this, okay? Can you read it? What does it say?"

"Hush now, everybody," said Kitty. "Go on now, Jess. Is it Paul Revere? Is it?"

"Yeah, well," said Jess. "Hold on, okay? It's like the journal. You have to get into it. But at least it's short." Her head was practically in the box, and her finger was moving slowly from letter to letter. Then she blinked a couple of times and sat up straight.

"What?" said Ellsworth. "What?"

She grinned.

"Come on!" said Ellsworth. "What does it say?"

"Okay," she said. "Okay. It says 1771. And then it says"—and she peered down for one more look—"it says, get this: 'From a smith to a Smith.'" And the first *s* is a small one, and the second *s* is big."

"'From a smith to a Smith,'" Ellsworth echoed. Then he stood up because he had to. It was like another bolt of lightning had just touched down on the table in front of him. "From a smith, because that's what he was, right? A silversmith. And then *to* a Smith, because that's who it was for. You get it? You *get* it? If Paul Revere really made this, he made it for us!"

41

All of Them

Elizabeth's back steps were beginning to feel like home. Ellsworth, full from a late supper, slumped sleepily against the left-hand newel post, TigerLily curled in his lap. His view of the Sward, with its litter of half-burned branches, was veiled by the wide floating expanse of Elizabeth's flowers. Refreshed now by rain, they gave off a fragrance that was almost visible.

He heard the screen door open and close and looked up as his father sat down beside him.

"Hi," he said.

"Hi," said Ben Robert. He touched the cats gently and they started to purr. "Happy little guys, aren't they?" He glanced at his son. "How about you, though? Okay?"

"Yeah," said Ellsworth. He stretched. It felt good, it felt really good, having Ben Robert finally there, on the steps, next to him, here.

Ben Robert relaxed slowly against him. "Yeah. I guess I am, too. It's been pretty crazy, though, this past week. And the Square sure laid on the fireworks this afternoon." His hand went back to the cats. "You like it here, though, don't you?"

"Yeah," said Ellsworth. He frowned, concentrating. He'd been thinking about it a lot the last few hours, ever since things had quieted down. "It's . . . different here. You know? Not like our other places. It feels . . . like, I don't know. Like they know me. Even though I just got here. Elizabeth. And Jess. And the cats. I like the cats. The pond, even. I'd been dreaming about it, and I didn't know. I didn't know it was *here*." There was only one important thing to say, really. "Dad? Do you think we can stay?"

Ben Robert didn't answer right away. He was staring into space, looking like he was trying to puzzle something out. "Well," he said finally, "Elizabeth sure wants us to. She says we can stay with her as long as we want. And then, there might be another house empty, soon, if she and Matthew tie the knot." He shrugged. "Hard to think of Elizabeth married, somehow. But Matthew seems like a good guy. And he's got a good job, that's for sure. Benefits even. That would sure be a change for her, to have some money coming in. She could finally get that knee fixed."

"They play Scrabble every Saturday," said Ellsworth. "You could play with them."

But his father was still thinking out loud. "But the ghosts, Zee. The memories. They're all so mixed up, the good with the bad. They probably always will be." He shook his head. "And then I'd have to find a job, and that wouldn't be so easy, either. There's not much work in these old mill towns."

He glanced at Ellsworth. "There's one funny thing, though, and it's only fair to say it. My book. It's almost done now. It's been almost done for six months, and my agent even thinks it'll sell. But I can't find the ending." His hands now were gripping each other tightly. "I know why. I've known all along, except I didn't want to know. If the answer's anywhere, it's . . ." His face twisted. "Yeah. Well, I still can't say it, can I? But it's not at the Lake Breeze, that's for sure."

Ellsworth shook his head. "The only thing at the Lake Breeze is Mr. Rocco, and he doesn't want us back."

Ben Robert almost grinned. "You're right about that, Zee. You're sure right about that."

"It was too noisy there anyway," said Ellsworth. "You were always saying that. The Square's quieter, you know? So I bet you *could* finish it here. I bet you could, and then you wouldn't need a job, right? Everybody'd buy your book and you could write another one . . ."

Ben Robert snorted. "First novels don't usually rake in the big bucks, you know. Second ones, either."

"Okay, then. What about the spoons? Won't we get some of that money, when they sell them?"

"Well, that sounds great, too, Zee, but that's not how it works. That money will go to the Square. For roofs and paint and tree men and taxes. For insurance. For heat. For electricity. For all the boring stuff that's let the family live here all these years. That'll help us to stay, I have to admit, if that's what we decide to do. But listen. We can be glad about one thing, anyway. Elizabeth was talking about it inside. Those spoons mean that we don't have to sell the picture."

"Yeah?" said Ellsworth. His heart lifted. "So we can always look at it, whenever we want? That's good. I want Trevor to see it, when he comes to visit." Then he had another thought. "But what about the box. Paul Revere's box? Are they going to sell that, too?"

Ben Robert grinned. "If I know anything about your cousin Kitty, that box is going to be on permanent display at the State Museum. And it's going to have a big sign on it, too, I'll bet: 'Courtesy of the original Smith family of Smiths Mills, New York.' No, I think we'll keep our hands on that one." Then he gave a short laugh. "Well, at least until the next big crunch. Because there're no more treasures to bail us out now, Zee. You pulled the very last one out of John Matthew's hat. So we're on our own now, aren't we? The Smiths . . . And that's probably the scariest thought of all."

"I don't know what's so scary about it," said Ellsworth. "You know, I was thinking, we could save a lot of money if we took down those houses. Not Richard's, that's still okay, and it's got all that good stuff in it, and maybe, Dwight was talking about it, we could make it a museum, even, with John Matthew's boxes and his toys and things. But the other two. They're dead, Dad. Even John says so. There's nothing in them, and they're falling down. And you said there's a river down there, so if the houses were gone, maybe we could plant some more climbing trees so we could see it. I'd like to see that port, you know? And maybe . . . "

Now, finally, his father was laughing. Ellsworth hadn't heard him laugh, really laugh, for a long time. It sounded good. Then, abruptly, Ben Robert got to his feet. He cupped his hands around his mouth. "You hear that, John Matthew?" he shouted. He shouted it out into the Square, and it bounced out against the trees and the houses, and then it came echoing back. "You hear that? You can go back to sleep, old man! You finally got it! You finally got what you wanted!" Then, still smiling, he turned back to his son. "Okay, Zee. At least I think it will be. I hope it will. And now maybe I'll go pass some of this conversation on to Elizabeth. She'll be over the moon."

"Okay?" The screen door, though, was closing and his father was gone. The cats looked up sleepily, still purring, and then squirmed down into a tighter bundle. "Really okay?" he asked them. They purred louder. Finally sure, almost sure, he settled back. Then he yawned. It was starting to get dark. What did it mean, anyway, "over the moon"? The clouds were almost gone and he could see it, the moon. His moon. The Square's moon. It was up there hanging. It was just a sliver. It was hanging now, where the pine trees weren't. Where the pine trees weren't . . . Where the pine trees weren't . . .

Something poked him gently in the ribs. "Wake up." He blinked, wiped his mouth, and sat up. Jess was hunched on the step beside him, her arms wrapped tightly around her knees. She was staring out into the dark.

"You know what?" she said finally. Her voice sounded dreamy, as though she'd been sitting there for a long, long time. "When I was little, we lived in these town houses, and there were so many kids, and there was this big open field out back, and every night we'd all go out there and just play and play until it got dark. It was the best time. And then we moved, and after that I was older, and it was mostly just me. And I told myself that someday I'd have kids, lots and lots of kids. So for them it would never be just . . . one. You know?"

Ellsworth nodded. He knew. John Matthew had known, too, hadn't he? Ellsworth again could almost see it, the Square, and how it must have been when all those kids had been little and rolling around together.

Jess pulled a folded piece of paper out of her pocket and put it on his knee. "You remember the initials? And how I always liked it in grade school, on holidays, making words? Because I was good, and I always got the most? This was different, though, because it wasn't the most. It was the right ones, the right words, and that was harder. Except I knew they were there. They had to be. John Matthew and Betsy, they wouldn't have just put them there. Not for nothing."

There was a dim light shining out through the screen from the kitchen. In it, Ellsworth peered down at the initials, the initials of those first Smith children. Jess had written them big. E. T. R. E. U. S. I. S. A. R. M. T. H. He studied them for a long minute and then shook his head. It just wasn't the kind of puzzle he was good at. He just never, probably, was ever going to be much good with words.

Shyly, Jess reached out her hand and flipped the paper over. Ellsworth looked at what she'd printed so carefully, and suddenly, in the cool damp night, he felt as though someone was reaching warm arms around him and holding him tight.

"SMITH TREASURE," she read softly. "It was the kids, right? That's what they were trying to say. In the house. Everywhere. The SMITH TREASURE was the kids."

"Yeah," Ellsworth said finally. "Yeah." The kids. The

first Ellsworth and Thomas, and Richard, and the rest . . .
Then John and Dwight and Kitty and R.C. . . . Then Ben
Robert and Emmy. Then Jess. Then him.

It was the Smith family kids.

It was all of them.

42

At Rest

It is a cool rainwashed summer night, and the sky is clear of everything but stars and a small scrap of moon. On the Square, a slight breeze lifts a corner of a curtain, touches the pages of an open book, ripples the edge of a water lily on the pond. In the cemetery, it nudges a last few drops from the pines that cluster over the family plot. They fall, some to pool with earlier ones on the modest markers, others to slide down blades of grass and then down farther to the waiting roots below.

All the Smiths are asleep. Some of them are dreaming, too, as they always will, but their dreams tonight are happy ones. The Smiths, tonight, are at peace.

They are at rest.

All of them.